A Hero for Christmas

JO ANN BROWN

D0126729

⟨H⟩ **HARLEQUIN**® LOVE INSPIRED® HISTORICAL

Recycling programs
for this product may
not exist in your area.

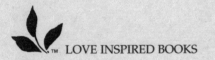 LOVE INSPIRED BOOKS

ISBN-13: 978-0-373-82993-4

A HERO FOR CHRISTMAS

Copyright © 2013 by Jo Ann Ferguson

www.Harlequin.com

Printed in U.S.A.

I sought the Lord, and he answered me,
and delivered me from my fears.
—*Psalms* 34:4

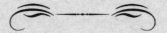

For Patrick,
who has brought such a new happy melody to our family

Chapter One

Meriweather Hall, Sanctuary Bay, North Yorkshire
November 1816

Shouts came from the entrance hall. Loud shouts. Startled shouts. What was going on?

Catherine Meriweather rushed toward the front of the house. She should be asking: What *else* was going on? Her cousin Edmund, who had inherited the title of Lord Meriweather from her late father, had let their neighbor Sir Nigel Tresting persuade him that it would be fitting for the new baron to reinstate the old tradition of a Christmas Eve masquerade ball. But why hold it this year when her sister Sophia was getting married just before Christmas? The last Christmas Eve ball at Meriweather Hall had been years before Catherine was born. However, Cousin Edmund had bought the idea completely.

And then promptly handed the planning over to the Meriweather women. Her older sister, Sophia, was busy with her wedding gown, and their mother had gone to York to visit her sister who was recovering from a broken leg. That left Catherine with the responsibility for the assembly, which made no sense. She was the one who often overlooked details, the one who never managed to get anything organized the right way, the one with her head firmly in the clouds…the one whose faith had grown weak, so she did not have God to turn to when she felt overwhelmed. That was most of the time now; yet to leave the matters in Cousin Edmund's hands would be a disaster, because he could not make the simplest decision.

But what was happening in the entrance hall?

"Get him!" That shout rang through the corridor, and she walked a bit faster.

Other voices came quickly. "I got him! No! He got away from me!"

"Grab him! Don't let him get behind you."

"He bit me!"

Gathering her skirt in her hand, she ran toward the commotion. Men stood in the doorway, shouting and pointing and jostling. They paid her no mind when she asked them to let her by. She gritted her teeth, stuck out her elbow and pushed her way past them.

"What is going on?" she asked.

A large dark blur raced toward her.

"No, you don't!" A hand reached out and grabbed at the blur. As it slowed, she realized it was a gangly black-and-white puppy.

Then she looked at the man keeping the puppy from jumping on her, and she gasped in astonishment. Jonathan Bradby was the tallest man in the entrance hall, even taller than Ogden, their butler. His ruddy hair had been blown every which way by the wind, and snow was melting on the shoulders of his dark greatcoat.

And he was the last man she had expected to see at Meriweather Hall today. Mr. Bradby had written in response to the note she had sent him, inviting him to Sanctuary Bay, that he was not able to come for either the wedding or the Christmas Eve ball. He had explained that his work as a solicitor prevented him from leaving Norwich, even for the wedding of one of his best friends. Catherine's sister and her fiancé had been disappointed, and so had Catherine. Mr. Bradby's jests during his previous visit had eased the pain in her heart whenever she thought of her late father or of her dear Roland who had died so far from home during the war.

"Mr. Bradby! What are you doing here?" she asked before she could halt herself.

"At the moment, I am trying to get this horse disguised as a pup under control." He looked toward Foggin, the blond-haired footman. "How badly did he bite you?"

Foggin flushed. "It is nothing. His teeth grazed my hand. He never bit down."

The black-and-white pup pulled away from Mr. Bradby and lunged again at Catherine, yelping in excitement. She sidestepped the ungainly dog before he could jump on her, and then cupped his head to hold him gently in place. He slobbered a kiss on her cheek.

"And who are you?" she asked as she wiped her face.

"An intruder," Mr. Bradby replied. "I would make mention of what the cat dragged in, but I daresay, it was the dog that dragged me in here from the courtyard."

Chuckling at his jest, she said, "I thought— That is, we thought you were not coming."

"I changed my mind when your cousin asked me to come here to advise him on some papers he intends to sign. As I was coming here anyhow, I thought I might as well attend the wedding. I know the banns have not yet been read, but I thought I should take advantage of more clement weather for my journey. As you can see, that did not go according to plan." He shrugged, and melting snow fell off his greatcoat. He pulled it off to reveal that he was dressed conservatively…for him. His coat and breeches were a somber black, but his waistcoat was an eye-scorching yellow with red-and-green embroidery.

"I know the feeling too well." Her laughter faded as her memory spewed forth the day Roland Utting and she had last made plans for their future. He had asked her to wait for him and told her that they would marry when he came back from the war against the French and the Americans. *That* had not gone as they had planned, because, though she had waited, he had never come back, dying in distant America.

"I am dripping on your floors," Mr. Bradby said, forcing away the image of the day when she had believed that God truly wanted her to be happy. "Are the rooms I used before available for me?"

Instead of answering him, she asked, "Who is this big guy?" She patted the puppy between his floppy ears as the footmen and Ogden returned to their duties. The pup rolled onto his back so she could rub his damp belly.

"A stowaway in my carriage."

She bent to pet the puppy's belly and cooed nonsense words, then asked, "A stowaway? I thought that was only for ships."

"I have no other idea how to describe him. He crawled into my carriage after I had stopped at a coaching inn one night. When I went back, the owner told me that the pup was now my problem. I think the inn-keeper was glad for an excuse not to feed him any longer. I stopped at a couple of villages along the way to see if someone wanted a puppy. No one wanted one this big, so he has traveled with me."

"What did you name him?"

"I just call him pup. He seems to like it."

Straightening, she smiled. "Because he knows no better. Don't you think he deserves a name of his own?"

"So far he has chewed one of my boots and two of my socks and swallowed a button that he threw up on my best waistcoat." His tone was grim, but his pale blue eyes twinkled with amusement. "He has left hair on the seat of my carriage and relieved himself on its wheels. I am not sure he *deserves* a name of his own." Despite his complaints, Mr. Bradby tethered himself to the dog with a leash.

Catherine squatted to pat the puppy again. "We shall have to see what name suits him." She stood. "Shall we talk in a warmer part of the house?"

"Of course." He motioned with the hand holding the leash for her to lead the way.

She took a single step before her heel caught on the rough edge of a tile. He grabbed her arm, and his other arm swept around her to keep her from falling. He held her up against his strong chest until she was steady on her feet; then he bent to pick up the leash he had dropped.

"Thank you, Mr. Bradby," she said as she carefully drew herself away from him without looking in his direction.

"I am glad to have been of service. So tell me, how are the wedding plans coming?"

"As well as one can possibly hope." That was not quite the truth, but she was not going to lay all her worries at Mr. Bradby's feet.

"Your cousin tells me that you will be going to London for the opening of Parliament. You must be excited."

She glanced at him, then quickly away. What would he think if she told him that she had a single reason to go to London? She planned to visit the new exhibit at the British Museum of the sculptured panels that once had graced the Parthenon in Athens. The Elgin Marbles, as they were commonly called. She was going to see them, not just for herself, but for Roland who never had the chance.

Dear Roland, the only man who ever understood her love for art and did not consider it worthless. The only man whom she had ever trusted with her heart. She blinked back tears. The two years since his death in battle had not lessened how much she missed Roland.

Instead of answering Mr. Bradby, she ruffled the pup's fur.

His tail wagged so hard it almost became invisible as he looked up at Cat with adoration.

"What do you say, pup," she asked, "if I take you to the kitchen and see what scraps Mrs. Porter has? You can chew on a bone by the fire tonight."

Mr. Bradby shook his head. "You don't need to impose on your cook. He can sleep in the stables with the horses. After all, he is about the same size."

"He may be big, but he is a puppy. It will be very cold outside tonight, and he will be far more comfortable by the kitchen hearth." She smiled at him. "Don't try to change my mind on this."

He grinned back. "Thanks for the warning, Miss Catherine, but to own the truth, I suspect that your cook will soon be begging you to send him to the stables."

"Why?

"He snores. Loudly."

Catherine laughed as they and the pup walked along the corridor toward the kitchen stairs. It *was* good to have Mr. Bradby's sense of humor back under their roof. She was sure to need it in the coming days.

Why was he here?

As Jonathan Bradby strode toward the grand staircase at the front of Meriweather Hall, he reminded himself that he could have ignored the request from Edmund Herriott. He could have remained in his comfortable home in Norwich, where he could admire the cathedral's spire from his office window. Instead, he had driven north along the coast to Meriweather Hall. The estate had been inherited by Herriott—no, he needed to think of him as Meriweather now that he had claimed his title—upon the death of his distant cousin…Miss Catherine's father.

Jonathan had, if he were honest with himself, looked forward to seeing Miss Catherine again. When he had visited the baronial estate two months ago, she had always laughed at his jests rather than looking at him with pity, as others did, when he acted silly.

Acted…

He ground his teeth as his jaw worked. Was he becoming just like the rest of his family? Their lives were one continuous illusion. His siblings played roles, changing like chameleons to attract an admirer with both title and wealth, as they took advantage of the social whirl. Creating such a persona was a skill they had learned from an early age, when their parents had chosen to live separate lives but maintain the image of the perfect family.

Now he had become like them, pretending that a lie was the truth. Everyone believed he was a hero who had saved his best friend's life on the battlefield. If he had spoken up the first time someone had lauded him for saving Northbridge, he would not have to be living now with the abhorrent lie. But he had not admitted that he had stumbled and slammed into the French soldier. It had been enough to keep the Frenchman's sword from slicing off Northbridge's head, leaving his friend only with a scar where the blade had glanced off his cheek.

But that did not make Jonathan a hero. It made him a clumsy oaf, as his father had called him so often, when Jonathan was struggling to get used to growth spurts that had him sprouting up two or more inches seemingly overnight.

He should have told the truth from the beginning. Now it was too late, and he had become the very thing he despised. An illusion that everyone accepted as the truth. He had no idea what his friends would think of him, if they discovered the truth now, but he also did not know how much longer he could live what both he and God knew was a lie. He often wondered if God had let him leave the battlefield alive in order to right the mistake he had made. If so, he was letting God down a second time.

"Bother!" came Miss Catherine's voice through an

open doorway just in front of him. "You didn't do that, did you? I cannot believe this!"

Jonathan waited to hear a reply, but there was none. Curiosity drew him to the door that was flanked by suits of armor. He looked in to see a fire dancing on the white marble hearth. Carved with vines and birds and lush grapes, it was too ornate for his taste. Books covered every shelf in the bookcases that lined the other walls, and more were piled on the floor and on the overstuffed chairs.

Cat stood by a rosewood desk covered with stacks of papers, her fists clenched on one pile. *Cat.* He had not thought of Catherine's childhood nickname since he had left Meriweather Hall, but it suited her. She was small, at least a foot shorter than his six-foot-four height, and her black hair was as sleek as a cat's fur. Instead of green eyes, she had earth-brown ones. Yet they sparked like a cat's when her emotions were high, as they were now.

"Is everything all right?" he asked from the doorway.

She whirled, her eyes wide.

"I didn't mean to startle you," he said.

"I was lost in thought." Her voice was filled with frustration. "I was doing some work for the Christmas Eve ball."

He stepped into the room. "And it sounds as if there is a problem."

"It would appear that Cousin Edmund forgot that he had asked me to send out invitations to the wedding and the assembly. I spent hours on them. If I had not had Vera's help, I doubt I could have gotten them done on time."

He nodded, recalling that Vera Fenwick, the vicar's sister, was Cat's bosom-bow. "I see."

"No, you don't." She pushed away from the desk and leaned her fists on the back of one of the chairs. "I am receiving replies from invitations that I did not send, people telling me that they are delighted to attend. All I can figure is that, after asking me to handle the invitations, Cousin Edmund went ahead and invited more people without telling me."

Jonathan tried to quell the smile that tickled his lips.

She must have noticed his efforts because she grimaced. "I know it sounds petty, but I had everything planned out. And now…"

"Now you have to make a change in plans."

"Yes, and that is far less simple than it sounds."

"Poor Meriweather," he said. "He cannot make up his mind whom to invite, so he invited everyone."

Cat's shoulders eased from their rigid line. "I didn't think of it that way. Oh, dear! What a muddle this has become! To say something to him would be cruel, so I will endeavor to make the adjustments without bothering him." She sighed. "I hope he will not regret avoiding that decision when the rest of our guests start to arrive, and we don't have enough room for everyone." She glanced toward the window. "Although if it keeps snowing like this, I wonder who will come."

"You sound hopeful."

Catherine smiled at his jesting tone. "I didn't intend it that way. I want everything to be perfect for Sophia and Charles."

He chuckled. "Would you like some advice I received from a very wise man?"

"I can use all the advice I can get." She sat on the chair and tilted her head back to look up at him.

Sitting in the chair that faced hers, Jonathan said, "A very wise man told me that nothing goes smoothly, but if the other party never sees the mistake, because you have remedied it, then the mistake never happened. At least in the other's mind."

"Who told you that?"

"Mr. Lippincott, the man I read the law with." He leaned toward her, putting his hands on his thighs, so her nose and his were an inch apart. His voice dropped to a rumbling whisper. "He gave me that counsel when I first began to work on my own. I was so afraid of making an error, I could do nothing. Once I took his words to heart, I found it much simpler."

"That is good advice." Her voice was uneven as she slanted away from him. "I will try to remember it, but I just want everything to be perfect."

He was astonished. He could not imagine any of his six siblings going to such lengths to help someone else. They had been derisive both when he had decided to study law and when he had bought his commission to serve in the army. That he had come home as a hero had silenced them somewhat.

If they knew the truth…

He pushed that thought aside and affixed a smile on his lips again. "Good, and never forget that, if the burden becomes too much to bear, you need not shoulder everything alone."

"I know. The household staff—"

He shook his head. "I was speaking of handing the problem over to God. With His help, there is nothing you cannot accomplish."

Cat looked down at her hands in her lap. They were clenched so tightly that her knuckles were white.

What had he said to distress her so? He waited for her to answer or to look at him. An icy chill flowed through him. Maybe he should offer to leave so someone else might use his rooms. When he said as much, she shook her head.

"No, don't even suggest that." She raised her eyes, and he was almost staggered by the pain within them. Had he caused it? He prayed not. "I know Charles and Sophia would be hurt if you departed before their wedding," she said.

"All right. I won't say that again, but, for what it is worth, I will be glad to do what I can to help you deal with these complications. If I could organize a company of soldiers, I daresay I should be able to help organize a party."

"Two, actually."

He chuckled. "Of course, I may make a complete muddle of any task you give me."

"You would do a fine job, but I cannot ask you. You are our guest."

"Northbridge and your cousin are closer to me than my brothers, so I don't consider myself a guest. More like family." He almost gagged on the word. He thanked God that Northbridge and Meriweather were not like his real family.

He had to own that one of the reasons he did not want to leave Meriweather Hall now was that his family might decide to come from London to spend Christmas with him in Norwich. Within hours of their arrival, someone would get into a brangle with someone else, and any chance of a pleasant Christmas would be lost…

as it had been since his boyhood, when his father and his mother had decided to live separate lives.

"In that case," Cat said, her smile returning, "I am sure I will be able to find so much for you to do that you shall regret your generous offer. You must promise me that, if at any time you grow tired of the planning, you will let me know straightaway."

"I shall, but I am glad to help with the ball and the wedding and the holiday planning."

"And the upcoming London Season."

His stomach tried to tie itself into a knot. "The Season? Are you planning to go to London for that as well as the opening of Parliament?"

"Yes. Cousin Edmund is arranging for a house for us, and Sophia and Charles will join us there. I hear one can go from one event to the next for weeks. It sounds quite exhausting. And the preparations?" She shook her head. "Hannibal got his elephants through the Alps with less trouble, but Sophia and Cousin Edmund assure me that all of it is necessary."

Jonathan stopped listening as he recalled his younger sibling, the baby sister of the family, Gwendolyn, and her dearest friend, Augusta Williams, saying much the same thing before their first Season. He and Gwendolyn were the youngest children in their family with a gap of almost a decade between them and their other siblings. Growing up, they had been as thick as peas in their pods. She had introduced him to Augusta, and their duo became a trio. And, as he grew from boy to man, Jonathan had lost his heart to pretty blonde Augusta.

Then the two young women had been fired off into the Polite World in London. Two warmhearted, sweet young girls had altered before his eyes into a pair of coquettes who were happy only when they had several men dangling after them. His sister had married a viscount with plump pockets, pretending she would have chosen him even if he did not have a farthing. Jonathan might have believed that if he had not overheard her bragging to their older sisters about how her husband was buying her a house on Berkeley Square where she could host the best gatherings in London.

And Augusta… No, he would not think about the woman who had broken his heart in the weeks before he had bought his commission and headed for the Continent—with the intention of showing her that she was wrong to dismiss him as no longer worthy of her time or interest.

Would Cat be beguiled by the illusions and rich rewards of the *ton* as his sister and Augusta had been? As his whole family had been? He should warn Cat, but as he raised his gaze to her animated face, he wondered if he would be wasting his breath. He had to try. For her sake. She had treated him with kindness, both on his previous visit and now.

He started to speak but halted at the clump of boots. Later, he promised himself. Later he would try to warn her about the way the Beau Monde could change a person. But would she heed him? Neither Augusta nor Gwendolyn had, and his heart still ached from the loss.

Jonathan stood and smiled when Edmund Herriott, now properly addressed as Lord Meriweather, walked past the door, paused, then came in. Jonathan's smile faded when he saw the dark gray circles under his shorter friend's eyes and the lines that had not been gouged into his face the last time Jonathan had visited. Was Meriweather's mantle of responsibilities as the new baron too much for him?

Then Meriweather grinned, and the anxiety vanished. He shook himself like a wet dog. Snow flew in every direction, and he pushed his tawny hair from his eyes as he came forward, his hand outstretched.

"Bradby! I see that you changed your mind and have come to join in the excitement. I thought if I offered you the right bait, you would bite."

Jonathan did not let his smile waver when Cat's eyes widened. Did she think that her cousin had used *her* as the bait to entice him to North Yorkshire? Or was she struggling to hold back her vexation with her cousin's impetuous act of sending out his own invitations to everyone he knew?

"Dashed cold out there," Meriweather continued as the two men shook hands, and Jonathan guessed he had not noticed his cousin's reaction. "But at least it has stopped snowing." He shrugged off his greatcoat, sending more flakes tumbling to the floor. "I left the carriage at Sir Nigel's. Once the roads have cleared, he will send it over with one of his grooms. I wanted to get back as soon as possible." With a laugh, he added, "You know how Sir Nigel can go on and on about absolutely nothing, especially when it comes to his paintings."

Jonathan grimaced. He had met the baronet only once, but that had been more than enough. Sir Nigel styled himself a great artist and displayed his work as if some great Renaissance painter had created it. The truth was the art lacked any semblance of skill that Jonathan could perceive.

He put the baronet out of his mind when Cat stood and asked them to excuse her. She fired a quick glance in his direction, and he guessed she did not want him to say anything to her cousin about the invitations Meriweather had sent. Whether she wanted to speak to her cousin privately, or she realized that there was nothing that could be changed at this point, he would acquiesce. He gave her a nod, wondering if she saw it as she hurried out of the room.

Meriweather took one look at the pile of letters on the desk and motioned for Jonathan to follow him from the room. He mumbled something about the room was better fit for ladies than the two of them.

Once they were a ways down the corridor, Meriweather said, "I didn't want to say anything in front of my cousin, but this time Sir Nigel did not prattle about his paintings."

"Because you discussed the smugglers?" During his previous visit, the smugglers in Sanctuary Bay had trespassed on Meriweather Hall lands, and he knew Meriweather was as determined to put a halt to them as his predecessor had been. It appeared that Meriweather's efforts had been as futile as those of the previous baron.

"We did talk about the smugglers. Some." He shuddered. "But his real interest was talking about his greatniece. I think he said her name is Lillian. He seems to believe that she would be very eager to marry a baron who lives close to her great-uncle."

In spite of his efforts not to, Jonathan laughed. "Some woman is always expecting you to marry her. First, the elder Miss Meriweather, whom everyone assumed you would marry after you inherited the title from her father."

"Not everyone, because Northbridge won her heart."

"True. However, there is now this unknown great-niece who has decided you would be a good husband. You have become, it would appear, quite the irresistible man."

"'Tis no joking matter."

"Quite to the contrary," Jonathan said. "It is highly amusing when *you* are the focus of the matchmaking."

"When I decide to marry, it will be *my* decision. No one else's."

"Not even the young lady's?"

Meriweather let loose a loud laugh. "Ah, Bradby, I have missed you and your bizarre sense of humor. Come in here."

He went into a chamber across from the dining room. The aroma of coffee wafted around them, but Jonathan paid it no mind as he looked at the center of the room.

An elegant billiards table claimed most of the space. The oak had been carved with the Meriweather family's crest, and additional images from the moors and the sea. A cast iron rack holding the cues was set in one corner. The balls were scattered across the table's top.

"I don't remember this from my other visit," Jonathan said.

"It was delivered last month." Meriweather draped his coat over a chair by the hearth.

"When did you decide to order it?" He was careful not to put emphasis on *decide* because he did not want to upset his friend, but he could not imagine how Meriweather had chosen to order a billiards table when he could not make any decision.

With a sheepish smile, Meriweather said, "Actually it was ordered by my predecessor. No one knew about it until the table arrived. The craftsmen were very slow workers, but they did a fine job, don't you think?"

Jonathan ran his hand along the smooth edge of the table. "I agree. Excellent work." Looking across it to his friend, he asked, "So don't you think it is time you tell me why you were so insistent that I come to Meriweather Hall?"

"I told you in the letter I sent. I could use your advice on certain matters to do with the estate and with my construction business."

"And that could not wait until after Christmastide?"

His friend's smile became a guilty one. "You have caught me out. You and Northbridge and I have been through so much together. I did not think we should abandon him on his way to the altar."

"You sound as if he is about to meet the hangman." He leaned against the billiards table. "I am surprised he didn't marry your cousin Sophia before he left for his estate."

"Sophia wished for her mother to be out of mourning, so she could attend the ceremony. Then there are all the plans the ladies like in order for everything to be as complicated as possible. Catherine is so focused on the events that the slightest problem or change can send her up to the boughs."

Jonathan bit his tongue to keep from saying that Meriweather was one of the reasons Cat was stressed. Rather, he said, "I am sure the wedding and the ball will be successes. I have offered to do my bit to help Miss Cat—Catherine."

"You are a braver man than I am, Bradby." He slapped him on the back. "But we knew that already, didn't we?"

Here it was. His chance to tell the truth. His chance to clear his conscience.

Again, as he had done too often, he hesitated. He should tell Meriweather the truth straightaway.

Unless...

He began to smile and nodded as his friend suggested a game of billiards. Going to the rack, he lifted out a cue. The solution was so simple that he was unsure why he had not considered it before.

He would never have to reveal the truth if he proved to everyone—and himself—that he deserved the title of hero. He hefted the cue and smiled.

After all, how hard could it be to become a true hero?

Chapter Two

The eaves outside Catherine's bedroom windows dripped in a steady rhythm two days after the snow had stopped, and Mr. Bradby had returned to Meriweather Hall. The sun glittered on snow that had fallen from the trees and bushes. Puddles were forming on the garden paths, and she guessed by late afternoon that most of the snow would have melted.

She looked down at her shoes and then paused. Between the sloppy snow and the sand along the shore, she risked ruining anything she wore on her feet. She needed footwear that would not work as sponges, so she reached into her cupboard and pulled out a pair of old boots.

She pulled them on, and thereafter she went to the closest window and opened it. Cold air swept her breath away. She hastily shut the window. She had not realized it was so chilly. The dripping eaves had suggested it was much warmer.

She pushed away from the window. No matter. She would go ahead with her plans to visit the beach below the village farther north along Sanctuary Bay. If her bosom-bow, Vera, did not want to leave her cozy fire and join her, then Catherine would go on her own.

Buttoning on a heavy pelisse and wrapping a scarf around her neck, while taking care not to knock off her wool bonnet, she then grabbed a pair of thick gloves from her dressing table. She smiled when she opened the door and saw a small pail waiting by her door. Ogden had remembered that she liked to search the beach after a powerful storm.

Catherine swung the wooden bucket by its handle as she walked down the stairs. She half-expected the puppy to bound up the stairs as he did each time she came down. Glancing into the large parlor, she saw the huge black-and-white pup lying in front of the hearth. He looked up, wagged his tail a couple of times and then went back to sleep. That was a relief because she did not want the pup along today.

She heard the rattle of harnesses and wheels, and smiled again, knowing the carriage she had requested to be ready this morning would be waiting for her. If only the plans for the wedding and the Christmas Eve ball would go as smoothly…

No! She was going to have positive thoughts today. If she found what she sought on the shore, then that would be one task she could cross off her list.

Foggin was waiting by the door and opened it for her when she approached. She urged him to shut it quickly, because he already looked half-frozen.

The closed carriage was waiting in front of her, and she rushed toward it. Before she reached it, she heard her name called. She looked over her shoulder to see Mr. Bradby coming around the corner of the house. He was bundled up as much as she was, and she recognized him because of his height and his red hair which peeked around a scarf that was the brightest orange she had ever seen.

"I did not expect to see you outside on this blustery day," he said when he was close enough, so he did not have to shout.

She was startled to have him address her. Since Cousin Edmund's return, Mr. Bradby had spoken less than a dozen words to her. She had caught a glimpse of him turning in the opposite direction when their paths through Meriweather Hall were about to intersect. He and her cousin had not dined with the Meriweather women for the past evenings, offering polite excuses. When she came down for breakfast, if Mr. Bradby was at the table, he hurried to finish and left after saying a cheery "Good morning." She had tried to guess what she had done to vex him, but nothing came to mind.

"Where are you bound?" she asked in lieu of a direct response.

He drew down his scarf so his face was visible. He gave her a smile that seemed to make the wind a smidgen less biting. "Just out to get some fresh air. I thought I might walk along the shore."

"Vera Fenwick and I are going to the beach. I want to pick up some mermaid tears."

"What?" His smile was replaced by puzzlement.

"That is what we call broken pieces of glass that wash up on the shore. The edges have been smoothed, so it reflects the light in a pretty way." She caught her bonnet before the wind could pluck it off her head and quickly retied it under her chin. "The best time to find them is the first low tide after a storm. That is in about an hour or so. Would you like to join Vera and me?"

"It sounds like fun. However, I don't want to encroach upon your outing."

"Nonsense! The more eyes the better." Maybe if she persuaded him to spend time with her, then she could ferret out why he had been avoiding her. "I have been collecting mermaid tears since Sophia and Charles announced their betrothal, but I need many more pieces to decorate the wedding breakfast tables."

He grinned. "Like I said, that sounds like fun. I will help you search for your mermaid tears." He glanced at the carriage. "Is Meriweather going somewhere again today?"

"I am using the carriage because the best place to find the glass is on the beach at the bottom of the village. We seldom find any pieces beneath the cliffs here. The currents wash all jetsam toward the village."

A gust of wind silenced whatever Mr. Bradby might have answered. Instead, he reached a long arm past her to open the carriage door. He held out his other hand to assist her in.

She thanked him with a smile and placed her hand on his. Some sensation that had no name but was undeniably pleasurable shimmered up her arm, starting at the very spot her palm sat atop his. As he handed her up onto the first step, he edged closer. All his usual good humor vanished.

She should withdraw her hand from his, but she could not make her arm move. She could only stare into his eyes that were level with her own. For the first time, she noticed the navy ringing the pale blue. She had never seen eyes like his. And she had never before felt like she stood on the very edge of the cliff and could tumble over at any moment.

With that thought, Catherine jerked her hand away so quickly she almost fell off the carriage step. He looked at her in astonishment, but, gathering what was left of her composure, she climbed in and sat on the black velvet seat. She stared at her clasped fingers on her lap.

Why was she thinking such thoughts? Jonathan Bradby wore his Christian faith proudly and spoke of prayer with ease. When she had lamented about wanting everything perfect for Sophia and Charles, Jonathan had advised her to turn her problems over to God as if he did so all the time. She did not want to imagine how he would look at her if she admitted her own faith had faltered. And he was a warrior just as Roland had been. Even though England was now at peace, there were still rumbles of discontent on the Continent. Napoleon had been exiled to Saint Helena, ten thousand miles from Sanctuary Bay, but he had escaped banishment once. If he did again, the war might flair up anew, and any man who answered the call to battle might not come back.

Just as Roland had not.

She must guard her heart as closely as the king's soldiers watched over Napoleon on that speck of an island in the South Atlantic. Risking it again for a soldier would be stupid. She could enjoy Mr. Bradby's company and his jokes, but nothing more.

It was a good plan, and it allowed her to smile when he stepped into the carriage. He closed the door and gestured toward the empty space beside her.

"May I?" he asked as the coachee set the carriage in motion.

She nodded. *Stick to your plan,* she reminded herself.

"First," she said, "we must stop for Vera, then go to the shore at the foot of the village."

"Down that steep, steep, steep and twisting, twisting, twisting street?" He gave an emoted groan and stretched his arm along the back of the seat.

"It is not the going down that bothers most folks, though I would never suggest we take a carriage down that steep street. It is the walking back up."

"Either way is bad. Whoever decided to put a village on the side of a curving cliff must have enjoyed seeing people suffer."

Catherine laughed at his droll expression. His eyes twinkled when he smiled more broadly. As he continued to joke, she matched him jest for jest. Soon both of them were laughing so hard that Catherine had to wipe tears from the corners of her eyes before the chill wind froze them there.

The journey across the ridge and back toward the church near the top of the sea cliffs went so quickly that Catherine was astonished. Usually she was impatient during the ride that could take an hour or more. With Mr. Bradby entertaining her with witticisms, the time had rushed past.

The carriage slowed to a stop in front of the flint vicarage half-hidden behind the squat stone church. Small windows were set deep into the walls, and the wooden door was in the need of paint. Nothing near the shore could keep paint on for very long, because the salt on the wind scoured it off like pots being scrubbed in the scullery.

Mr. Bradby assisted Catherine out, but did not hold her hand any longer than propriety allowed.

Catherine knocked on the vicarage's door, then wrapped her arms around herself as a gust of wind sifted through her coat and scarf. Maybe going to the beach today was not such a good idea. She hoped the high cliffs edging the bay would lessen the wind along the shore.

A curtain shifted in the nearby window, and Catherine saw her friend's face. Moments later, the door opened.

"Come in, come in," Vera called in her cheerful voice. "Mr. Bradby! I hadn't heard that you had returned to Sanctuary Bay. Do watch your head."

Catherine knew the warning was not for her. She was short enough so the low rafters in the vicarage's ceiling presented no problem for her. Though her tall sister Sophia's head just cleared them, Mr. Bradby had to duck. Even so, his shoulder bumped a hanging lamp, sending light and shadows ricocheting around the room. Comfortable, well-worn furniture along with stacks and stacks of books and papers were lit, then lost again to the shadows.

He reached out to steady the lamp and apologized. "Sorry."

"Think nothing of it," Vera said as she retrieved her coat. "I keep asking my brother to move it, but though his intentions are good, the needs of the parish always demand every moment of his time."

"Vera," Catherine said, "I would be glad to send someone to handle small tasks like that for you."

"I know, but I never think of it until someone hits the lamp."

"If you would like," Mr. Bradby said, "I can move it for you. All I need is a hammer, if you have one."

"I do." Vera dimpled before she disappeared past a curtain hanging in a doorway. Even before it stopped rippling, she pushed back into the room. "Here you go."

Mr. Bradby removed his gloves and stuffed them into his greatcoat's pocket. He took the hammer in one hand as he lifted the lamp off its hook with the other. When he offered the lamp to Catherine, he jerked his fingers back as a spark jumped between them.

"Ouch!" they said at the same time.

He grinned. "Warn me next time before you decide to play flint to my steel, Miss Catherine."

Warmth climbed her face. She hoped it was from the fire on the nearby hearth and not from a blush. She moved out of the way as Mr. Bradby made quick work of removing the hook that had held the lamp and then hammered it back into the spot over a pair of chairs that Vera pointed to. He held out his hand for the lamp, and Catherine gave it to him, taking care not to let his fingers graze hers again.

He smiled as he hung it, holding his hand under it until he was sure it was secure. "There. Better?"

"Mr. Bradby, you are clearly a man of many talents," Vera gushed as she took the hammer and set it on the kitchen table beside a piece of paper with her brother's name on it. Vera always let her brother know where she was going and when she expected to return.

He wove his fingers together and pressed them outward before bowing toward her. "I appreciate your commendation, Miss Fenwick."

"Thank you so much for helping. You most definitely are a hero of the first color."

Catherine saw a ruddy tint rising up the back of his neck. She had not guessed that Vera's compliment would put him to the blush. Hoping to ease his discomfort, she hurried to say, "We should not delay any longer, if we want to find the mermaid tears before the tide starts coming back in."

"An excellent idea," Vera said.

"Ah, that steep hill." Mr. Bradby's grumble set them all to laughing.

Catherine's eyes were caught by his, and she saw his gratitude in them. She was unsure why, but asking might be the most want-witted thing she could do.

Jonathan was pleased that the wind was not as vicious along the shore. It was blocked by the high cliffs and the houses clinging to the ess-shaped street that dropped down through the village. Waves thundered against the stones at the bottom of the street, and melting snow made rivulets down the cliffs to pool on the sand. The fishermen's deep boats, which were called cobles, had been pulled out of the tide's reach, their single rudder tilted up to keep it out of the water and sand. Fishing nets were draped over every surface, even hanging from the cliffs where the water from the beck oozed out where the small stream had been redirected under the houses.

He nodded toward the fishermen who were mending their nets and cleaning their boats. Gulls hopped around and soared overhead on the sea wind, waiting for any morsel of fish they could snatch. When one of the fishermen dunked a rag in the small stream of water emerging from under the nets and flowing into the sea, Jonathan wondered exactly where it ran beneath the village. He remembered learning on his last visit that the beck, which is what the locals called a stream, had been built over in order to allow for more houses in the crowded village. He also recalled the elder Miss Meriweather's dismay at the thought of investigating the waterway, because it was rumored there was also a passage the smugglers used for moving their illegal wares.

"Don't you find it curious," he asked quietly, "that everyone knows there must be a tunnel near here but everybody acts as if it does not exist?"

Miss Fenwick clamped her lips closed as her gaze shifted to the fishermen.

Cat said only, "I do not have to see something to know it is there."

"So you *do* believe the smugglers have access under the village?" he asked in a near whisper.

She put her finger to her lips. "Don't speak of that here. Too many ears could be listening." She glanced toward the fishermen and then at the houses rising above them on the cliff.

Jonathan had no idea which houses in the village—maybe only a few or maybe all of them—sheltered smugglers. He looked from Cat to Miss Fenwick, who wore a fearful expression, then nodded. "We will save the discussion for Meriweather Hall. Why don't you show me how to find mermaid tears?"

"It is simple."

"Then I should be well suited for the task." His jesting brought smiles back to both women.

Could finding the tunnel and exposing the route the smugglers took be the way to prove he was a hero? Jonathan discounted that idea immediately. Not a soul along Sanctuary Bay doubted its existence, so uncovering it would not earn him the legitimate title of hero.

Lord, there must be a way to make this lie into the truth. Please show me how. His steps were lighter as he raised the prayer up. Surely God would not want him to live falsely.

As he followed Cat south along the curve of the beach, Jonathan stared across the wild waves to the headland where Meriweather Hall stood like the bastion it once had been. Pirates and other raiders had come from the sea and across the moors, and the great house had provided a refuge for nearby farmers and fishermen. Now the sun glinted off the hall's many windows as if stars had fallen from the sky to take up residence in the walls.

"Show me what I am supposed to do," he said.

"Finding mermaid tears," Cat replied, pulling off her gloves and dropping them in the bottom of the bucket, "requires you to walk very slowly with your head down while you scan the sand. When you see a sparkle, check to see if it is glass."

"Like this one!" Miss Fenwick bent and picked up something from the sand. "Oh, it is only a piece of shell." She tossed it back to the ground.

"Where do you want me to look?" he asked.

Cat pointed to small stones that had been left in a line along the beach. "Why don't you start there? I will follow the other line of stones closer to the water, and Vera can search next to the cliffs."

Even though he would have preferred to walk beside Cat so he could admire her pretty face, Jonathan moved to the strip of stones. "This is a great length of beach," he called over the rhythmic crash of the waves. "How long do we have before the tide comes in?"

Cat put her hand to her forehead to shade her eyes. "At least a couple of hours. I can still see the scaurs even though the waves are high."

He copied her motion so he could see through the sun's glare on the waves. "What is a scaur?"

"That rocky ridge in the harbor, the one the waves are breaking over." She walked toward him so they did not have to shout. "Papa told me that the word derives from a Viking one for rock. *Scaur...*" She said the word slowly as if tasting how it felt on her lips.

He quickly looked away. He should not be thinking of her lips or any woman's. Not while he clung to his lie. He repeated his prayer silently, hoping he would be shown the right path soon.

"Found one!" Cat held up a piece of glass no bigger than his smallest fingernail. "A green one."

"May I?" asked Jonathan.

She placed the mermaid tear in his hand. The edges were as smooth as if they had been ground by a machine. Its time in the sea had given it a milky color. When he held it up and looked through it, he could see it had been pitted and scraped by salt and sand.

"Isn't it lovely?" Cat asked.

"I had no idea that glass would look like that after being in the sea." He dropped the piece in her hand and watched as she put it with care into the bucket. "Are they all that size?"

"All different sizes." She motioned along the beach. "And various colors, so don't assume it is not glass simply because it is white or brown."

For the next hour, Jonathan walked along the beach

between the two women. He had a difficult time concentrating on his task. Rather than look at the stone-strewn sand, he would prefer to admire Cat. Her cheeks were burnished by the wind, and her laugh lightened his heart. Each time she glanced in his direction, he hurriedly shifted his gaze back to the ground.

Why hadn't he told her about his concerns with her embarking on a Season in London? He had had the perfect opportunity when they rode from Meriweather Hall to the vicarage. He should have said something, but he had enjoyed laughing along with her too much to bring up the dreary subject. And what could he have said? *Don't go to London and let the Beau Monde change you as it changed my sister. As it cost me the one woman I loved.*

But it had taught him an important lesson. He would be a cabbage-head to lose his heart again to any woman who was part of the *ton*. If his heart had half the sense God gave a goose, it would lead him to a sensible woman like Vera Fenwick, who had no aspirations of a Season in London. Or perhaps he should emulate his mentor Lippincott and become a confirmed bachelor.

He needed to concentrate on the task at hand, but he found himself growing more frustrated. Because he did not find any mermaid tears? Or because he was close to Cat but too far away to chat with her without shouting?

As if she had heard his thoughts, she called, "Have you found anything?"

"I think," he said, "I need to borrow some of the pieces *you* have found, so I might make a pair of spectacles out of them." He paused, pretending to be deep in thought before adding, "Though it might not be wise to don what so many call barnacles when yon fishermen are scraping one and the same off their boats."

That set both Cat and Miss Fenwick to laughing. Jonathan joined in, but his own laughter was forced. The jokes flowed off his lips without him being able to halt them. He would prefer to speak to Cat of things that mattered to her and to him. Instead, whenever he longed to say something serious to her, a jest burst from him.

Bowing his head, he continued to walk along the shore. Now he wanted to escape his own weakness, a legacy from the war that no medicine could cure.

He gave an exultant shout a short time later when, for the first time, he picked up a glittering tidbit and found it was a mermaid tear. Putting it in his pocket, he went on, becoming more adept at determining which pieces were glass and which were broken shells.

He heard a sharp cry. A gull? He looked up, but did not see any of the sea birds overhead. They still circled around the fishermen, eager for an easy meal.

Miss Fenwick yelled and pointed at the sea. Shading his eyes again, he looked in that direction. Something dark bobbed on the waves. A seal?

The cry came again, and he saw arms waving next to the dark spot on the water.

It was a child!

Being swept out to sea!

Jonathan did not hesitate. Here was his chance to prove to God and himself that he was worthy of being called a hero. Shrugging off his coat, he shoved it into Miss Fenwick's hands as she ran toward him.

"Don't dump the glass out of the pockets," he warned, as he yanked off one boot and then the other.

He threw them onto the beach and ran toward the water. He heard shouts behind him. The only voice he recognized was Cat's, but he did not slow. The child might be dragged down by the next wave.

The icy water froze his toes within seconds, and he gasped with the shock of the cold when he dove beneath the next wave. He fought the water's pull that tried to send him back to the shore. Cutting as fast as he dared through the water, he heard more shouts. The words were lost to the wind and the sea. He looked up every few strokes to make sure he was headed in the right direction.

The child was being pulled out to sea faster than Jonathan was swimming. He sliced through the next wave and did not pause to raise his head. Ice seemed to be forming around his toes and fingers, and he had to fight to keep them moving. He could not slow. He had to get to the child. He had to save the child. Then he would be a hero.

Save the child.

Be a hero.

Save the child.

Be a hero.

He kept repeating that in his mind in time with his strokes to keep himself from slowing as the cold water began to gnaw at him.

Something splashed in the water beside him. The child! Had he reached the child?

He raised his head, shocked by how much energy the simple motion demanded. Instead of a child, he saw a coble.

A hand appeared in front of his nose, and he halted.

"Hey up, mate," called a voice from above him. "Grab on and climb up."

"Save the child," he said. Or he tried to say it, but the words blurred through his chattering teeth.

The four fishermen in the coble must have guessed what he meant because one said in a heavy Yorkshire accent, "The barn is gat."

"What?"

"The barn is gat." The hand gestured toward where the child had been.

He saw another boat there. Two men were lifting the youngster out of the water and into that boat.

With a sigh, Jonathan nodded. The man's strange words must have been telling him that the child had been saved. Grasping the man's hand, he let himself be pulled up into the boat. He shivered in the bottom of the deep boat until someone tossed him a blanket that stunk of fish scales and sweat. He did not care, as he pulled it around his shoulders.

He said nothing, as the men rowed back to the shore where Cat and Miss Fenwick paced uneasily. What was he going to say to them? Now he recalled Cat's shout. Most likely she had been trying to tell him that the fishermen were far more experienced than he was in saving someone in the sea. Not only had they rescued the child but him.

This hero stuff was going to be harder than he had guessed.

Chapter Three

As soon as the coble was pulled up on the beach, Catherine ran toward it, pausing only to pick up Mr. Bradby's boots. She reached the boat at the same time Mr. Bradby was stepping over its high side. He wobbled, and she grasped his elbow to keep him from collapsing to the sand. A tingle swept up her arm, just as it had when he had handed her into the carriage back at Meriweather Hall, but this time she did not release her hold on his arm. Ignoring the delightful sensation, she focused on him.

He was dripping, even though the blanket had soaked up some water from his clothes. His sleeves were already stiffening from the salt and the chilly wind. When she proffered his boots, he snatched them and upended both to shake any sand out.

"That was the bravest thing I have ever seen," Catherine said.

He tried to reply, but his words were garbled by his chattering teeth. When triumphant shouts came from closer to the village, he looked past her.

She turned, not letting go of his arm, to see another

coble sliding onto the stones at the bottom of the street. A little boy was plucked out of the boat and handed to his mother who hugged him close, even as she scolded him for going too close to the water. Both mother and son were wrapped in more blankets as the rescuers led them up the steep street.

The men with Mr. Bradby slapped him companionably on the back. They started to make a few jokes at his expense but stopped at a firm look from Catherine. Or it might have been the pastor's sister coming to join them. The fishermen put their fingers to the brims of their floppy hats, before they pushed the coble back into the waves and rowed toward the village.

Vera draped Mr. Bradby's coat over his shoulders. "Can you walk?"

"Of course." His words were clipped.

When he did not move, Catherine asked, "Do you need help with your boots?"

"I can manage quite well on my own." He looked at her for the first time since he had come ashore. Anger blazed from his eyes. "If you would be so kind as to release my arm…"

Catherine jerked away, startled as much that she still held on to him as by his terse words. When he swayed again as he pulled on first one boot, then the other, she grabbed his arm before he could fall on his face. She let go quickly, but he still glared in her direction before stamping away along the sand. He started to pull on his coat, then slung it over his shoulder.

"What is upsetting him?" Vera asked as she and Catherine followed.

"I have no idea. Maybe he is annoyed that he didn't get to rescue the child himself."

"What does it matter who saved the child? We must be grateful to the good Lord that the child is safe along with Mr. Bradby and the other brave rescuers. God is good to heed our prayers."

"Yes." She envied Vera's unshakable belief that God listened to each of her supplications.

Vera frowned. "I never imagined Mr. Bradby using such an icy tone. When last he called at Meriweather Hall, he was jolly and joking. Now he is grim."

"I know." Catherine had no other answer. She was as baffled as her bosom-bow.

Something must have happened out in the water that they had not been privy to on the shore. She could not imagine what that might be nor could she ask Mr. Bradby when fishermen still gathered at the foot of the street.

When the men called out greetings to Mr. Bradby, he nodded in their direction but did not speak. He remained mute as they climbed the steep street. A trail of drips marked his uneven steps. Several times Catherine had to steady him, and she heard exhaustion in his breathing as they crossed the bridge over the beck. He muttered something when Catherine linked her arm with his when he stumbled yet again.

"You may be petulant if you choose," she said, giving him a frown as fierce as his, "but *I* choose not to see you fall on your nose."

Vera looped her arm through his other arm, silencing any further protests from Mr. Bradby.

They reeled up the steepest part of the street, which seemed as vertical as the cliffs beyond the village. Catherine doubted Mr. Bradby could have made the climb on his own. His steps slowed, and he was panting by the time they reached the top. With the coachee's help and Vera's, Catherine assisted Mr. Bradby into the carriage. He sat heavily and leaned his head back against the seat.

Vera caught Catherine's arm before she entered the carriage. Catherine looked at her, surprised, and asked, "What is it?"

"I will walk to the vicarage," Vera said, as she dug into her pocket and pulled out a handful of mermaid tears. She placed them carefully in Catherine's hand. "You are welcome to bring him there, if you wish."

"I think it would be for the best to take him to Meriweather Hall where he won't have to go back out in the cold again, just as he is getting warmed up."

"I agree." She glanced at the carriage. "I thought you might want a haven, too."

Catherine smiled. "I am sure his usual good humor will return once he has dry clothing and something warm inside him."

Vera nodded but did not look convinced.

Rightly so, Catherine discovered, when she climbed into the carriage. Mr. Bradby neither looked in her direction nor did he speak all the way back to Meriweather Hall. The damp wind coming off the sea was cold but not as frosty as the silence in the carriage. Catherine tried to start a conversation once and then gave up. Even when the carriage turned through the gates of Meriweather Hall, he said nothing.

She got out on her own and directed the footman who came to greet the carriage to assist Mr. Bradby. Hurrying inside, she gave instructions to another footman to have tea and bottles filled with hot water delivered to his chambers.

Only when she was going upstairs did she remember that she had not thanked Mr. Bradby for helping her and Vera collect mermaid tears. Her steps faltered, but she kept going. She did not have the courage to face him again, when he was in such a snappish mood.

She was going so quickly that she almost ran into her sister who was coming in the opposite direction at an equally determined pace.

"Where have you been?" asked Sophia. "I have been looking everywhere in the house for you."

"I was—"

Her sister gave Catherine no chance to explain. "You should have told me where you had gone," said Sophia, usually so calm, as she rubbed her hands together anxiously. Everything about the upcoming wedding seemed to leave her on edge. "Mme. Dupont is furious that you have missed another fitting. You know we have barely six weeks to get everything done."

Catherine sighed. "I forgot about this morning's fittings. We went down to the beach, and our appointment with Mme. Dupont slipped my mind."

"The beach? Why would you go to the beach on such a blustery day?"

"For your wedding breakfast. I know how you love mermaid tears, so I've been collecting them since you announced your betrothal. Think how pretty they will look scattered on the tables."

Sophia's eyes grew round. "What a wonderful idea! Oh, I wished I had your artistic imagination. I never would have thought of such a thing." She swept her sister into a big embrace. "I'm so glad to have you overseeing the wedding breakfast. It will be unforgettable."

"Yes, it will." She hoped it would be memorable for

the right reasons, rather than the fact that she had made a muddle of it. "We were able to find quite a bit. Vera joined us looking for the pieces of glass."

"Us?"

"Mr. Bradby helped, too."

A smile brightened Sophia's face. "So that is how he got soaked! I saw him coming into the house, dripping wet. Ogden had one of the maids trailing Mr. Bradby with a cloth to wipe up the floors. Did a big wave splash him?"

Catherine walked with her sister along the corridor as she gave a quick explanation of how Mr. Bradby had jumped into the sea to save a child. "He paused only long enough to give Vera the mermaid tears he had found. Which gave the fishermen a chance to launch their cobles and reach the boy before Mr. Bradby did."

Sophia turned the corner toward the hallway that led to their rooms. "What a brave man!"

"That is what I said, but he brushed aside my words as if he didn't want to hear them."

"Heroes can be like that. They do something amazing but don't want to talk about it afterward."

Catherine considered her sister's insight. Was that the reason Mr. Bradby had been tight-lipped? Her efforts to draw him out had been for naught, and if he had not spoken with Vera too, Catherine would have wondered if she had distressed him somehow.

And the anger she had seen in his eyes. Vera had been right. That fury seemed to belong to someone other than Jonathan Bradby, who had always been ready to make them laugh. What else lurked in the depths he had hidden so successfully? She needed to talk with Cousin Edmund, who had known him during the war. Maybe her cousin could offer some insight into Mr. Bradby's peculiar behavior.

That would have to wait until she endured the fitting she had missed. The *modiste* jumped to her feet when Catherine followed Sophia into her sister's room. A book dropped to the floor, and Mme. Dupont quickly picked it up and shoved it into her bag.

Catherine bit her lower lip to keep from smiling when she saw the author's name emblazoned on the cover: *Mrs. Ross*. She hadn't guessed the seamstress read gothic novels where even heroes and heroines went into decline and died before the end of the story. Such fanciful stories for a woman who insisted on acting practical at all times.

"I am sorry to keep you waiting, Mme. Dupont," Catherine said to cover the *modiste*'s embarrassment.

"Non, non." Mme. Dupont was once again determined to be in charge. "You are my customer. You have—how do they say?—no need to apologize to *moi*."

Catherine tried not to roll her eyes at the seamstress's fake French accent. To do that would chance making Sophia laugh, and they both would earn another scowl from the self-styled Mme. Dupont. The seamstress's name was probably a very English one, but she clearly thought posing as a French *modiste* was good for her business.

Mme. Dupont waved her hand at the middle of the room. "Come, come, mademoiselle."

Catherine had to admit that, despite her charade, Mme. Dupont was skilled with a needle. The wedding dress she was making for Sophia was the most beautiful Catherine had ever seen. It was unblemished white with delicate lace accenting the modest neckline, and the design was perfect for a tall, slender woman like her sister. The sketches Mme. Dupont had made for the gown Catherine would wear to the wedding had different lines because she was more than six inches shorter than Sophia.

"Get up on ze box," Mme. Dupont continued, "so I can measure you for ze gowns."

"Gowns?" asked Catherine, surprised. "I need only one for the wedding."

"But," her sister argued, "you need a full wardrobe for your Season in London. You will want to catch eyes when you attend soirees and assemblies."

She nodded, though she doubted she would be there long. *Only long enough to go to the British Museum to view the Elgin Marbles.* What would her sister and Cousin Edmund think if she spoke of her plans and how she had no expectations of any man proposing to her? Even if one did, she would have to decline his offer of marriage. The idea of losing someone else she loved was too painful even to think about. Tears welled up in her eyes, but she was unsure if they were for Roland or her father or both.

"We want you to look your best, Cat," Sophia went on.

"I thought you agreed not to call me that."

Sophia put her hands on Catherine's shoulders. With Catherine standing on the box, her sister's eyes were level with hers. "I'm sorry, but I know how important going to London is for you."

For a moment, Catherine believed that her sister had discovered the true reason for her longing to visit London. Then Sophia began to talk about needing several gowns for afternoon calls as well as riding clothes for Hyde Park and undergarments.

"All the clothing must be ready before Miss Catherine leaves for London," Sophia said to Mme. Dupont who was making hasty notes. "Lord Meriweather intends to go up to London for the opening of Parliament at the end of January, and my sister will be traveling with him. Will it be possible to finish everything in time, Mme. Dupont?"

The seamstress looked aghast. "Miss Meriweather, you know I will try my best, but the end of January is only a few weeks after your wedding."

Sophia's voice grew whetted. "I know we have asked a lot of you and your seamstresses. Be honest with us, Mme. Dupont. If you cannot do this, you must graciously step aside. My sister must not be held up for ridicule by the *ton* because her clothing is unworthy of her position."

Catherine was not astonished by her sister's uncharacteristic vehemence. The London Season remained a prickly topic for Sophia. Her only Season had been cut short when a man she had thought cared for her had instead humiliated her in front of the Polite World. That had hurt her so deeply that she had fled back to Sanctuary Bay and had made her so suspicious of men that she almost ruined her relationship with Charles.

Maybe Catherine should be square with her sister. If Sophia understood that Catherine did not anticipate a match in Town, then that might set Sophia's heart at ease.

"Sophia, that's not necessary," Catherine said.

"But it is."

Glancing at Mme. Dupont, who was listening avidly, Catherine knew she could not speak the truth now. "I will need only a portion of these items when I leave. The rest can be delivered when Mme. Dupont has completed them."

"That is true. Let me decide what the absolute minimum is you will need when you leave with Cousin Edmund." Sophia tapped her chin with a single fingertip, then picked up the list she had compiled. She placed checks next to some items. When she was done, less than half of the items had been ticked. Handing it to Mme. Dupont, she asked, "Can you finish these in time for my sister's departure?"

"Oui," the seamstress said, after she had studied the page. "As well as a few other items."

"If you can complete the ones I marked before Miss Catherine travels to London, then I'm sure my sister will commission you to do the rest."

"Oui, oui, oui." The *modiste* nodded her head in time with her agreement. She aimed a gleaming smile at Catherine.

The normally prattling Mme. Dupont said very little during the rest of the fitting. Catherine was equally quiet, abiding without comment the inadvertent prick of the pins as Mme. Dupont checked the seams and adjusted them. Finally she was done. She gathered her supplies and left, saying that she had all she needed for finishing Catherine's gown and would be back on the morrow for a fitting with Sophia.

Catherine dropped onto the chaise longue by her sister's biggest window and leaned her arm against her forehead in an exaggerated pose. "I'm not sure how much longer I can endure Mme. Dupont's attention."

With a laugh, Sophia pushed Catherine's arm away

from her head. She sat beside the chaise longue. "She said she was finished with you."

"On one gown only. Once you are satisfied with your wedding gown, her attention will be fully on me again." She sat up. "Really, Sophia, I don't need a complete new wardrobe for this short trip up to London."

"Short?"

Catherine looked away from her sister's abrupt frown, as she scolded herself for speaking without thinking. "Sophia, you warned me that time goes quickly during the Season with all its events and calls."

"True." Her sister's smile returned. "I want everything to be perfect for you. I have noticed Mme. Dupont annoys you. With the promise of more work, she will be on her best behavior."

"I appreciate that."

"You are doing so much for me. How could I not do something for you?"

Catherine embraced her sister. Dear Sophia always took such good care of her! It would be so different once her sister married and moved to live with her husband at Northbridge Castle in the south of England. For the first time, other than Sophia's own abbreviated Season, the two sisters would be apart. Catherine realized how lonely it would be without having her sister to turn to. Vera would be nearby as would Cousin Edmund, but it was not the same.

And, also for the first time, Catherine could not be completely honest with her sister. If she told Sophia her fears, her sister would urge her to pray and seek guidance. That only worked if God listened to her prayers, and He had not in more than a year since her father's death. Even before. He had not seemed to heed her pleas for Roland to return safe from the war.

Catherine must continue on the path she had chosen. Once she fulfilled her promise to Roland and visited the Elgin Marbles, she would come home with the sketches she had made of the ancient figures, knowing that she had done the best she could to honor the memory of the only man she had ever loved. She hoped then that her heart would begin to heal. She was certain she would never risk it enduring such pain ever again.

"Am I late?" asked Cousin Edmund as he entered the small parlor where Sophia had arranged for hot chocolate and cakes to be brought that afternoon for him and her sister.

"Right on time." Catherine folded her hands on the pale blue of her gown as she smiled at her cousin.

When he had first arrived at Meriweather Hall in the autumn to claim the property that had come to him with his title, so many, including Catherine, had assumed he would offer for her sister. That way, the late lord's family would not lose their home to a stranger. Shortly after Sophia had announced her betrothal to Cousin Edmund's good friend, he had told Catherine that he doubted he would be a good match for either of the late baron's daughters. Catherine had appreciated his honesty, and their uneasy relationship had developed into a friendship.

"I was pleased to get your invitation," Cousin Edmund said. "After the bad experiences your sister and I first had with strained conversations during tea, I doubted either of you would ask me again."

Catherine smiled as she motioned toward the tray. "Hot chocolate."

"Let's see if I do better with hot chocolate." He sat facing her and took the cup she held out to him. "I knew winters are fiercer in North Yorkshire than in the midlands, but I guess I didn't realize how much colder until now."

"And the winter solstice is still weeks away."

"We must make sure there is a lot of cocoa in the house then."

Catherine laughed with him. When he asked how the plans were going for the Christmas Eve ball, she gave him noncommittal answers. She did not want to ask him to stop trying to help, because he was making her more work, nor did she want to admit that she was overwhelmed by the tasks.

"Alfred told me that a suitable log has been found for our Yule log." Cousin Edmund reached for a cake. "I have forgotten to tell Sophia how much I appreciate her recommendation for Alfred to assume his late father's duties as gamekeeper. Please remind me to tell her."

"If I don't forget…"

He took a bite of the cake, then set the rest on the plate by his half-emptied cup. "I know you have a lot on your mind right now. Was there something in particular you wanted to discuss with me?"

"Yes." She decided to be forthright. "I wanted to talk to you about Mr. Bradby."

"Is there a problem?" His easy smile fell away, and she caught a hint of the man who had been such a good leader on the battlefield. Now he was ready to leap to the defense of his friend.

"I wouldn't call it a problem. I am baffled by something that happened today."

"Him jumping in to save a boy when there were fishermen ready to go to the rescue?" His good humor returned. "That's Bradby. Always ready to be the hero."

"But when I praised his efforts, he gave me a look that could have frozen a fire."

"What look?"

She described the anger she had never seen in his eyes before, how it had pierced through her, even icier than the sea wind. "But the fury didn't seem to be aimed at us. It was turned inward." She looked steadily at her cousin, hoping he had an answer for her. "Cousin Edmund, I knew from the beginning there has to be more to Mr. Bradby than the jester he often portrays. Such a man could not be successful as a solicitor."

"That intense expression was one that we once were well familiar with." Cousin Edmund took a sip from his cup and then balanced it on the knee of his black breeches. "We saw it often early on in the war. Bradby has an acute sense of fairness, and when he believed anyone was being treated unfairly, he was ready to do battle."

"A true Don Quixote."

"Truer than you may guess. He seemed to break into two parts of the character after the battle where he saved Northbridge's life. On one hand, he has become like the silly man who believed a downtrodden woman was his queen. On the other, he is willing to joust with windmills, if that is what it takes to do what is right."

"But what about the anger?"

"It's always there, simmering behind the laughter." He put his cup back on the table and clasped her hand between his. "Cousin Catherine, one thing you must know. Whenever Northbridge or I have tried to speak to him about what fires that anger, he has gone mum."

"As he did today."

He nodded and sighed. "We learned we must act as if we never saw any sign of what he's trying to hide."

Catherine wondered how that was supposed to help their friend, but their plan had worked for more than a year. Even though every instinct warned her not to acquiesce, she nodded. Her cousin and Charles knew him far better than she did. She hoped she was doing the right thing.

As he walked through Meriweather Hall, Jonathan sneezed once, followed by a second time and then a third. He hoped his beef-headed heroics that morning were not going to leave him with a head cold. That would be the ultimate joke on him and his scheme to be a true hero.

"Bless you," he heard from the small parlor to his left.

He paused and looked in to see Meriweather and Cat slanting close to one another. Were they holding hands? When they hastily moved apart, Cat busied herself with the tea tray, as if she could not bear to look in his direction.

"See, the conquering hero comes!" crowed Meriweather as he came to his feet and motioned for Jonathan to enter.

Jonathan pretended to find his host's comment amusing. With a terse laugh, he said, "I didn't realize you were a fan of Handel's *Judas Maccabaeus*."

"Is that where the quote is from? I had no idea." He

waved toward the table. "Would you like something to warm you after your dip in the sea?"

"There is hot chocolate," Cat said, standing with the lithe motion that always drew his eyes. "I find it comforting on a winter afternoon. If you would prefer tea, I can ring for it."

"Hot chocolate sounds perfect." Jonathan saw the twinkle in Meriweather's eyes and looked away.

Yes, he had made a fool of himself this morning by diving into the sea when dozens of fishermen were standing by their cobles. He wished everyone would forget the incident. Or were Meriweather's eyes bright because he had been holding Cat's hand? *That* was what Jonathan wanted to forget.

Meriweather is your friend, and you should want him to be happy, an annoying little voice whispered from the back of his brain. *And you have nothing to offer Cat other than a lie.*

Even so, he was unable to meet his friend's eyes as he took the cup Cat held out to him. He took a sip. It was delicious, but it could not warm the cold at his core when he thought of her hand in Meriweather's.

Lord, give me the strength to do what is right for Meriweather and Cat. They deserve a better friend than I have been. It is bad enough that I am a fake hero. Do not let me become a false friend, too.

"You will have to come back in the summer," Meriweather said, still grinning. "It should be a bit warmer for bathing in the sea then."

"Actually the North Sea stays cold all year." Cat sat as gracefully as she had risen.

"Then maybe your dip in the sea wasn't so wantwitted, after all." Meriweather chuckled.

The familiar fury rushed through Jonathan. For once, it was not aimed at himself. If Meriweather thought to belittle him in front of Cat, then he was not the friend Jonathan had thought him to be.

"What would you have me do?" he fired back. "Stand there trying to decide whether I should help or not while a child was drowning?"

He realized his voice had been too heated and his words poorly chosen when color drained from Meriweather's face and Cat gasped. Meriweather put his cup on a nearby table. Pushing past Jonathan, he walked out of the room. The door slammed in his wake.

"Oh, my!" Cat whispered. Her face was as pale as Meriweather's had been.

Jonathan strode toward the door but halted when Cat called out to him. He turned. Distress dimmed her eyes as she slowly rose again.

"How could you say that?" she asked, each word lashing him. "How could you make a joke about his inability to make a decision?"

He almost snapped back that she had not come to *his* defense when Meriweather was jesting about *him*. Then he recalled that neither Meriweather nor Cat understood how Meriweather's humor sliced into him. They had no idea that he was a fake hero who needed to prove his worth.

He sighed. Upsetting everyone was not his intention. It was his fault that he had been such a beef-head earlier. It was also his own fault that he had been foolish now. How could he foist his blame on his friend?

"I meant him no insult," Jonathan said, wondering if Cat would believe him.

"You don't need to explain that to me." Her voice was strained. "You need to tell my cousin that."

"Miss Catherine, I trust that *you* know that I meant him no insult. He is one of my dearest friends."

She walked to where he stood and tilted her head back to meet his eyes. "Of course I do, and, deep in his heart, Cousin Edmund knows, too. He is frustrated at how the war changed him."

He tried to comprehend her words, but it was difficult when her face was at the perfect angle for him to lean down and brush her lips with his. He shoved that thought away. Already he had wounded his good friend. He did not need to hurt her, as well.

"At least you have a few good memories of what you experienced," she went on when he did not answer.

"Very few." He thought of the camaraderie he had enjoyed during the war.

"You can always recall that you saved Charles's life. My cousin doesn't have that to comfort him." She looked past him to the door. Her amazing eyes were the color of the hot chocolate and just as warm when they focused on him again. "I hope when we go to London, it is not too much for him. He plans to take his seat in Parliament, and the other lords will expect him to vote on issues brought before them."

"While you enjoy all the events of the Season." He managed to keep the bitterness out of his voice.

"I don't know about *all* the events, but I am excited about going to London."

"I am sure you are." He bowed his head toward her. "If you will excuse me, Miss Catherine, I need to make my amends to Meriweather."

If she replied, he did not hear her, as he rushed from

the room before he gave in to the temptation to grasp her by the shoulders and try to instill some good sense into her. He despised the idea of charming, innocent Catherine Meriweather changing as his siblings had to meet the expectations of the *ton*.

Maybe he could talk her out of going. He had no idea how, but he must try before Cat's life became an illusion just as his sisters' lives had.

Just as his was.

Chapter Four

"Catherine?" Meriweather grumbled under his breath and loosened his cravat to begin tying it again in front of the glass in his grand bedchamber. "Of course I like her. She is my cousin."

Jonathan sat and watched. He doubted his friend would ever get the complicated arrangement of his cravat to his satisfaction. He could help, but that was not the reason he had come to speak with him at such an early hour.

Meriweather's valet stood to one side, eager to offer his assistance. The short, pudgy man clasped his hands behind his back only to suddenly reach out to assist his lord, but then drew his hands back and clasped them again.

"Lane, that will be all," Meriweather said without glancing at his valet.

Lane bowed his head before leaving.

"The servants are too loyal here," Meriweather said. "They listen at doors in hopes of serving us better."

"Or to have some tidbit of gossip to share in the kitchen."

Meriweather chuckled, then grew somber as he drew on his waistcoat and began buttoning it. "You know, I never had a manservant before. I was quite capable of dressing myself, but I have come to depend on Lane to lay out my clothing and assist me."

"As you should, now that you hold the title of Lord Meriweather." Jonathan pretended not to hear his friend's frustration. Meriweather was more distressed about not being able to decide which clothing to wear each day than having a man to brush the lint from his coat.

"You aren't here to discuss how I've become accustomed to the life of quality. You didn't bring the papers with you, so you are not here to have me sign them."

"If you are ready to review the lease, I can get the paperwork now." Jonathan started to rise. He wondered why he had not put the facts together before he had arrived at Meriweather Hall. He should have guessed when Meriweather arranged to lease a house on a fashionable square in London that he intended to fire off his cousin into Society.

"Not now." He motioned for Jonathan to sit again. "What is bothering you, Bradby?"

"Your cousin."

"I usually would say you must be more specific, but I have eyes, and I have noticed how often yours are on my cousin Catherine." He buttoned up his dark blue waistcoat. "Not that I can blame you, for she is charming and lovely. I assume you find her that and more."

Jonathan considered his words with care. He knew the power of words from his law work. "Odd that you should say that after what I witnessed."

"Witnessed? Speak plainly, man!"

"I saw you holding her hand."

"Me? I never—" His eyes widened. "Of course. In the small parlor the other day. She asked my advice and was distressed by what I told her. What you saw was familial affection. Nothing more." He turned from the mirror and grinned. "Do you have another type of affection for my younger cousin?"

"I barely know her, and she barely knows me."

"She appears to know more about you than you suspect."

That shook Jonathan. He had been certain that his secret was so well hidden that nobody would perceive it. His friends had not, because they thoroughly believed the lie that he was a brave hero. How had he betrayed the truth to Cat?

"If I may, can I ask what she sought your advice about?" he asked.

Meriweather gave his cravat a final twist before he answered. "You."

"Me?"

"She was bothered by your darker side, which she had not encountered before that morning on the shore."

Jonathan was brought up short. He had not guessed that Cat had been so distressed by his anger at himself.

"And there may be more," Meriweather said as he considered his cravat. "She may have been troubled by your attempt to rescue that child."

"What?" He came to his feet. "You cannot believe she would ever allow a child to be endangered."

Meriweather faced him. Raising his hands, he motioned for Jonathan to sit again. As soon as Jonathan had complied, Meriweather said, "You mistake my meaning. It is not your actions that would have upset her. Just the fact that both you and the child were in danger in the sea." He went to where his brightly polished boots waited by a stool. "I have heard enough in the past couple of months to know that she was involved with a young man before the war. His name was Roland something-or-other. He joined the navy and died in battle." He sat and tugged on a boot, grimacing. "I probably should say no more."

"Probably not."

Meriweather stood to stamp his heel down in the tight boot. "Or maybe you should know. Help me here."

Jonathan stepped forward to grasp the top of the boot so his friend could force his foot into it.

"Not with the boot!" Meriweather stamped away, his foot partially in the boot. "Help me with deciding if I should tell you or not. Rip me! I can't even make the simplest decision." He sat and slumped in a nearby chair. "Will I ever stop doubting myself?"

"You are asking me for more help than I can give." His heart ached for his friend, and he knew of only one solution. "If you take this problem to God, He will help you."

"Don't you think I have already done that? Every night and every morn, I pray for God to show me His mercy and help me rediscover how to make even the simplest decision." Meriweather waved his hands to halt Jonathan's reply. "I know what you are about to say, because it is what I would say if our situations were reversed. God's time is different from man's. We must be patient."

"That is what I would say," he replied, though he thought of how often he was impatient for the chance to prove that God had been right to let him survive the battlefield.

Meriweather finally jammed his foot all the way into his boot. Resting his elbows on his knees, he looked up at Jonathan. "I thank God that one of us came through war relatively unscathed."

Jonathan gulped so loudly he was surprised his friend did not react. He should tell Meriweather the truth that haunted him. He could not. He turned on his heel and walked out. He was halfway down the stairs before he realized Meriweather had not told him about the young man who had touched Cat's heart. It served Jonathan right not to hear the truth when he could not speak it himself.

The breakfast-parlor was empty when Catherine entered it. Two days had passed since she had sought her cousin's advice, and that afternoon had splintered with anger. Despite Mr. Bradby's determination to speak immediately to her cousin, she had seen no sign of any mending of the differences between them.

Not that she had seen either of them often. Her fitting sessions with Mme. Dupont were aimed at providing her with the best designs possible for her sojourn in London, but most of the gowns the *modiste* suggested were, in Catherine's opinion, silly. Yesterday she had told Mme. Dupont that she had some ideas of her own and would bring them to the session today. She suspected the seamstress agreed only to placate her. Mme. Dupont was due for a surprise when she saw the patterns Catherine had completed late last night after spending the evening scanning magazines from London. *La Belle Assemblée*, *Ackerman's Repository* and

The Lady's Magazine had given her ideas, and she had added her own touches for clothing that would be both useful and beautiful. She focused on one gown, which she could wear to the British Museum for her visit to the Elgin Marbles. It must be a shell pink, because that was the color she had imagined wearing when she and Roland went to visit the ancient carvings. He always told her that she looked her best when she wore pink.

Before she showed the designs to Mme. Dupont, she wanted Sophia's opinion. She had hoped Sophia would be at breakfast when she arrived.

Catherine put her sketchbook on a chair at the table and then went to the sideboard where steaming servers held eggs, oatmeal, muffins and more than a dozen other choices. Taking a plate, she spooned some eggs onto it, and then selected sausages that smelled of apple cider and black pepper.

At the sound of boot heels behind her, she looked over her shoulder. Her smile wavered when Mr. Bradby entered the breakfast-parlor. He wore a bright blue coat and a yellow waistcoat over black breeches. When he moved past a window, his ginger hair caught fire.

He walked to the table. If he espied her sketchbook, he was sure to ask her about it. She did not want to admit to her love of art and chance that he would think of it as a waste of time, as one young man had coldly described her work when he had called at Meriweather Hall. Also there were articles about the Elgin Marbles, clipped from newspapers, pasted into the back of the book. If he saw those, he was sure to be curious why she was intrigued with the ancient Greek sculptures. She wanted to avoid speaking of the promise she had made to Roland until she had fulfilled it. Maybe she should pull out the pages with her sketches for Mme. Dupont before she showed them to Sophia.

But for now... She gave a moment's thought to rushing to the chair where she had left her drawings, then halted herself. Acting so out of hand could draw his attention to her sketchbook.

"Good morning," Catherine said, hoping her voice sounded carefree. "Either we are very early or very late."

"The former." He met her eyes steadily. The rage she had seen after their time on the shore was now gone, replaced by regret. "Your cousin should be down in a few minutes."

She set her plate on the table, then poured herself a cup of coffee. *Casual. Just act casual.* She carried the steaming cup to where she usually sat. Placing it next to her plate, she drew out her chair and sat, sliding the sketchbook onto her lap.

She had no idea if she betrayed her tension somehow, or if Mr. Bradby had extra-keen eyes. "What is that?" he asked as he sat across from her.

She put the sketchbook on the floor by her feet, putting the toe of one slipper on it. "A book I have been enjoying." That was the truth, and she hoped he would not question her further. "Did you get one of Mrs. Porter's blueberry muffins? They are a rare treat."

"I did." He looked down at his plate. "May I give our thanks for this wonderful meal?"

"Of course."

He bowed his head, and she did the same, hoping—as she did each time someone said grace or she attended church—that she would again feel God's comforting presence. The loss of Him in her life added to her grief from losing Papa.

"Lord," Mr. Bradby said, "we thank You for Your benevolence in bringing us to this table on the beautiful morning You made. We are grateful for the food we are about to eat, and we are grateful for having each other in our lives."

Catherine was glad her head was down so he could not see her amazement. After how he had acted the last time they spoke, she had not expected him to speak of having her in his life, especially in prayer that should come from the heart.

"Amen," she said after he had. "That was lovely, Mr. Bradby."

She reached for her fork, but paused when he asked, "Would you be offended if I asked you to call me by my given name in exchange for permission to address you as informally?"

She smiled. "Is that a very convoluted way of asking me if I'd feel comfortable calling you Jonathan?"

"I am a solicitor. Not too long ago in the past, my ilk was paid by the word. It is a habit that has been passed down ever since." He leaned one elbow on the table and smiled. "But, Miss Catherine, you have yet to give me an answer to my question."

"If I understand your question—and that is a mighty *if*—then, yes, I would be pleased to have you call me by my given name, and I shall do the same when I speak with you." She pushed his elbow off the table. "Solicitor, one must mind one's manners here."

"Truly?"

She laughed, glad that he was once again the funny man whose company she had enjoyed during his last visit. "If my mother was here, she would be shocked by a gentleman with his elbow on the table."

"I shall endeavor to make sure my manners are the pattern-card of perfection by the time Lady Meriweather returns." He stood and bowed deeply to her, sweeping out his arm like a grand courtier.

"Are we too late for the dance?" asked Cousin Edmund as he and Sophia walked into the breakfast-parlor.

Jonathan laughed. "We were just being silly."

She looked from her cousin to Jonathan and back, relieved when they both smiled. Cousin Edmund must have accepted Jonathan's apology. For that she was very grateful. Christmas was the time of year for good spirits, not angry ones.

The light conversation continued while her cousin and sister served themselves and came to the table. Catherine let the others chat while she listened. Later she would show Sophia her sketches. For now she would enjoy the companionable meal.

She looked up startled when Cousin Edmund's voice took on a sharper edge as he talked of more serious matters. "Those curs dared to threaten Alfred Demaine and his mother."

Alfred had been appointed by Cousin Edmund to take over the position as gamekeeper on the estate. He was not yet twenty, but he had learned the job from his late father, who had held it for more than thirty years.

She gripped the edge of the table, horrified that anyone had menaced Alfred and his kindly mother whose cottage was beyond the stables. Jonathan mumbled something under his breath, and she glanced at him. He was appalled by the threat to the Demaines. Even though he was not part of Meriweather Hall, she remembered Cousin Edmund saying that fairness was important to him.

She had no doubt who had bullied the Demaines. "Why would the smugglers do that?"

"To keep them close to their cottage," Cousin Edmund replied. "It happened last night. The lad was so terrified to leave his mother alone that he didn't come to tell me until after dawn. He knows the smugglers usually seek their holes as soon as the sun rises, so he believed that she should be safe. I am not as certain as Alfred is that the smugglers are abroad only after dark."

"If he spoke with them…" Jonathan began. The smugglers were becoming too bold. Maybe their overconfidence would be the route to their downfall.

He looked around the table. Both Cat's and her sister's faces were blanched. Meriweather's mouth was a straight line, and fury radiated from him.

"I know what you're hoping, Bradby, but no," Meriweather said. "He cannot identify them by either their voices or by their clothing. There were four men. They wore work clothing, but with kerchiefs pulled up over their faces, and their caps drawn low. Alfred said one man spoke in a low growl that sounded more like a beast than a human."

"To frighten them more." Cat fisted her hands on the table. "This must stop!"

"I agree." Meriweather's face was grim. "I know your father tried to work out an agreement with them to stay off the lands of Meriweather Hall, but that failed. Even if it had worked, it is not my intention to let bullies have their way."

"So what do we do?" asked Miss Meriweather.

Cat got up and went around the table to give her sister a hug. Jonathan sighed. No wonder Miss Meriweather was distressed. She had nearly had a run-in with the smugglers a couple of months ago, and the incident had scared Cat's usually courageous sister who had feared for Northbridge and his children.

"That is the question, isn't it?" asked Meriweather.

Jonathan clenched his hands in his lap. They had reached the impasse again; the place where his friend needed to make a decision, and he was unable to do so. Wishing he could think of something to say to help him, Jonathan looked away.

His gaze connected with Cat's. She was as discouraged as he was about Meriweather, and he wished he could offer some solution.

Lord, he prayed, *Meriweather is a good man. Help him trust himself again.*

"What about going to Sir Nigel?" asked Miss Meriweather.

Jonathan looked reluctantly away from Cat as Meriweather said, "He has offered to help, but he has not done anything."

"Maybe if he learns of this threat to our people, he will consider doing more," Cat said. "It could be his people next."

"What do you think?" Meriweather asked Cat and Sophia. "Is it worth talking to Sir Nigel again?"

"We must take care that no one belonging to Meriweather Hall comes to harm." Miss Meriweather glanced at her cousin, then back at Cat. "Unless you have a better idea, I say we should reach out to Sir Nigel one more time. Perhaps Lord Ashland, as well."

"That sounds like a good idea, though I have no eagerness to call upon Sir Nigel again so soon." Meriweather looked relieved that someone had made the decision for him. "I shall give Lord Ashland a call in the coming week. Maybe he will have some good ideas."

"We could," Jonathan said quietly, "pray that God freezes the sea, and that will keep the smugglers from their nefarious deeds."

Catherine laughed as she walked around the table past Jonathan and sat. "I daresay they would simply use the ice as a path to bring their goods ashore."

"True."

She felt around with her toes to find her sketchbook. Where was it? Had it slid away when she got up to go to her sister? She could not bend down to peer under the table. That would bring more questions, which she wanted to avoid.

Poking about with her toes, she found nothing. She stretched out her leg, soundlessly tapping the floor. When her foot struck something solid, she lowered her eyes when Jonathan looked up in surprise. She had not intended to bump her foot into his.

She breathed a silent sigh of relief when her toes discovered the sketchbook to the left of her chair. She drew it closer to her. She carefully avoided Jonathan's eyes as he began to talk to her cousin about when they should call on Sir Nigel and Lord Ashland and demand their help against the smugglers.

A shout came from outside the breakfast-parlor. Jonathan's black-and-white pup rushed in. He ran to Catherine and put his nose on her lap. Before she could react, he hurried to her sister. He looked up at her with absolute devotion, then loped around the table to Cousin Edmund before finally hurrying to Jonathan.

He grasped the puppy by the scruff and set himself on his feet.

"Forgive me, Meriweather, ladies. I will insist that this mongrel stay in the stables."

"Nonsense," Sophia said, patting the puppy's head. "Charles and the children will be arriving any day now, and I know that Gemma and Michael will be thrilled to have such a playmate."

"He can stay out there until they arrive."

"Jonathan," Catherine said, "it would be better if the puppy stayed inside. A barking dog will be less welcoming than a gamekeeper and his mother should the smugglers arrive here."

His eyes narrowed, and she almost recoiled before the formidable rage in them. She wondered how many of Napoleon's men had quailed before him.

"We must keep everyone safe," she added quietly.

"I agree." He released the puppy who ran to Catherine again, as if he understood that she had kept him from being sent outside.

Slowly Jonathan sat. He pushed his plate away and stared at the middle of the table.

Into the silence, Sophia asked, "What do you call him?"

When he did not answer, Catherine said, "Jonathan has not yet decided on a name."

"Really?" Sophia gave her a single pointed glance, and Catherine knew her sister was expressing her surprise at how Catherine spoke of Mr. Bradby. "As we are all among friends here—" She shot Catherine another questioning look. "I think we can come up with a name for him."

"We could call him what he is perhaps. Big Bother," Catherine said with a strained laugh as she snuck the puppy a piece of sausage. She wished Jonathan would say something.

"How about Star? He has a star marking on his forehead," Miss Meriweather offered.

"That sounds like the name for a horse," Cousin Edmund said. "You could always call him Jobby."

"Why?" asked Catherine as she held out her hand under the table. The dog's tongue brushed it lightly, and another piece of sausage vanished.

"Jobby dog is a Town term for someone who likes to have a good time, and I daresay, few of God's creatures enjoy themselves more than this one."

"I think that is a fun name." She slid her own plate toward the center of the table, directly into Jonathan's view.

He blinked and raised his head when she asked him what he thought of calling his dog Jobby. He agreed, but she wondered if he had heard anything they had said. His gaze was turned inward. She could not help thinking how he had looked exactly the same before he had dived into the sea.

Cousin Edmund asked Sophia to help him once more with the accounts before her wedding. She agreed and suggested Catherine come with them.

"I think I will take Jobby out for some air," Catherine said.

"I can do that," Jonathan interjected. "You must have more important things to do."

She did not want to admit that he was right. She had

planned to spend the morning with the footmen as she outlined where she wanted holiday greens hung in the great hall, but she had not finished her sketch for that.

"I could use some fresh air myself," she replied. "A brisk walk along the shore would be wonderful. It will be pleasant to stroll without looking for mermaid tears."

"You should not have to handle that great beast on your own." He squared his shoulders. "I will be glad to go with you if you would like company."

"I had planned to ask Foggin," she said with a smile and a glance toward her sister who gave her a slight nod of approval, "but I suspect he would be happy to have someone to help him keep Jobby under control. Let me get my wraps, and I will meet you in the garden."

The hint of a smile returned to his face, and warmth spread through her as if she had stepped out into summer sunshine. He took her hand and bowed over it. His thumb brushed her palm, a tentative exploration that delighted her. As he raised his head, his gaze fused with hers. She could not have looked away, even if she had wanted to. She did not. She wanted to study his blue eyes that changed shade with each emotion. Now they were as deep a blue as his coat, shining brightly.

He hastily released her hand and stepped back. "In the garden then. I shall send for Foggin, if you would like."

"Thank you." She struggled to say those two words without her voice splintering.

If Sophia had not come over to link her arm with Catherine's, she doubted she could have moved. She yearned to return to the moment when he held her hand, lightly caressing her sensitive palm.

Her sister said nothing as they went up the stairs and to Catherine's room. Sophia sat while Catherine put away her sketchbook and sent Hubbard, the maid who served them both, to collect her outerwear. The dark-haired young woman must have guessed something was amiss, because as soon as she brought Catherine's dark navy pelisse as well as her bonnet and gloves, she excused herself to tend to a task in Sophia's room.

"You and Mr. Bradby are becoming good friends, I see," Sophia said as soon as the door closed behind their maid.

"He is a nice man and an intelligent one." She pulled on the pelisse and reached for her bonnet. "Did you know that solicitors used to be paid by the word?"

Sophia ignored her attempt to change the subject. "Just be careful. I don't want to see you hurt again."

"Hurt? Jonathan would never hurt me."

"Not intentionally, but his attempt to rescue that child has given me pause."

"Why?"

"He saved Charles's life, but I wonder if being proclaimed a hero hasn't changed him. He may feel an obligation to repeat his great deed. After all, he jumped into the sea when the fishermen were far more prepared to save the child."

"I thought that was something he should be lauded for."

"It is, but I can't forget how Roland Utting was determined to prove that he was brave, too. He ended up dead."

Catherine's numb fingers somehow tied her bonnet ribbons, but she could not hook the frogs on her pelisse. She had never told her sister how Roland had asked her to wait for him, because he had asked her to say nothing to her family until he could return from the war to obtain her father's blessing on their plans to marry. She had asked why they could not marry before he left, but he had been determined to prove that he was worthy of a baron's daughter, and if he had been part of the push to defeat Napoleon, he believed he would win the respect that was so important to him. Nothing she had said had budged him from that opinion.

So he had left and never came back.

For the first time, she wondered if Jonathan had yearned to be a hero before he went into battle. Her fingers tightened on the braided frogs. Had he been desperate to prove himself to a woman he loved? But if that were so, that woman might still be in his life, even though he had not mentioned someone special.

All the more reason for her to remember her plan to make sure Jonathan became no more than a friend to her. It was a good plan, and it was one she found simple to follow...until she spent time with him, and he made her laugh and remember how it felt to be light-hearted again.

Standing, Sophia came over and began closing Catherine's pelisse for her. "Listen to your big sister. Don't get involved with another hero. It will only break your heart anew. Mr. Bradby is a nice man, and I will be grateful to him every day of my life for saving Charles's life, but I don't want to see you as sad as you were when the news of Roland's death reached us. I don't want you to be so hurt ever again."

Embracing her sister, Catherine whispered, "I don't intend to be."

Chapter Five

Jobby raced around the garden, first chasing a squir-rel up a tree and then taking off after a rabbit in the bushes. Each time the pup rushed back when Jonathan called to him.

"What a smart dog!" Catherine crowed before Jobby ran across the garden again, chasing a leaf that bounced along the ground.

"Occasionally." Jonathan chuckled when the pup barked at the leaf that was no longer moving. "One thing is for sure. He has a lot of energy." He offered his arm to Cat.

She did not hesitate. Not only was Foggin standing discreetly on the stone terrace where he had an excel-lent view of the whole garden, but she was sure that the layers of wool between her and Jonathan would blunt her reaction to being close to him. As soon as she placed her hand within his arm, she discovered how wrong she was. That lightning buzz sped through her anew. He put his gloved hand on hers as he led her over some uneven ground toward where Jobby still barked at the motionless leaf.

She looked up at his face while he laughed as he related the puppy's other bird-witted antics. She saw no sign of either the unsettling intensity or the silliness. He appeared more at ease than she had ever seen him. Was this how he had been before the war?

She kept that question to herself, wanting to enjoy this peaceful moment. She drew in a deep breath of the cool fresh air that was flavored with the tang of salt.

"I am glad that you and Cousin Edmund are in good pax again," she said.

"He accepted my apology and forgave me for being cantankerous, whether I deserved it or not." He paused by the huge boulders that jutted up out of the earth and marked the outermost edge of the garden. "I half expected him to ask me to take my congé."

"He is happy you are here. I think he misses having other men to speak to. Before he inherited Papa's title, he spent a lot of time among men with his construction work. Now he has to leave Meriweather Hall to find male company, and as Sir Nigel is the closest…" She grimaced.

Jonathan chuckled. "Your cousin wants to avoid Sir Nigel because he apparently is eager for Meriweather to meet his great-niece." His smile dropped away. "Oh, I shouldn't have said that."

"Why not? Sir Nigel has always been a meddler, so I'm not surprised he wants to play matchmaker."

"So you don't mind?"

"Of course, I mind, but nobody will ever change Sir Nigel." She looked directly at him, pushing back one side of her bonnet that the wind tried to curve around her face. "And my cousin can be stubborn when he wishes to be. He may have trouble making decisions, but he knew his heart when he stepped aside so my sister can marry Charles."

Jonathan nodded, and she noticed the tips of his ears were red. That was no surprise when the wind blustered cold from the beach. He picked up a stick and tossed it across the garden. Jobby took after it at top speed.

"You sound as if you don't like Sir Nigel," Jonathan said as the puppy pounced on the stick and began chewing on it. "Not that I would blame you if you didn't. The man is too much in love with the sound of his own voice, and, coming from a solicitor, that is saying a lot."

"I don't like or dislike him. He is a neighbor, so I must treat him kindly."

"Now that sounds even colder than your first words."

"You are right." She gave him a quick smile. "I need to choose my words more carefully."

"Or your neighbors."

She laughed as she had not since before her father had became ill. Jonathan's droll tone along with his somber expression tickled her.

"I don't dislike Sir Nigel himself," she said. "It's his art."

He grinned as they continued strolling through the garden.

"What's so funny?"

"Your lip curls as you spit out *his art,* as if you took a bite of something foul."

She watched Jobby pick up the stick and run with it; then she turned her gaze to Jonathan. His easy grin made it impossible not to smile back.

"Did you see what his latest 'innovation' is for his art?" she asked.

"I only gave the pictures a cursory look during that ball he gave back in the fall."

"He mixed real sand with his paint. To give the scene more texture was what he told me when I asked him about it last month." She rolled her eyes. "Have you ever heard of anything so addled?"

"I did get the feeling your neighbor is more than a bit harebrained. There are not many people outside the Royal Academy of Arts who invite people in to view their own work."

"The Royal Academy of Arts!" Why hadn't she thought about visiting the Royal Academy and its school while she was in London? It was on the Strand, not too far from Mayfair where she would be staying with her cousin. Like the British Museum, the work displayed there could inspire her to look at her own in new ways.

"What about the Royal Academy?" Jonathan asked.

Catherine chided herself for risking the secret she had guarded closely. Hoping her laugh sounded natural, she said, "I had not considered it before now as a place that might be fun to visit while I am in London."

His face closed up, and she wondered why. There had been enough truth in her words to make them easy to say.

When he said nothing, she went on. "Of course, before any trip to Town, we have the wedding and the Christmas Eve ball to look forward to. So many people have said they intend to attend both. I suspect there are few who can resist a wedding celebration and a masquerade."

"Masquerade?" He halted and faced her. "Are you saying the ball is a masquerade?"

"The invitation stated so."

He grimaced. "I didn't look too closely at it, because I assumed I would not be attending."

"And if you *had* noticed that it was a masquerade, you would have definitely decided not to attend."

"That is true, though I doubt Meriweather would have accepted my excuse."

"Which is?"

"I feel silly wearing a small mask that is supposed to conceal my identity, when I am betrayed by my height."

She tapped her finger against her chin. "There may be a way to disguise your height. I can ask Mme. Dupont to make you a costume. All we need to decide is what you want to come as."

"Your *modiste* is busy making a wedding gown for your sister. She won't have time for any other projects."

She smiled. "You don't know Mme. Dupont. She is not happy unless she has a dozen things going on at once."

"That chaos would drive me mad."

"All the more reason for you to meet with her soon, because as the time gets closer to the wedding, everything will be even busier." She raised one brow. "Unless you want to go as a soldier or a solicitor."

"I think not. I have had enough of the first, and most people have had enough of the latter."

Laughing, she said, "Then you have no choice but to submit to Mme. Dupont's measurements and fittings."

"You make it sound dire."

"I have to own that I make every excuse I can to avoid a fitting, but Mme. Dupont will be here shortly after the midday meal. Why don't you come to Sophia's rooms around two?"

"You are not going to offer me any way to avoid this, are you?"

Catherine laughed along with him as they turned back to the house. He whistled, and Jobby came running. Jonathan promised to meet her at Sophia's room as the long-case clock struck the appointed hour.

But later, as the clock chimed the half hour past two, Catherine tried not to tap her foot against the floor. Where was Jonathan? She had not guessed he would keep her and Mme. Dupont waiting. From inside Sophia's room, she heard the *modiste* telling Sophia that she needed no more measurements until the final fitting.

A sudden motion from the far end of the hallway caught Catherine's eye. Jonathan hurried toward her, his coattails flapping. She shifted her sketchbook behind her, so he would not notice it. Even though she had planned to rip out the pages to show Mme. Dupont, she could not bring herself to tear apart her precious sketchbook. She hated subterfuge, but she was not ready to trust him with her innermost secret that had sent other men rushing for the door.

"Forgive me for being late," Jonathan said, panting as he stopped beside her. "I have no excuse other than I lost track of time. Meriweather and I were playing billiards, and he demanded a chance to beat me at least once."

"That sounds as if you were doing well."

"Very." His grin broadened. "But one learns that it is not wise to win all the time when playing one's host. I trust you will accept my apology."

Why had she never taken note of that dimple in his left cheek? It was endearing yet did not distract from his tautly carved face. She was unsure how long she would have stared at his dimple if he had not asked her if she thought it was wise to keep Mme. Dupont waiting any longer.

She tore her eyes away from him, but not before her gaze was caught again by his compelling eyes. Now they appeared a paler blue than ever, but there was nothing cold about them. In fact she was suffused by that pleasing warmth again.

Somehow she groped for the door and opened it. He motioned for her to precede him. She did and discovered Mme. Dupont gathering up lace scraps from Sophia's wedding gown. Sophia came from behind a screen set up along one side of the room.

"Mr. Bradby, I hope we didn't leave you in the hallway for too long," she said.

"Not at all." He winked at Catherine. "The timing was perfect."

"Excellent." Sophia motioned toward the *modiste* who was staring at Jonathan, her mouth agape at the garish colors the rest of them had become accustomed to. "Mme. Dupont, Mr. Bradby needs a costume for the Christmas Eve ball. I would consider it a great favor if you would make it."

Mme. Dupont regained her composure. "Ah, M. Bradby, it is a *très bonne* pleasure to meet you."

"Enchanté, madame," he replied. *"Vous êtes bon pour faire un costume pour moi quand vous êtes tellement occupé avec la robe de la mariée. Je vous remercie à l'avance."*

Catherine averted her eyes when she saw the bafflement and dismay in Mme. Dupont's eyes at Jonathan's effortless French. If the *modiste* saw Cat's attempts not to laugh, Mme. Dupont would be even more embarrassed. Taking pity on the seamstress, she said, "Jonathan, English please. My French is regrettably far less skilled than yours, and Mme. Dupont doesn't have time to translate for me."

"Of course," he said. "I said that she was kind to make a costume for me, when she is so busy with preparations for the wedding and a wardrobe for you."

"Thank you for explaining." She did not add that she had easily understood every word he had spoken. Even though England had been at war with France for most of her life, she had learned to speak the language because many art books she wanted to read were written in French.

Mme. Dupont motioned to the box in the middle of the floor. "I must make ze… How do you say it?"

"Measurements?" suggested Catherine.

"Oui!"

"We will stand over here," she said. "Once your measurements are complete, Mme. Dupont, we can discuss the best costume for Mr. Bradby."

Sophia muffled a laugh as she and Catherine went to the door. In a whisper, her sister said, "I must speak with Mrs. Porter about tonight's meal. *Bonne chance.*" She hurried out, closing the door behind her.

Jonathan heard Cat's sister wish her good luck before she left the room. He wished he could have gone with Sophia, but he squared his shoulders and said nothing when Mme. Dupont instructed him to stand on the middle of the box. It was absurd because she had to get a chair to reach his shoulders. He began to understand why Cat found her fittings ludicrous.

Jonathan stared straight ahead as the seamstress whipped the string around his chest and waist. She made quick knots in the string with each measurement. He wondered how she knew what each knot was for, because he saw no hints of how she identified one from the other.

Mme. Dupont was as professional as any knight of the needle. She made her measurements with quiet efficiency and then rolled the string around her wrist when she was done. She called to Cat, who put down the book she had been paging through and came back over.

His eyes narrowed. That appeared to be the same leather-bound book she had had at breakfast. He was curious about its topic, because she clearly found it so fascinating that she kept it with her. If he knew what she found interesting, it could give him insight into her. He longed to know her better.

"I have just ze thing *pour vous,* M. Bradby," Mme. Dupont said, pulling his attention back to her.

"And what would that be?"

"You should go as a wolf." Her eyes twinkled. "You are a tall man, and a wolf is a large creature. You are a former soldier, so you know how to hunt as a wolf does."

"Mme. Dupont," Cat said, and he wondered if she had seen how he had flinched at the *modiste's* cheerful explanation. "Mr. Bradby's time is valuable."

Jonathan flashed Cat a grateful smile. He had no other demands on his time, but he did not want to hear that a soldier was like a wolf stalking its prey.

"Oui, oui," Mme. Dupont said, before going on as if Cat had remained silent. "I can create a mask that will have whiskers and a wolf's ears. With a coat of

gray or even black and a sedate waistcoat, you will portray a wolf well."

"Sedate?" He had not brought with him a waistcoat anyone would deem as *sedate*.

"Dark colored," Mme. Dupont said. "Anything else will ruin the costume. It is something I can make for you, if you have a need." She eyed him, and he knew that she found his bright waistcoat too garish.

"I had hoped for something that would make me less visible. Cat—Miss Catherine," he hurried to correct himself, "suggested you might make a costume that disguised my height."

"You can hunch over." Mme. Dupont gave a very Gallic shrug. "Zat will disguise you, M. Bradby."

"Hardly." He stepped off the box.

Cat turned to him. "That you are wearing such grim colors may be your best disguise, Jonathan."

He wished he could capture her beautiful smile that rose to sparkle in her dark eyes. He wanted to take the image with him when he left Meriweather Hall and was again alone.

"And what costume will you wear?" he asked, returning her smile.

Mme. Dupont looked up from where she leaned over a piece of paper. "Mademoiselle will be a shepherdess."

"A bit of a cliché, no?" he asked, arching a brow at Cat.

"True, for many women dress as shepherdesses for masquerades," Cat said. "But this is the first time that I have had a chance, and I have a wonderful costume. Do you think we should dress Jobby up as a lamb?"

He laughed. "Only if you want the whole ball disrupted."

Though he wanted to continue their lighthearted conversation, Mme. Dupont asked Cat for her opinion on the sketch of his costume. It was simple, and he doubted he would be able to decipher any of the lines drawn on top of each other. Cat seemed to have no problems because she pointed to one part of the odd costume, then to another.

"You will need to use a stiff fabric to make the mask stand up," Cat said. "Will you use linen stiffened with paste?"

Mme. Dupont nodded, an expression of relief easing her tense face. "That is exactly what I will do." Gathering up the pages, she added, "I have all I need for today, M. Bradby. I will return by week's end with ze first pieces for your costume. Then we shall make zem fit *vous* perfectly."

He struggled not to smile at her fractured French as he said, "*Merci beaucoup,* madame."

Again the seamstress started, but then comprehension brightened her face. She nodded and began to sort through her supplies on the other side of the room.

Jonathan went to where Cat still studied the drawing Mme. Dupont had made. As he neared, she picked up the book she had been carrying and held it under her left arm, obscuring its title.

"Are you enjoying that book?" he asked, knowing he might be overstepping the boundaries of good manners.

"Yes." Color flared up her face, and she shifted the book to her other side, away from him.

He considered asking another question, then remembered that he had no right to probe into her life when he was keeping such a vital secret himself. But he could not refrain from thinking about the young man Meriweather had mentioned. He should ask his friend the whole story, but he did not want to discompose Meriweather again.

Behind them, the *modiste* muttered to herself as she spread some pearl gray silk on a table. For his costume or for something else?

In little more than a whisper, Cat murmured, "You should not tease her by speaking French."

"I know. It is not a Christian act, and I will apologize to her."

She grasped his coat sleeve as he turned to go to where Mme. Dupont was now scowling at the silk. "Don't! That will show her that you do not believe her illusion of being a French *modiste*."

"But you and your sister know the truth. Why keep pretending?" He fought to keep his voice low as vexation bubbled up inside him. Another illusion intended to impress others. He had endured enough of that with his family.

"Because it matters to her, and that should be reason enough to comply."

He was about to fire back another sharp retort but halted himself when he saw the dismay on her face. He admired her tender heart that had made him feel welcome at Meriweather Hall. Yet to allow another delusion to continue… For Cat, he would say nothing.

He nodded, and was rewarded by her scintillating smile that seemed to reach inside him and ease the iron bands wrapped so tightly around his heart.

"You will be happy with your costume," she said.

"She didn't know what to do with the mask until you made your suggestion."

Cat picked up the pencil and drew a few lines on the

page. "For the past ten years or so, Sophia and I have created the effigies for the annual Guy Fawkes Night bonfire in Sanctuary Bay, and we learned to use paste and thin fabric to mold the shapes we needed."

"What changes are you making?"

"Nothing much." She folded the drawing and secured it with the pencil. "You looked upset when Mme. Dupont mentioned a sedate waistcoat."

"I assure you that I can dispense with my peacock colors for one night." He hesitated, then said, "It might start a new trend for me. Even I get bored with gaudy colors after a while."

"Then why wear them?"

"If I didn't, Meriweather would be disappointed. He enjoys laughing at my bright waistcoats."

"You are a good friend."

"Because he is. I appreciate how your family has made me feel welcome here." As she looked up at him with her luscious eyes, he added, "Very welcome."

She quickly lowered her gaze. "You are free to go, Jonathan, but I must remain for my fitting. I dislike these initial fittings the most."

"Initial? The wedding is not much more than five weeks away. If she isn't finished with your gown for that, she should not be wasting time making me a costume for the ball."

Cat laughed, surprising him. "This fitting is for a riding habit for me to take to London." Her nose wrinkled. "Having a whole wardrobe made here to go to Town seems so silly."

Jonathan swallowed hard, feeling as if she had just driven her fist into his gut. Was he wrong about Cat? Even though she had not reached London yet, she already was acting as if, once she was fired off, anything from the country could not be worth a fig.

Would he lose her, too, to the world of delusions woven through the Season?

Chapter Six

The long-case clock marked the hour with a single chime, and Vera stood and rubbed her lower back. "I must get back to the vicarage, Catherine. Gregory planned to spend the day making calls on sick and elderly parishioners, and I like to have a good meal waiting for him after such a long day."

"Thank you for coming and keeping me sane." Catherine stared at the pile of papers in front of her. "If I had an excuse to flee from this jumble, I would, too."

"If you need me to stay—"

"Nonsense. We have made such little headway during the past two hours, there isn't much hope we would make much more in another hour."

Vera gave her a quick kiss on the cheek and then left.

Catherine considered scooping up the pages and tossing them into the air. Maybe they would make more sense when they were scattered on the floor.

She dropped into the chair behind the desk and stared at the pages. Some had been simple to sort, but others refused to fit into any of the categories she had devised.

"Why such a grim expression?"

She smiled when she saw Jonathan in the doorway. His ginger hair was windblown, so she knew he must be just back from the call Cousin Edmund and he had made on Lord Ashland. When he walked in, cool fresh air wafted from him.

"I have made a complete muddle of the plans for my sister's wedding and the Christmas ball," she replied.

"That is a grand statement, and one I find impossible to believe."

She flung out her hand toward the cluttered desk. "Look at this mess. I have tried to sort these pages out, so I can deal with them more efficiently, but it is hopeless." She leaned forward and propped her forehead against the heels of her palms. "Or maybe I am."

"What did you tell me about elbows on the table?"

"This isn't a table." She did not feel like being teased out of her dreary mood. "It is a desk."

"So the rules are different?"

In spite of herself, Catherine grinned as she raised her head. "You aren't going to allow me to wallow in self-pity, are you?"

"I have done enough of that for everyone in North Yorkshire, so no, I shan't allow that."

"Why have you been pitying yourself?"

His cheerful smile did not match the intensity in his eyes, but his voice remained light. "That is no topic for a sunny afternoon. The wind is light, and the air is the warmest it has been since I arrived at Meriweather Hall. Let's take a walk."

"But you just came in."

"From a long and disagreeable call on Lord Ashland. Your company will be far more pleasant. What do you say?"

"I say that I would agree to just about anything to avoid looking at these papers." She stood and came around the desk.

"Good." He crooked his arm toward her. "Taking the air will clear your head."

Catherine put her hand on his arm and knew he was mistaken. Just standing close to him and touching him, even chastely, made her head spin. Every breath she took was flavored with the scents that were uniquely his—the soap his shirt had been washed in, the lush aroma of his wool coat, the woodsy tang left from his ride through the evergreen trees toward Lord Ashland's estate. When his lips tipped upward, she smiled, too. Being with him made her feel lighter, as if her burdens had fallen away.

She matched her steps to his as they went into the hallway. When he stepped away to give a footman instructions to fetch her wraps, she was astonished by the strength of her regret. It was almost a physical force.

Catherine made sure her face was serene when Jonathan turned to her. He smiled and suggested they bring Jobby with them. Nothing more than friendship was visible in his expression. And why should she expect more? He had been the pattern-card of bonhomie since his arrival. Even when he could not hide more potent emotions, he made every attempt not to trouble her or anyone else with them. He was the perfect guest.

But he had created a facade to hide the real Jonathan Bradby. She could not help wondering why and what part of him he felt he must conceal. Both her cousin and Charles spoke of him with the greatest admiration.

"You could have warned me," Jonathan said, drawing her out of her thoughts, "that Ashland is a high stickler. He barely deigned to speak to either Meriweather or me."

"He keeps much to himself." She tried to remember when she had last seen the viscount, but could not. "You shouldn't be offended by his lack of welcome."

"I'm not, but your cousin's nose was put out of joint."

"I will assure him that Lord Ashland's attitude has nothing to do with him."

Jonathan grimaced. "Maybe you can persuade him that Ashland was within his rights to decline helping to halt the smugglers."

Catherine did not answer as the footman had returned with her wraps. While Jonathan held her gloves and bonnet, she drew on her pelisse. Poor Cousin Edmund! He was determined to put an end to smugglers intruding on Meriweather Hall lands. He must be furious at Lord Ashland's response.

She focused on closing the frogs on her pelisse. The idea that Jonathan would need to help her, standing so close that she would be aware of each breath he took, threatened to undo her already shaky composure.

"I will talk to Cousin Edmund," she said as she took her bonnet from Jonathan.

"Give him time to simmer down. He is near his boiling point."

"I will." She smiled as she pulled on her gloves. "It sounds as if we all need to clear our heads."

She followed him out of the house with Foggin in tow. Another footman was sent to bring Jobby out to join them.

Jonathan had been right. It was a lovely day, too

lovely to remain indoors while she and Vera tried to make sense of the papers. When the puppy rushed up, tail wagging with excitement and jangling, she asked, "Is he wearing bells?"

"Some of us," Foggin answered quietly, "believe it will be easier to keep track of him if he wears a belled collar."

"And he looks quite stylish," Jonathan added.

Bending, she saw a leather collar with three bells hanging from it hooked around Jobby's neck, almost lost in his thick hair. She petted his head. "Aren't you a handsome chap?"

His tail wagged even more vigorously in answer.

"Do you want to stay in the garden or go farther afield?" Catherine asked Jonathan. "We could walk down to the beach."

He smiled. "So you can look for mermaid tears?"

"As I told you, we seldom find any on the beach below the headland, but who knows?"

Jobby ran ahead of them and then back as Catherine led the way down the steep curving path to the beach. The footman remained at the top of the cliff where he would have them in view all the time. Several times the dog almost knocked her or Jonathan off the path, so she was relieved when they were on flat ground again.

The beach was beautiful in the bright sunshine that sparkled like hundreds of individual diamonds off the low waves. In the distance, the village clung to its cliff, but it was too far away for any sounds to reach them. A ship sailed out near the horizon, barely little more than an outline of its sails.

Catherine tried to commit every detail of the scene to memory, so she could draw it before she went to sleep. The time she once used for prayers was now used for drawing. She did not understand how, but spending time with her art made her feel closer to God. He had given her a love of art, a true gift she treasured. She reminded herself of that each time she felt the void left since her father's death and the memory of how distant God had become when she had prayed to Him.

Jonathan picked up a stone and tossed it along the beach. The puppy sped away, sending clumps of sand high in the air. He caught the stone on the first bounce. Catherine was astonished when the pup came back, tail wagging like a jaunty flag, and dropped the stone by their feet. Mouth open, tongue fallen over the side, he looked from the stone to Jonathan and back with a clear message to throw it again. Jonathan did. Over and over as they walked along the sand. Jobby never tired of chasing and retrieving it.

"Silly dog," Jonathan said, ruffling the dog's hair, as they turned to retrace their steps.

"You need never worry about losing a rock, because he will bring it back to you straightaway." Catherine laughed.

"I have to say it was never a skill I looked for in a dog." He did not add more until they reached the top of the cliff. Winded, he added, "I thought it was difficult going *down*. This path is even steeper than the street in the village."

She pressed her hand over her heart as she slowed her own breathing. "As children, Sophia and I raced up and down. I never considered one of us might fall."

"That is the way children are." He held out his arm. As she put her hand on it and they began walking toward the house with Foggin falling in behind them, he added, "When we are young, we know we are in God's hands and safe. Only as we grow, do we come to recognize that, even though He is always there with us, our way may not be safe."

Her fingers tightened on his sleeve. How easily he spoke of God in his life! She missed knowing that He was never far away when she needed to turn to Him. Instead she felt as distant from Him as that ship on the sea had been from the shore.

"I'm sorry," Jonathan said when she remained silent. "I didn't mean to upset you."

"You didn't," she hurried to say.

"Then what is wrong? Your face was shining with a smile moments ago, and now the happiness is gone."

She had to tell him something. "I am thinking of the work I left on the desk."

"You truly are overwhelmed, aren't you?" He walked beside her as they re-entered the garden. Jobby raced past them and vanished among the shrubs.

"As much as I hate to admit it, I am."

"I don't understand why."

She shrugged. "I am not an organized person, but I had hoped to become so by overseeing the wedding breakfast plans and the Christmas Eve ball. I wanted to give Sophia time to concentrate on her gown and the wedding service itself. But if I make a complete jumble of it, I will have only succeeded in adding to her anxiety."

"I understand *that*," he said as they followed the path made of broken seashells. "But what about mermaid tears?"

She paused and faced him. "Now I don't understand."

"You have collected that glass, and you intend to use it to decorate tables for the wedding breakfast. Isn't that correct?"

"Yes."

"Then you must have a plan on how you will do that."

"Yes, but why are you talking about that, when I need your help in sorting out the mess I have made with the wedding and ball plans?"

He took her gloved hand in his and gave her that boyish grin that always made her heart take an extra flutter. "It is simple, if you break any task into small pieces and focus on one facet at a time. First you had to find the mermaid tears. Then you had to clean them and sort them."

"True." A motion caught her eye, and she pushed past him to go around the boxwood hedge to their left. She scanned the wood beyond the garden. Nothing.

"What is it?" Tension sifted through Jonathan's question. His smile had vanished, replaced by a forbidding frown.

"I thought I saw something."

"Or someone?" He put his hand up to shade his eyes.

"Yes. Over there. Just inside the wood."

"Wait here." He started past her.

She grasped his arm. "Have you lost your mind, Jonathan? What if I saw a smuggler?"

"I am assuming you did." His mouth tightened. "They are foolish to come so close to Meriweather Hall. I—"

A sharp and urgent barking came from the wood.

"Jobby!" Catherine shouted. "They will kill him if they think his barking can betray them."

"Stay here." He put his hands on her shoulders, but it was fierce gaze that froze her in place. "I mean it, Catherine! Stay here. Promise me that you will."

Jobby barked again. It reached a higher pitch. Was the puppy in danger?

"Go! I will stay here," she said.

Drawing her hands into the sleeves of her pelisse, she watched as Jonathan's long legs made short work of the distance between the garden and the wood. Her sister's warnings rang in her ears. *Don't get involved with another hero. It will only break your heart anew.*

He disappeared among the trees. She flinched when she heard Jobby's excited barking. Oh, how she wished her prayers for both Jonathan and the dog's safety would be heard!

Will You listen to my plea for help today? She ached to hear that soft answer within her heart. *Keep them safe.*

Nothing sounded within her heart, but the puppy burst from the wood, followed by Jonathan. She ran to meet them. Foggin rushed past her and was nearly bowled over by Jobby. He caught the dog by the collar and kept him from jumping on Catherine. She knelt and threw her arms around Jobby. She was so glad that both Jonathan and the dog were safe.

Jonathan nodded his thanks to the footman who was watching Cat hug the puppy. Jonathan walked over closer to Cat, who looked up at him with a fearful expression. He ached to pull her into his arms and soothe her by promising that he would never allow the smugglers to harm her or her family. But it was not a promise he was certain he could keep.

"Are you all right?" she asked.

"Yes, both of us are. Thank God for those bells on his collar." He nodded grimly to Foggin again, hoping the footman would pass along his gratitude to his fellow servants. "Between the jingling and his barking, I was able to find him within seconds."

"Did you see what he was barking at? Was it a squirrel or a deer?"

He shook his head, sorry to have to dash her hopes. "There was a man in the wood, but he took off when Jobby gave chase." He held up a piece of fabric. "Not quite quickly enough. Someone will need to patch his breeches tonight."

"May I?"

He offered the torn material to her. When she rubbed it between her fingers, he asked, "What are you doing?"

"This was made for wear, not for comfort. As well, it is stiff with salt as if it has been dunked into the sea and dried." She looked up at him, and her eyes were dim with dismay. "Jobby got his teeth into a smuggler."

"Good dog." He squatted and rubbed the dog's sides until Jobby's tail was a blur. He chuckled when the dog licked him twice on the cheek. Wiping his face with his sleeve, he stood. "I shall alert the men in the stables to keep an eye out for other trespassers."

"Tell them not to confront the smugglers." She shivered and wrapped her arms tightly around herself. "After they threatened the Demaines as they did, I doubt they would hesitate to hurt one of the stablemen."

"I will tell them not to face the smugglers on their own. Meriweather and I—"

"No!"

He arched a brow, and she closed her eyes and sighed.

"Jonathan, you and my cousin have already fought in too many battles. You are both lucky to be alive. You don't need to risk your lives again."

"But God didn't spare our lives so we could waste His gift by allowing these criminals to terrorize Sanctuary Bay." His voice was sharper than he realized because she turned away, but not before he saw a glimmer of tears in her eyes.

Slowly she nodded. "I know, and I appreciate your fervor, but I cannot bear the thought of losing someone else."

He saw how her cheeks had blanched, and he wondered if she spoke of her father or the man named Roland. A man she apparently had been in love with. Edging so he faced her again, he motioned for Foggin to take the puppy to the kitchen. He waited until the footman was out of earshot before he added, "We will do nothing foolhardy, Catherine. But, if something isn't done to stop these smugglers, they will be running tame through the corridors of Meriweather Hall soon."

Chapter Seven

Jonathan waited for Cat to say something as they walked into the house. What a bumble-bath he had made of the afternoon! He had hoped to lighten her spirits, and their outing had ended with her in the dismals.

"Would you like me to go through the papers with you?" he asked, hoping to ease her distress.

"If we must, we must."

He grinned as they took off their coats and gave them to a waiting footman. "Sounding like a martyr does not become you."

"It is just that I would rather do anything else, even another fitting with Mme. Dupont." Finally she smiled. It was a faint smile, but it was better than the fear he had seen on her face in the garden.

"I had no idea you found the situation that appalling."

She walked to the desk where pages were separated into about a dozen different piles. "I hate to admit defeat, but I don't even know where to begin. At least when I collect mermaid tears, I know where to start looking."

"May I?"

"If you think you can make some sense of that mess, please do."

He scanned the pages and understood why she was baffled by the invoices from various merchants, both local and in York. More than half included information for the wedding, the wedding breakfast and the Christmas Eve ball. Then there were pages of information about the events mixed in with the invoices. Some, like the plans for where guests would sleep, were lumped together.

"May I?" he asked again as he pulled out the chair.

"Of course."

"Do you have ink, so I may make notes?"

"Wait here."

Jonathan paused sorting the pages to watch Cat leave. He was in awe of how she seemed to float on air, each step as light as if she walked on invisible clouds. She was petite, but she possessed a presence that filled any room she entered. Everything about her seemed genuine, carefree and honest. Even when she was weighted down with worry as she was now, she possessed a sense of freedom he envied.

You could be as free, if you released your grip on the lie you have let take on a life of its own. He recognized the voice of his conscience, for it had repeated those words to him countless times in the past year and a half.

He was a coward. If he needed any proof, there it was. He was not brave enough to risk his friendships with Northbridge and Meriweather. More important, his friendship with Cat. Any of them, hurt at his deception, would be well within their rights to evict him from their lives. He had other friends in Norwich and even a few in London, but none like the ones here in Sanctuary Bay.

When Cat returned with the ink, he bent over the desk and began working. She left him alone to make whatever progress he could.

He continued sorting the pages but was aware of her on the other side of the room, paging through a book. There was something so cozy about being there with her, even if the span of the room separated them. He thought about his house in Norwich. The rooms there were beautifully appointed but held no warmth. He had thought he preferred his surroundings to be like that. He had been bamblusterating himself.

This was what had been missing from his life. A feeling of connection to another person, the comfort of being in the same room with that person and knowing that he had no need for illusion. Once he had believed his parents had such a relationship, but they had created such a scene—only when others beyond the family were present. When alone, his parents were happiest in separate parts of England, the farther apart the better. Had they ever been in love? He had believed he had loved Augusta, but that had died just as his parents' love for each other had. Maybe love itself was the greatest illusion.

Regret clamped his heart. He looked at the stacks of paper. While he was at Meriweather Hall, he would enjoy Cat's company, knowing how fleeting their time together must be. After the wedding and the Christmas ball, he would return to Norwich.

That was easy to plan, but it was more difficult not to imagine Cat traveling there with him. What would she think of his cozy house? Would she even be willing to be so far from the sea? Mermaid tears could not be found along the river that cut through the city.

He bent his head over his task. It would be better if he kept his focus on the present. The future would come soon enough, and he needed to enjoy this time when Cat was part of his life.

Jonathan did not look up again until the clock in the hallway chimed four. His stomach grumbled, and he thought of a sturdy tea. That would have to wait.

When he called Cat's name, she came to the desk. He handed her a page where he had listed all the papers and separated them into columns for each event. He quickly outlined what he had done.

She listened closely. When he was finished, she said, "I understand. I should have seen this before, but you have made it simple, Jonathan. May I keep this list?"

"I made it for you."

"Thank you. I will refer to it often." She laughed.

He laughed along with her, but the sorrow that he had tried to ignore pushed forth again. Her teasing reminded him of how his sister Gwendolyn's bosom-bow, Augusta, had once spoken to him. Lighthearted. Genuine. Never intending to hurt. Then Augusta had embarked on her first Season, and everything had changed.

"I thought you would want something to eat," she said as a footman came in with a large tray.

She took Jonathan by the sleeve and drew him to where she had been sitting by the fire. If he shifted his arm, could he draw her within his embrace? Would she come willingly?

He shoved away those enticing thoughts as he noticed the footman lingering by the door. All he was doing was torturing himself. It would be better to enjoy their friendship than risk losing it.

A generous tea was spread across the large tray. In addition to the usual bread, butter and jam, there were small meat pies topped with cheese. The pungent smell of pickled vegetables made his mouth water. Pieces of dried fruit waited on another plate.

"Help yourself," she said with a smile, and he knew he had betrayed himself with his eager gaze.

"Thank you." He took a small plate and handed it to her before picking up another for himself. "This is a generous tea, but, from what I saw on some of those invoices, you are planning an equal bounty for the wedding breakfast. How many people are coming?"

"Everyone who belongs on the estate plus the village residents and friends and family."

"Everyone?"

Cat selected a piece of cheese and nibbled on it. "It is a long-standing tradition for every bride and groom at Meriweather Hall to throw open the doors for the whole estate and the village. Any who wish are welcome at the Christmas Eve ball, as well."

"Do your traditions include inviting those involved with smuggling?"

"Without knowing who hides behind the smugglers' masks, we must open the door to everyone."

"Do you think that is wise?"

"Actually I do." She poured tea for both of them.

"You do?" He was so shocked he did not see the cup she held out to him until the saucer brushed his hand.

"Yes, if they are here, they won't be taking advantage of everyone being distracted to go about their illegal business. Anyone who doesn't come will be noticed, so the smugglers will be here, and we don't have to worry about them beyond our walls."

He tipped the cup in a salute to her. "Brilliant! You are a great strategist."

"I wish it wasn't necessary." She stirred sugar into her tea. "Someday the smugglers will find it expedient *not* to be in Sanctuary Bay."

"Keep praying for that day to come soon."

She reached for another piece of cheese. "Cousin Edmund says your family spends most of the year in London."

"They do." He was not surprised she had changed the subject abruptly. The topic of the smugglers rubbed against her the wrong way. Any further discussion about having the smugglers inside Meriweather Hall must be between him and Meriweather. He did not want to distress Cat.

"But you live in Norwich," she said. "That is a good distance from London."

He slathered a piece of bread with jam. What would she think if he told her that the reason he had chosen Norwich was because it was far enough from London to make it inconvenient for family to visit? He doubted she could even imagine wanting to put space between her and her family. She and Miss Meriweather and Lady Meriweather had welcomed Edmund Herriott because he was family. Then they had offered the same cordial reception to Jonathan and Northbridge, because they were Meriweather's friends.

"True," Jonathan said, knowing he owed Cat the courtesy of a reply.

"So you do not see your family often?"

"No."

"Now I understand."

"You do?"

She smiled, and he guessed his bafflement had been displayed on his face. "Why you were reluctant to come for the wedding. It means that you will be unable to spend Christmas with your family." Her smile disappeared. "Oh, Jonathan, it was wrong of Cousin Edmund to insist. If you want to be with your family, I'm sure Sophia and Charles would understand."

"I appreciate you saying that, but it's not necessary."

"Do you have plans to be with your family for Twelfth Night?"

He shook his head. "No."

"That was very definite."

"Yes."

When she arched a brow, he realized she was not going to be satisfied with a terse answer. There was no need to hide the truth from her. Once she reached London, she would learn it from the *ton*.

"My mother insists," he said, "that she be the first hostess of the New Year each year, so she holds a big assembly on the very first night."

"Why?" She tasted her tea, then added more cream.

"It is believed among the *ton* that whoever hosts that first party is the premier host or hostess of the year."

"So it is a matter of prestige."

"In her mind, it is. She guards her position as the

first hostess of the year as closely as the Yeoman Warders do the Jewel Tower in London."

"What an image!" She laughed. "I hope she doesn't insist on keeping ravens nearby, too, as they do at the Tower of London."

"Not likely. She considers them dreary, noisy birds that upset the serenity of her gardens."

Cat set her cup on the table and pushed a strand of hair back from her cheek. His own fingers itched to exchange places with hers so he could be the one touching her pretty face.

He looked down before she saw the truth in his eyes. He selected a meat pie and said, "One year, when I was no more than twelve, a neighboring peer's wife tried to usurp my mother by sending invitations to a ball to be held earlier on New Year's Day. So my mother decided to pay this woman a call."

Her eyes widened. "Ah, the plot thickens."

"Not really. After that short call, the lady switched her ball to later in January and blamed her secretary for putting the wrong date on the invitations."

"The poor secretary."

"He didn't lose his position, and I suspect, from what I heard afterward, he was well rewarded for taking the fall for his employer's wife."

"All's well that ends well, then."

"That is what Shakespeare says. After the war, I decided I preferred the quiet of my own company to such drama, so I have not attended the New Year's Day assembly."

She picked up her cup and smiled. "And this year, I'm sure your family understands that you would have a long journey from Meriweather Hall."

"They will be very pleased to hear that I am attending the wedding of Lord Northbridge to your sister." He kept the resentment out of his voice, but he knew his family, especially his mother, who would retell the story over and over of how her son the solicitor was counted as a friend of an earl with an esteemed and ancient lineage.

Cat began to talk about various Twelfth Night celebrations at Meriweather Hall, and he let the music of her soft voice envelop him. It created a wall that separated him from his vivid memories of celebrations at his mother's estate. His memories were not as filled with joy as hers, and he had no intention of spending the upcoming Twelfth Night, or any other, with his family.

Cat woke to a white world. The gentle breezes of the past week had been banished several days ago, replaced by an icy wind off the sea and snow piling up on the windowsills. Even the air inside her room had a crisp freshness to it, and she shivered as she quickly dressed in a burgundy wool gown. Its long sleeves were not stylish but were warm.

A knock was set on her door. She went to open it, expecting her sister. She was surprised to see Ogden on the other side. He was dressed impeccably as always, even at this early hour, and she was curious when he found time to sleep.

"Demaine, the gamekeeper, is here. He says he will take you to the wood today, if you wish, to view our Yule log."

She glanced at the window and realized frost had whitened the window, not snow. Holiday excitement pulsed in her as she told Ogden to let Alfred know she would be down soon. As the butler went to deliver her message, she rushed to her cupboard and dug deep within it to find her warmest gloves and a knit hat to wear beneath her bonnet. It would not be *à la modality,* but London was far warmer than North Yorkshire.

Wearing a lighter coat beneath her pelisse and taking her heaviest cloak, she hoped she would be warm enough. She needed, for excursions like this one, a heavier coat like the men in the stables wore. Maybe, after she returned from London, she would speak with Mme. Dupont about having one made.

Catherine hurried down the stairs, not wanting to keep Alfred waiting, when she knew he had many chores to do each day. He would not want to be gone from the cottage long, because he feared for his mother's safety when the smugglers were growing bolder with each passing day.

She smiled when she saw Alfred talking with Jonathan. She had not been told that he and Cousin Edmund were back from calling on landowners along the coast. They had hoped to obtain the additional help of the other landowners along the shoreline in halting the smugglers from transporting their goods inland.

Both men looked up as she came down the stairs. She was surprised to see Jonathan was only an inch taller than Alfred, who seemed to sprout up another hand's breadth every week. She noticed that in the moment before her gaze focused on Jonathan. With his hair mussed by the wind and a day's growth of beard edging his strong jaw, he had never looked more handsome.

As she reached the bottom of the steps, she said, "Good morning, Jonathan, Alfred."

"Good morning," Jonathan said while Alfred put his fingers to his forehead and gave a quick nod. "Demaine tells me that he is taking you to inspect the Yule log."

"You are welcome to come with us." She hoped he would agree, because it would be fun to share this important custom with him.

"You are going to freeze, and you would like me to do the same when I have not had a chance to get warmed up yet?"

"Yes." She could not keep from giggling. She hoped his good mood signaled that all had gone well during Cousin Edmund's calls.

He pulled on his gloves. "Then let's be on our way. The sooner we go, the sooner I can return and sit in front of a roaring fire."

"Cousin Edmund might want to come."

Jonathan's easy smile faded. "He has other matters to concern him. I doubt he wishes to be disturbed."

Questions tumbled through her head, but she did not ask any of them when Alfred could hear. The cold air hit her like a fist as she stepped outside. When Jonathan laughed and told her that he had warned her, she laughed, too, pushing away her dreary thoughts. Jobby rushed to join them.

"Miss Catherine," Alfred said, frowning at the puppy, "it would not be wise to have him digging up the animals' dens. That would disturb the creatures, and they could die from the cold."

"But he will warn us if any *creatures* come nigh," she said quietly.

The gamekeeper's face turned as white as the ice frosting the grass. He gulped hard and nodded.

"Here." Jonathan held out a leather strap that could be used as a leash. "Good luck getting him to stand still long enough to hook it to his collar."

It took the gamekeeper a half-dozen tries before he managed to get the leash on the excited puppy. Jobby yanked as far as the leash would go in one direction before running the opposite and doing the same.

Alfred did not complain. Each time the pup ran past him, he spoke to Jobby calmly. That serenity must have cut through the puppy's exhilaration, because Jobby slowed and walked alongside him into the wood.

"Astounding," Jonathan said as he followed with Catherine. "No wonder Meriweather asked him to stay on as gamekeeper. He has a definite way with animals."

"Just as his father did." She hesitated, then asked, "How did your calls go?"

"About as we expected."

"Is that good or bad?"

"Mostly it is no change. Too many worries and not enough guts."

Catherine nodded. Here in the open, where anyone might hear, she could not get more specific. It did not sound as if the help Cousin Edmund had hoped for would be forthcoming.

"I am sorry to make you look sad, Cat…" He quickly apologized again, adding, "I know you haven't given me permission to address you so. Forgive me."

"There is no need to forgive you," she replied automatically, then realized it was the truth. The name that had annoyed her when she had left childhood behind seemed somehow special when he spoke it. "Sophia uses it regularly, and Cousin Edmund even did before you returned to Meriweather Hall."

"But I presumed..."

"Nothing, Jonathan." She hooked her arm through his as they stepped within the even cooler shade of the wood. "Let's enjoy what this day has to offer."

He agreed and was the most charming and amusing companion she could have wished for. Even Alfred, who was stilted in her company, chuckled at Jonathan's silly stories of people he had encountered in Norwich.

They walked about a quarter mile before the trees thinned ahead. Alfred grinned and nodded when Catherine looked in his direction.

"I cannot wait to see it!" She ran to the center of the clearing where a huge trunk had been stripped of most of its branches. Only smaller ones and a few golden leaves remained.

She walked around the oak log, staying out of Alfred's way as he cut off more of the smaller branches with an ax that had been leaning against the trunk. The tree, when it had been standing, must have been more than forty feet tall. What was left was at least ten feet long. It would burn throughout the Christmas Eve ball and long into Christmas itself.

"It is huge," Jonathan said as he paced around it as she had.

"Only one of the hearths in the old great hall can accommodate it."

"How will you get that in the old hall? If you take it through the house, every piece of furniture in the hallways will have to be moved and the floors will be scraped."

"Jonathan, Meriweather Hall has stood for centu-

ries. Don't you think someone devised a way to bring a
Yule log into the great hall? Some of the windows can
be easily removed." She continued to examine around
the tree trunk. "Alfred, this will make the perfect Yule
log."

The gamekeeper grinned as he chopped more
branches off the trunk. "I am glad you like it, Miss
Catherine."

"You will oversee it being brought in, won't you?"

"Aye, if you wish me to."

"You found it," she said with a smile, knowing the
men considered it an honor to be in charge of setting
the Yule log on the hearth. "You should oversee the
job. Do make sure your mother comes to Meriweather
Hall before you return here to get the log. She won't
want to miss a moment of it."

"Aye." He lowered the ax, then tipped his cap to her.
She guessed he understood what she could not say in
the wood. With his mother in the great hall, he did not
have to worry about the smugglers paying her a call
on Christmas Eve.

Alfred was about to add more when Jobby gave a
great tug and pulled out of his collar. The puppy took
off with the gamekeeper in pursuit.

"You won't catch him!" Jonathan called, but Alfred
was already gone from sight. With a shrug, he picked
up the ax the gamekeeper had dropped and swung it
at the branch Alfred had been cutting.

Catherine watched as he sliced off one branch after
another. His face was set, and his eyes narrowed. Each
motion was sharp and precise...and powered by frustration.

The meetings must have gone even more poorly

than she had guessed. No wonder Cousin Edmund had shut himself away as soon as they returned. Without everyone standing up to the smugglers, nothing would change.

Without a word, she gathered up branches he and Alfred had cut off. She dropped them on top of others at one side of the clearing. They worked in silence for more than a half hour while they waited for the gamekeeper or Jobby to come back.

She was scooping up more debris when something sharp pierced her thumb. "Ouch!" She yanked off her left glove.

"What is it?" Jonathan asked, putting down the ax.

Instantly, as she heard his alarm, she felt silly. "It is only a small cut. Probably a splinter."

"Let me look."

"Jonathan, it is nothing."

Cupping her hand in his, he tipped her palm toward him. "Where is it?"

"My thumb."

He bent toward her hand. His breath was gentle and warm against her skin. That warmth seeped into her veins and spread through her like liquid sunshine. Her knees threatened to melt. He would catch her if she stumbled. His strong arms would keep her safe. Even when her greatest danger was her craving to kiss him. She had watched his lips in every mood. Happy, sad, angry, reverent. Would they have a different flavor for each? Oh, how she yearned to find out!

"It is gone," he said quietly and raised his head.

"Thank you," she whispered as she looked into his eyes which were so close to hers. A single motion by either of them would bring their lips together.

His hand rose to curve along her cheek as tenderly as he had held her palm. She leaned into his gloved fingers. Closing her eyes, she savored his touch.

"Cat?" he called softly.

"Yes?"

"Look at me."

She did and smiled as he tilted her mouth toward his. She held her breath, waiting for the delight of her first kiss.

But it was not to be. Jobby, barking wildly when he caught sight of them, burst into the clearing with Alfred surprisingly close behind. The gamekeeper wrapped his arms around the puppy and pulled the collar over Jobby's head.

Catherine was unsure if she or Jonathan or both of them had jumped away at Jobby's first bark. All she knew for certain was that the moment when he would have kissed her was past.

She was curious how much Alfred had witnessed, because both he and Jonathan made every effort to act normally. They talked about Jobby and bringing the Yule log to the house and everything except how Jonathan had been standing so close to her. If they noticed her silence, neither of them made any mention.

A carriage pulled through the gate as Catherine and the men reached the rear of the house. It was a heavy closed carriage. Shades were pulled over the windows, and, in the box, the coachee was hunched with the cold.

"I wonder who is calling on such a cold day," she said.

"Sir Nigel." Jonathan's answer was curt, and she wondered what their neighbor had said when Cousin

Edmund and Jonathan went to him for his assistance against the smugglers.

It looked as if she were about to find out.

Chapter Eight

Sir Nigel Tresting stood by the hearth in the larger drawing room, looking as comfortable as if Meriweather Hall were his domain. He was almost as round as he was tall, and the buttons on his navy waistcoat looked ready to pop. His white hair was perfectly coifed, and he wore thick gold rings on almost every finger. With boots that shined almost as brightly as the rings, he was the picture of a country squire who enjoyed good food and good company.

As Catherine walked in with Jonathan, she was startled to see a young woman sitting close to where Sir Nigel stood. Cousin Edmund was perched on a nearby chair, looking as if he was eager to escape.

"Come in, come in!" Sir Nigel pushed away from the hearth and crossed the room to bow over Catherine's fingers. "A pleasure, as always, Miss Catherine."

"Thank you." She gave no sign of her curiosity. Why had Sir Nigel come to Meriweather Hall? Had he changed his mind and was offering his help against the smugglers? From the strained expression on her cousin's face, she doubted that.

"Bradby." Sir Nigel's eyes slitted as he appraised Jonathan.

"Sir Nigel," Jonathan responded in an identically cool tone.

The baronet faltered, then his broad smile returned as he looked back at Catherine. "Please allow me to introduce my great-niece, Lillian Kightly. She has come to live with me until the Season begins. I wanted her to meet at least one other young woman who would be part of this Season. Lillian, my dear, this is Catherine Meriweather and Mr. Bradby." He added the last almost as an afterthought.

The young woman stood. She was classically beautiful with pale golden hair and large blue eyes. The fingers of her hand as she raised it to take Catherine's were slender and graceful.

"I am glad to get to meet you, Miss Catherine," she said in a lilting voice. "My great-uncle has sung your praises often during my visit."

"I hope you will make yourself at home at Meriweather Hall."

Sir Nigel interjected, "How kind of you to say that, Miss Catherine. I had hoped you would feel that way."

"Which way?" Catherine asked, clearly nonplused.

"Having Lillian feel at home here." His smile got even wider. "She finds my house boring, so I thought I would bring her here where she could enjoy the company of people her own age." He smiled at all of them, but his gaze focused on Cousin Edmund.

Catherine fought her instinct to step between the men and break that steady look. She suspected her cousin would appreciate her interference, but adding tension to the already taut moment might embarrass Sir Nigel's niece.

"Of course, it is not for me to say." She was glad her laugh sounded sincere and hoped nobody noticed her fingers curling tightly into her palms. How dare Sir Nigel try to back her into a corner like this! "This is Lord Meriweather's house."

"Most certainly. Most certainly." Sir Nigel put his arm around his great-niece's shoulders and herded her toward where she had been sitting.

Sympathy rushed through Catherine when she saw Miss Kightly try to edge away from her great-uncle. No doubt the beautiful young woman had been put to the blush by Sir Nigel's outrageous request. When Miss Kightly sat and faced them again, her hands folded on her lap, her face was a brilliant crimson.

Cousin Edmund must have seen Miss Kightly's embarrassment, because he invited her to stay as long as she wished. Her cousin's face eased into a smile when Catherine offered to escort Miss Kightly to one of the guest rooms near where she and her sister slept.

"Excellent," Cousin Edmund said. "That will allow us men to talk about less pleasant topics." His gaze shot daggers at Sir Nigel, but the round man seemed oblivious as he began to expound about one of the paintings on the wall.

Miss Kightly seemed ready to run as Catherine led her out of the parlor. Pausing only long enough to tell the footman by the door to have Miss Kightly's bags brought to the yellow guest room, Catherine led the way up the stairs.

"Please forgive my great-uncle," Miss Kightly said as they climbed the stairs. "He gets an idea in his head, and he cannot bear to let it go. When I decided to explore his house and the gardens, he took it in his head that I was bored, so he brought me here."

"We are familiar with Sir Nigel's ways." That was the most diplomatic way Catherine could reply. "He and my late father used to have some frightful rows, but then Sir Nigel would extend an invitation for Papa to go shooting with him or to watch him paint or to walk along the shore."

"And your father went?"

"For the walks along the shore, if I remember correctly." Catherine laughed. "I don't remember about the others. To own the truth, I have been so caught up in the details for my sister's wedding that I barely remember my own name, Miss Kightly."

"I would be happy to help you, Miss Catherine."

"Please call me Cat." She smiled when she said that. Cat. The name she once had hated, she found wonderful, because Jonathan used it.

Miss Kightly dimpled. "And you must address me as Lillian. I hope we can become friends."

"That would be lovely."

"I didn't plan to come to Uncle Nigel's house." She sighed. "My mother recently remarried, and her husband wanted some time for the two of them alone. Mother suggested I come to stay in North Yorkshire until the beginning of the Season." She glanced under her lashes at Cat. "Was Uncle Nigel correct when he said you would be going to London for the Season, too?"

"Yes." She did not explain further.

"Excellent. Now, at least, we will each know a friendly face there. I am glad you are agreeable to

my great-uncle's plans. Sometimes, when he thinks
he knows better than everyone around him, he can be
imperious."

"You are worrying needlessly. As I said, I have
known your great-uncle my whole life, so having him
bring you here was not a surprise."

"Really? You aren't just trying to ease my fretting?"

"Ask anyone in the house, and they will tell you that
a Meriweather daughter has never hesitated to speak
her mind."

"Good. I am accustomed to that after staying with
my great-uncle. He never curbs his tongue."

"So I have noticed."

Laughing, they continued up the stairs as Lillian
prattled about her plans for the upcoming Season. Cat
let her chatter, glad Lillian did not ask about Cat's
plans. She could not share with anyone that her only
reason for going to Town was to do as she had promised Roland before he left Sanctuary Bay to fight and
never return to her to make her his wife.

Cat pointed to the farthest window in the great hall.
"That is where the orchestra should go, Ogden."

The butler listened without comment.

"Do you think they should go somewhere else?" she
asked, recognizing his way of disagreeing without actually saying anything.

"When a Christmas Eve ball was held here, Miss
Catherine, that back corner was where the refreshments
were placed. There is a door nearby that is convenient
to the kitchen." He looked at a spot beyond her as he
said in his ever-so-correct voice, "Of course, you may
arrange the room as you see fit."

She laughed. "Please, Ogden, be honest with me. I wasn't born yet the last time Meriweather Hall hosted a Christmas Eve ball."

"And I was a footman." The butler unbent enough to smile. "I remember every detail of the first time I served at the famed Meriweather Hall Christmas Eve ball."

"Will you tell me?"

As the butler spoke, talking about the glorious greens that had been draped from the high ceiling, the joint roasting on the largest hearth, and the traditional music for singing and dancing, Cat closed her eyes. She imagined women wearing beautiful dresses with full skirts and waistlines far lower than the empire style that was popular now. The men's evening wear would have been decorated with gold lace and brilliant buttons with more lace at the throat. Their voices would have woven through the music and their laughter bright bubbles bursting throughout the hall.

Ideas filled her mind, and she could not wait to return to her room. She would draw them in her sketchbook. Combining her ideas and more conventional designs would make a beautiful setting for her sister's wedding breakfast. They need only add the orchestra, more candles and greenery for the Christmas Eve ball.

"Thank you, Ogden," she said when he finished reminiscing. "You have helped more than you guess."

"I am glad to be of service, Miss Catherine." He was once again the rigidly correct butler, but she caught a glimpse of a smile in his eyes as his gaze swept the room. And a glimpse of the young man he had been during his first Christmas Eve ball at the house, excited and impressed and resolved to do the best possible job.

She spent the next hour in her room, sketching her plans for the great hall. Sophia was busy with fittings for her trousseau, and Lillian never rose before midday. Neither her cousin nor Jonathan had appeared in the breakfast parlor while she ate, so she had no idea where they were.

That gave her the freedom to design the greenery in the great hall. Great swaths of ivy and holly over each window. More holly, with its bright red berries, would brighten the windowsills. She had heard tales of how the great hall was bedecked with fruit and candles, and she wanted to use both for the wedding breakfast and the Christmas Eve ball.

It was so easy to imagine exactly how it should be and then draw it.

It is simple if you break any task into small pieces and focus on one facet at a time. Jonathan's voice whispered in her mind, and she smiled. How kind he had been when he had helped her with the muddle she had made of the accounts!

She wished she could return the favor and help him with whatever made his expression grow grim. If only she knew what bothered him. At first she had thought he was embarrassed when someone lauded him as a hero. Cousin Edmund believed that, too. But she had seen signs that the root of his sadness was because of something else. The few times they had spoken of his family, his smile had wavered. In addition, any mention of her going to London bothered him.

Maybe she should be honest with him about her plans for London. She looked down at her sketchbook. Slowly she closed it, spreading her fingers across the leather binding. To open the book to him could unleash too much of the truth. He already knew she was hapless when it came to managing the wedding breakfast, and she had heard how fervently he prayed. There was no doubt in his voice that he would be heard, and his prayers answered. If he knew of her distance from God, would he be distressed that she had pretended nothing was amiss?

Cat avoided the unanswerable when Sophia opened her door and peeked around it. "Ah, here you are!"

"Come in." Cat opened the top drawer of her dressing table and slid the sketchbook inside. She wanted Sophia to be surprised by the decorations.

"No." Sophia hooked a finger toward her. "You come out. The pond has frozen, and we're going skating."

"The pond has frozen already?" Her eyes widened. "It never freezes before January."

Sophia gave an emoted shiver. "Haven't you noticed how cold it is? We barely had a summer."

"I guess I have become accustomed to the chill."

"I wish I could." She shivered again, this time for real. "Do you want to come?"

Cat nodded. She loved ice skating. Gliding along the ice while the cold air nipped at her cheeks was great fun. After they would return to the house and enjoy a hot drink and laugh about the spills they had taken.

As Cat dressed in her warmest clothes, Sophia listed who was joining them at the pond that was set on a cliff south of the house. Cousin Edmund and Jonathan had returned from wherever they had gone earlier, so they were coming along with Lillian. Vera and her brother, the vicar, had been invited, too. Several of the footmen and a pair of maids had volunteered to come as well, ostensibly to be there to help, but Cat knew they loved the chance to skate. The collection of skates kept in the stables would be waiting at the pond.

Soon Cat was walking with Sophia and the servants through the wood. The trees gave way to the windswept top of the cliff where the spring-fed pond had become a grayish-white. When she saw Jonathan sitting on a log as he lashed on a pair of skates, something quivered in her center. He had both her cousin and Lillian and the nearby servants laughing at some joke he had made.

But she could see past the jesting man who always had a witty word. She saw his gentle heart. Why did he always try to make people laugh? Did he fear others would see beyond his affability and discover his pain?

Tears began to flood her eyes, but she blinked them away before they could fall and freeze on her cheeks. Making sure she wore a cheerful smile, she greeted the others and took the skates Cousin Edmund held out to her. She lashed the leather straps around her ankles and listened to the lighthearted conversation.

Cousin Edmund sneezed, then grinned as they all said, "God bless you," at the same time.

"I hope we don't suffer from Christmas compliments this year," he said.

"What?" asked Cat.

"A head cold, as they say in London."

"The *ton* has a language of its own. I doubt I will be able to understand half of what is said once I get to Town."

"Which may not be a bad thing," Jonathan muttered. His face was tight, as it was when anyone mentioned London or the Season or the Beau Monde. What troubled him about those?

Sophia stood and stepped onto the ice. "Last one across the ice is a doleful donkey." She laughed as she skated away.

Cat followed. When she heard a thump, she looked back to see Jonathan sitting on the ice. She skated to him.

"Hurry!" she said. "You don't want to be a doleful donkey, do you?"

"I am afraid I must be." He did not move.

"Let me help you." She held out her hands.

"Go ahead with the others. I will catch up."

"Nonsense!" She grasped his hands and brought him to his feet. "The only way you are going to catch up with us is to let me help you."

He chuckled. "You hold me in low esteem, I see."

"Only your skating ability. Otherwise I hold you in the highest esteem." Her eyes widened as she realized she had spoken boldly.

Her sister skated to them. "Don't go to the far side of the pond. The ice isn't stable there."

"I doubt," Jonathan said, "I will make it that far."

Cat took his hands in hers. Slowly skating backward, she towed him. "Move your feet. No! Don't pick them up. Just let them slide. Good. Good."

He stared at his feet as he inched forward. His mouth was set in a determined line. He clearly intended to master the skill.

"Look up," she urged. "It is easier when you keep yourself in a straight line."

"Easier for you maybe."

"Trust me, Jonathan."

He raised his head so their eyes were level. As they

slid along on their own momentum, he said, "You know I would like nothing more than that."

She held her breath, waiting for him to continue. Was he about to tell her, on the frozen pond, what had hurt him so that the shadows of pain never left him? That thought sent a frisson of fright through her. If he were to be so open, could she be, too?

His arms windmilled, and she realized she had released his hands. She must have pulled back without realizing it. Reaching for his fingers again, she missed as he dropped to the ice.

"I am sorry," Cat said.

"Don't apologize. I should be able to stand on my own two feet." As Jonathan pushed himself up again, he said, "I don't know why I thought I would be less clumsy on ice than I am on solid ground."

"You are not clumsy."

He smiled grimly. "It is kind of you to say that, Cat, but the truth is that I spent half of my time on the Continent tripping over my own feet."

"Because you were hurrying here and there. You haven't been clumsy at Meriweather Hall."

"As far as you know."

His tone was so dreary, she had to laugh. "Skating is like dancing. Move your feet and the rest of you will come along."

"I am a very unskilled dancer."

"All you need is an excellent partner."

His voice dropped to a caressing whisper. "Is that you, Cat? Will you stand up with me for the first set at the Christmas Eve ball?"

Her heart thudded with joy. "Yes!"

"Good. I—"

Whatever else he might have added went unsaid when Sophia skated to them. She smiled as she circled to a stop. "You are doing well, Mr. Bradby."

"You are too kind. Way too kind." He laughed, once again the jolly man who acted as if he did not have any cares. Cat was astounded by the transformation, though she had seen it many times.

He inched away on his skates. His arms were out at his sides as if he walked on a tightrope, but he stayed on his feet. When he looked over his shoulder and called out that Cat was a good teacher, his feet slid out from beneath him, and he hit the ice with a crash. He waved help away and struggled to his feet.

Sophia grabbed Cat's hand, and they skated around the center of the pond. Lillian waved from where she sat on a log. A thick blanket covered her knees.

"I wish she would join us," Sophia said. "I tried to persuade her."

Cat matched her sister's pace. "Maybe *you* should not have been the one to try to persuade her." She looked across the ice to where Cousin Edmund was waiting for Mr. Fenwick to put on his skates. Beside him, Vera smiled at something their cousin had said. Cat was amazed, because she had not even noticed their arrival while she helped Jonathan.

"Cousin Edmund asked Miss Kightly to skate, but she suggested it would be better if he sat with her on the log."

"She acts smitten with him, taking any opportunity to sit beside him or talk to him." Cat waited until they had skated past their cousin and the Fenwicks before she added, "I hope it is not only because she wants to make Sir Nigel happy. Cousin Edmund deserves better than that."

"I wouldn't worry. Cousin Edmund is being a good host. Nothing more. If she has a calf-love for him, she must wait for him to take notice of her as more than a neighbor's great-niece."

"And if Sir Nigel truly wanted to smooth the road to true love, he could be more forthcoming with help to halt the smugglers."

Sophia's laugh rang across the pond. "Oh, Cat! You have the most wonderful way of getting to the heart of the matter."

A sudden spate of loud barking announced Jobby's appearance. He loped out of the woods, but he was not alone. Three forms emerged from the trees, two short and one much taller.

"Charles!" Sophia scrambled across the ice and almost tumbled.

Her fiancé rushed forward to catch her before she could collapse. Twirling her about as he kept his balance effortlessly, he kissed her, as if they were the only two people on the pond.

Cat looked away, startled by her response to their kiss. She had seen them in each other's arms before, but never had she felt the prickle of envy as she did now. She yearned to be part of something as wonderful as her sister had found. She had thought she had that with Roland, but she had been wrong. He had been so determined to do his duty and prove he was worthy of her that he never seemed to notice that she believed he already was, and he did not need to demonstrate that to her. He had helped her believe in herself and her art. She could not imagine anything else he could have done that would please her more, but that was not enough for him. He had been absolutely certain that her father would not approve of their match unless Roland was acclaimed for his role in the war. Had Roland taken foolish risks simply to assure her father's respect? Risks that led to his death? If so, it had been unnecessary, because the previous Lord Meriweather had spoken highly of Roland even before he had enlisted.

If only Roland had heeded her when she had told him that.... He had not, and all she had left was her grief at the waste of his life and the love they could have shared.

She glanced at Jonathan. He was inching toward them, his arms flung out to help him keep his balance. At least he had nothing to prove. Everyone already knew of his heroics. She was glad he would not throw his life away needlessly as Roland might have. To lose someone else she cared about... She could not bear the thought.

Small arms were flung around her knees, almost knocking her off her feet. She reached down and picked up Michael. The three-year-old gave a squeal as she spun around with him in her arms.

"Teach me," he said as she placed him on the bank again. "I want to do that."

Charles ruffled his son's hair. "As it happens, I brought a pair of skates just your size." He smiled. "And a pair for you, too, Gemma. They're in the carriage's boot."

The little boy and his seven-year-old sister gave an excited shout and ran ahead of their father to Meriweather Hall. Sophia waited until they returned and

Charles had tied on his skates, then both of them helped the children. With Charles holding Gemma's hand and Sophia gripping Michael's, the four of them began skating slowly.

"They look like a family," said Cousin Edmund.

Was that envy she heard in her cousin's voice? If so, she understood the feeling all too well.

"That is," Jonathan said as he tottered closer to them, "because they are. Even before Northbridge had the good sense to ask your cousin to marry him, they were becoming a family."

Jonathan stood to the side as Mr. Fenwick and Miss Fenwick stepped onto the ice. For a moment he considered asking the vicar if he could have a few minutes alone with him. Mr. Fenwick might have some advice for him on how to deal with the burden of his lies, a way that would guarantee that he did not lose his friends.

But now was not the time. Not when everyone was on the ice, laughing and enjoying the day. Everyone but Miss Kightly who seemed content to sit on the log and drink hot tea provided by one of the footmen.

He watched the others skate, but his gaze focused on Cat. Her innate grace served her well on the ice, and her face was appealing pink with the cold. She laughed, the sound as sparkling as the chilly air. He thought of how happy she had looked when he had asked her if he could be her partner for the first dance at the ball. His sister's friend Augusta had been as open with her emotions in the weeks before she had left for London and then changed into a haughty predator eager to win the attentions of the highest ranking man in any room.

He did not want that to happen to Cat, but he could not imagine any way to halt her from going to Town. She spoke of her visit eagerly, and he found it impossible to forget her dismissive tone when she talked about not needing much of a country-made wardrobe for the Season.

Sitting on the edge of the bank, he took off his skates. He suddenly did not feel like making more of a fool of himself.

A child's scream sliced through the air. He looked up to see Gemma at the far end of the pond where Miss Meriweather had said the ice was too thin. Jumping to his feet, he ran around the pond at top speed. He saw Northbridge and Meriweather turning toward the little girl, too, but Jonathan jumped down on the ice and went skidding in her direction.

Beneath him the ice cracked. He threw himself forward, spread-eagle on the ice, to distribute his weight. His momentum carried him toward the little girl.

"Grab my hand," he said, stretching his arm as far as he could.

"Why?" she asked, puzzled.

The ice broke beneath him, and cold water rushed up around him as he hit something hard. In astonishment, he realized he was lying in the mud on the bottom of the pond. The water was less than an inch deep.

He pushed himself up. More ice broke, but it did not matter. The water was shallow.

Behind him, he heard a laugh. He looked back as he pushed himself to his feet. Meriweather was laughing so hard that he had to lean forward and put his hands on his thighs. His whole body shook. Beside him, Northbridge grinned as he reached past Jonathan and set Gemma on the shore.

"Sophia warned you not to come over here, Gemma," Northbridge said with a stern tone that was lessened by his grin. "Go back with Sophia and your brother. Don't come over here again."

"Or else," Meriweather said with a smothered chuckle, "Bradby will try to rescue you again." He laughed so hard he had to sit in the snow on the shore.

"Bradby to the rescue," Northbridge said, clapping him on the shoulder. "No one can accuse you of not being willing to risk life and limb at any time."

Jonathan wiped at the mud freezing to his clothes. Stepping out of the pond, he tried to suppress the rage boiling up within him. Not at his friends. They had every reason to tease him. He had acted like a nick-ninny, rushing to save the little girl without checking to determine the circumstances first. Thunder! He was a trained solicitor and a trained soldier. Both should have taught him to look before he leaped. Instead he had heeded his craving to prove he truly was a hero.

He mumbled something about going to the house and changing out of his filthy clothes. He doubted his friends heard, because they were laughing too hard. As he strode around the pond, Cat called his name. He did not stop. He could not face her after his stupidity.

Jobby bounded up to him, but ran to the others when Jonathan ignored him and kept on a straight course for the wood. A hand seized his filthy sleeve as he stepped between the first trees. The tingle that raced up his arm told him, without looking, that Cat stood beside him.

"Jonathan, wait a minute," she said.

He kept walking.

"Talk to me!" she cried.

"And say what?" He did not slow. "That I have made myself a laughingstock for trying to save a child who didn't need saving."

"If she had, you would have been there."

"But she didn't need saving. Isn't that the point? Or do you think I acted like a Tom-fool simply for everyone's entertainment?"

She pushed her way in front of him, forcing him to stop before he plowed her down. The quick comment he had been about to speak died on his lips when he lost himself in her dark brown eyes. No hint of amusement glistened in them. Instead they were bright with unshed tears.

Thunder! Not only had he made a fool of himself, but he had ruined her outing. The thought thrust a sharp pain into his heart.

"Forgive me," he said. "I am being silly, as usual."

"You are not usually silly. Funny at times, but I don't think I have ever seen you do something truly silly."

His fingers wanted to cup her cheek, but his gloves were caked with mud. If he kissed her... That would be truly foolish, because then her clothes would be dirtied, too, and everyone would know what they had done.

He turned away before he could no longer fight the need to pull her close, no matter the consequences. As he stepped around her, she walked alongside him. She was waiting for him to say something, but the only words on his tongue were of how much he longed to kiss her.

"What is that?" Cat asked.

He glanced in the direction she pointed, then looked more closely at something that hung from a tree. Not high up. Exactly on eye level, so someone passing by would not fail to notice it. He reached up and scowled as he saw the breeches with a hole ripped in the back. The material was identical to what Jobby had had in his mouth when he had chased the intruder.

Jonathan pulled the hanging material off the branch, then grimaced as two things fell out of it. He picked up one and stared in disbelief. It was a crudely made stuffed toy in the shape of an animal.

"It is a dog." She gasped. "A dog with the same color as Jobby. An effigy like the ones we made of Guy Fawkes for bonfire night."

Jonathan reached down for the other item. It was an old knife. When he looked from it to the stuffed dog, he saw a slit in the toy the exact shape of the knife.

"Oh, sweet heavens!" Cat whispered.

He turned the rusty blade over and over. The haft was gritty with salt. "Heaven has nothing to do with this."

Chapter Nine

No one spoke.

The only sound was Miss Kightly's soft sobs, as she leaned her head on Meriweather's shoulder. His pats on her arm were awkward, but he was doing his best to calm her. Opposite them, Cat sat between her sister and Miss Fenwick. Northbridge paced on one side of the room, and the vicar did the same on the other. Northbridge's children were upstairs with a kind nursery maid named Alice, who was making them feel at home.

Jonathan stood by the door, leaning back against the wall, his arms crossed in front of him. He had tried to begin a conversation more than once, but each time either Meriweather or Northbridge shut it down with a few sharp words. It was clear that they did not want to discuss what he and Cat had found when the ladies were present.

That made no sense, because none of these women, with the exception of Miss Kightly, had given any indication that they were faint of heart. How long were they going to wait to talk about what they should do?

As if he had asked that question aloud, Cat and her

sister rose. He did not see any visible signal among the
ladies, but Miss Fenwick came to her feet, as well. Miss
Meriweather went to where Miss Kightly sat and dis-
entangled the young woman from around her cousin
so smoothly that Jonathan was amazed. Miss Meriweather and Miss Fenwick helped the sobbing woman
from the room.

Cat followed, pausing long enough to whisper, "Jonathan, don't let them do something foolish. If there was
any doubt before, it's clear now that the smugglers will
stop at nothing."

"I know," he said softly. "Jobby—"

"I have already given instructions that he must not
be allowed outside without a leash."

He gave her a swift smile. "He won't be happy."

"Better unhappy than dead."

He nodded as she stepped past him. He caught her
arm, surprising himself as much as her. When she
looked up at him, he said, "Advice we need to take for
ourselves as well, Cat."

She flinched but nodded.

Reluctantly he released her so she could catch up
with the others. Did she have any idea how much he
wanted to hold her close, while he kept her safe from
every danger in the world? One look deep into the
dark wells of her eyes and he would gladly lay down
his life to protect her. Only now when the threat surrounded them could he admit that he was beginning
to care for her deeply.

He almost laughed at the irony. The man everyone
believed to be a hero was ready to sacrifice his life for
a woman he should not dream of making his own, until
he proved he was a true hero. And if he became a real

hero by facing the mass strength of the smugglers by himself, he would end up dead. That was the warning left in the wood. What a mess he had made for himself with his web of lies!

"We cannot let these smugglers think they scare us," Northbridge said.

"Even if they have." Meriweather set himself on his feet. "Catherine has already alerted the staff to stay out of the wood and not to let any of the animals wander in there."

"That is wise." Mr. Fenwick remained sitting, but his eyes were narrowed with an anger that Jonathan had never expected to see on a clergyman's face. "I will speak to those in the village with children."

"And let the smugglers know of our plans?" Jonathan demanded as he pushed himself away from the wall. Save for the vicar, this conversation could have been one of the many they had around low-burning fires the night before a battle. He had not expected to fight another war once Napoleon was defeated.

He closed his eyes, and the image of the French soldier raising his knife toward Northbridge burst into his mind. Everything had frozen in perfect clarity in that moment, searing the whole attack on his brain. He could recall each detail, the smells of fear and death, the cries of battle and the dying, the way his muscles tensed as he saw the knife flash toward Northbridge.

"What plans?" asked Northbridge, yanking Jonathan out of his horrific memories. "All we have decided so far is to be cautious."

Jonathan nodded, annoyed for letting himself be sucked back to memories of when Northbridge had almost died. Jonathan had been known as the calm one when they had faced the French, but then Cat had not been involved. Admiration for Northbridge filled him anew. His erstwhile commander gave no sign of the distress of having the woman he loved and his beloved children caught up in this invisible war with the smugglers.

"Caution is the most important step," Jonathan said.

Northbridge smiled tautly in his direction. "I am glad to see we are of one mind on that. This is not the time for heroics. This is the time for thoughtful discussion and careful decisions."

"You know this situation better than we do, Mr. Fenwick." Jonathan looked at the vicar. "Do you have any advice for us?"

Slowly the vicar stood. He put one hand on Northbridge's shoulder and the other on Meriweather's. "I do not, but Paul the apostle does when he wrote to the Philippians. *'Finally, brethren, whatsoever things are true, whatsoever things are honest, whatsoever things are just, whatsoever things are pure, whatsoever things are lovely, whatsoever things are of good report; if there be any virtue, and if there be any praise, think on these things.'*"

"You are right," Jonathan said. "We should not act in haste."

Northbridge scowled. "The only way to kill a snake is to chop off its head. Declaring war on the poor fishermen in the village who have been coerced into helping or being silent or both will do nothing but create anger and fear and resentment."

"You saw the result of that today," the vicar said.

"So we need to find their leader and deal with him?" Jonathan rubbed his hands together, but nothing could ease the sudden cold cutting through him. He had thought he was done with war, but another battle awaited them.

"Yes," Mr. Fenwick said with regret. "The late Lord Meriweather planned to do that, and I have no idea how close he came to success."

"Not close enough to halt them." Jonathan glanced from Northbridge to Meriweather and then to the vicar. "It appears we must take on the task and finish what he began. What do you say?"

Northbridge smiled coldly. "I say aye."

"Meriweather?"

Their host nodded, and Jonathan suspected Meriweather was relieved that his friends had already made the decision before asking him.

"So what do we do?" Meriweather asked.

"Listen," Jonathan said. "When we were on the Continent, some of the best information we obtained was simply by listening. Here, we can listen in the house, in the village, on the shore and at church."

Mr. Fenwick smiled and nodded. "An excellent plan, and one I can help with, gentlemen."

"So is it agreed?" Meriweather asked.

They nodded, and Jonathan dared to believe that he would have a chance to halt the smugglers *and* prove himself to be a hero in truth.

"I publish the Banns of Marriage between Charles Winthrop, earl of Northbridge of Northbridge Castle, Sussex, and Sophia Meriweather of Sanctuary Bay, North Yorkshire. If any of you know cause, or just impediment, why these two persons should not be joined together in holy Matrimony, ye are to declare it. This is the first time of asking."

Sophia's face glowed as brightly as the candles on the altar. Cat took her sister's hand and squeezed it. On the other side of the pew box, Charles was smiling and trying to hush his exuberant son at the same time.

Jonathan, who sat beside Charles, picked up Michael and sat him on his lap. He bent and whispered something in the little boy's ear. Michael nodded, then edged off his lap and sat with his hands folded on his lap. He did not shift or make another sound.

Cat wondered what Jonathan had told the little boy. As if she had asked the question aloud, his eyes shifted toward her. She did not look away. She should, but she met his gaze steadily. When a smile uncurled along his lips, she smiled back. It was a day for joy. One of his best friends and her dear sister were eager to share with the world their love for each other.

There had not been much reason to smile since the discovery of the effigy. The men had searched the wood, but found nothing else. Even so, like Jonathan, Cat had no doubt it had been put up by the smugglers as a warning not to let Jobby loose in the wood again.

Lillian had been so distressed that she had taken to her bed and had not risen until this morning to join them coming to church. Cat had half expected her to return to Sir Nigel's estate, but she appeared more at ease this morning. Or maybe it was that she had stayed close to Cousin Edmund, letting him hand her into the carriage and sitting beside him on the way to church. Cat had heard her tell her uncle, who had attended the

Sanctuary Bay church this morning, rather than his own parish's church to the south, that her visit to Meriweather Hall was going well.

Mr. Fenwick announced that the banns were being read in Charles's parish church as well, and that the second reading would be next Sunday. Once they had been announced a third time, Sophia and Charles could marry.

Cat listened to the rest of the service, trying to absorb Mr. Fenwick's erudite lesson. He challenged them with quotes from Scripture and from scholars. She often wondered what the villagers thought of his sermons. They treated him with respect, and she suspected they were proud of their learned vicar.

She bowed her head during the prayers and sang the hymns. She waited, hoping for the welcome of God's presence, but it did not come. Even though she smiled along with the others as they thanked Mr. Fenwick for an excellent service, she was sad. She had no idea how to persuade God to be with her again.

Jonathan was pulling on his gloves beyond the church's porch. She walked over to him, hesitant, because they really had not talked since the skating party. When he gave her a warm smile, she asked, "What did you tell Michael?"

"That he needed to be quiet during the reading of the banns, because someone might think he was protesting that your sister and his father shouldn't marry. That way she might never become his mother." He chuckled. "That child adores your sister, and he cannot wait to be able to call her 'mama.'"

"How clever of you!"

* * *

Jonathan did not feel clever, but he liked the idea that Cat believed he was.

As if they had called the little boy's name, Michael ran to them and pulled on Jonathan's coat. "I was quiet, wasn't I?"

"You were wonderful," Jonathan said. "Do you think you can be quiet two more times while the banns are read?"

Putting his fingers to his mouth, he turned them as if he held a key. Eagerly he nodded.

Jonathan ruffled the little boy's hair, glad that Northbridge's children had come to love their father. Before the war, Northbridge had been unsure how to act around his children whom he barely knew after so many years fighting the French on the Continent. Sophia had taught him to open his heart to his children at the same time he had fallen in love with her. Now, young Michael adored his father, and his sister did, too.

It was so important, Jonathan knew, for a young boy to have his father in his life. He wished his own had been in his life more often, but the discord between his parents had prevented that.

As the others gathered around him and Cat and the boy, the conversation was lighter than it had been since they went skating. Parishioners interrupted them often to offer congratulations to Sophia and Charles.

"Thank you," Sophia said to each one. "I feel blessed."

"The community of Sanctuary Bay is thrilled to have the late Lord Meriweather's daughter marrying well," Jonathan said.

"And happily." Lillian batted her lashes at Meriweather in a clear hint that *he* should think of marrying soon, too. Color rose up his friend's cheeks, and he ducked his head.

"There are some," Cat said to fill the uncomfortable silence, "who say that, after all you soldiers have been through, you are due every bit of happiness."

"I like how you think," Northbridge said as he gave a half bow toward Cat. He smiled at his betrothed. "Your sister is, my dear, a very wise woman."

"Only because she agrees with you." Sophia held her hands out to the children. "But I do agree that you have done your duty." She glanced at Jonathan, and tears filled her eyes as they did each time she spoke of him saving her future husband's life. "And some of you have done even more."

Jonathan excused himself. He had to get away before he choked on the truth that he should speak.

Someday.

Not today on the day his friend was looking forward to his wedding. Not even to cleanse his soul would Jonathan ruin what should be a perfect day for Northbridge and his family.

When he saw Mr. Fenwick speaking with his sister, Jonathan made a decision. He was not ready to divulge the truth today, but he could not wait any longer for some guidance on how best to tell his friends when the time was right.

He greeted Miss Fenwick, who looked festive in her bright green pelisse. Then he turned to the vicar. "May I speak with you, Mr. Fenwick? Privately?"

Mr. Fenwick nodded. "It would be my pleasure, Mr. Bradby. Will you give me a few minutes to get everything in order after the service? Then I can give you my full attention."

"Of course." What else could he say? That he needed to speak with the vicar *now*. Before he lost his nerve.

"Why don't you meet me at the vicarage? I shall be less than five minutes here."

"I don't—"

"Mr. Bradby, come with me." Miss Fenwick motioned toward the simple flint cottage. "Gregory has to close up the church and make sure everything is put away properly."

He offered her his arm. What else could he do? Turn tail and run? He had started down this path, so he must see it to its end.

When Miss Fenwick put her fingers on his sleeve, he felt none of the delightful feelings that Cat's touch evoked. But Miss Fenwick was pleasant company, talking about nothing important, as if she sensed the weight he carried. He should have guessed a clergyman's sister would be insightful.

At the cottage, she opened the door. "You can sit anywhere, Mr. Bradby. Gregory will be here as soon as he can. If you will excuse me…"

"Of course," he said automatically, but was surprised when she turned and walked back the way they had come.

Jonathan lowered his head as he stepped into the cottage. He saw the lamp he had moved hanging by the hearth, and he thought of how pleased Miss Fenwick had been with his help. Cat had been even more so, and he had delighted in being able to make her happy with such a small deed.

He chose a seat by the hearth which had burned

down to embers. Rising, he put more logs on the fire and stirred it up, so the cottage would be warm when the Fenwicks entered. He sat again and waited with little patience. He wanted this conversation started. He wanted it over. He wished he could avoid it altogether.

Maybe he could have if he had not come back to Meriweather Hall. No, it was not the place that had compounded his guilt. It was Cat. She was open and guileless and believed the foolish story of his heroism. Each time she mentioned it, or someone else did in her hearing, he wanted to crawl away like the worm he was.

He needed forgiveness. God's and his friends'…and most of all, Cat's. He knew how to ask God for forgiveness and he had, but knew he had to own to the truth to his friends before God absolved him of what had started out simply as a misunderstanding before blossoming into this lie that consumed him.

The door opened, and Mr. Fenwick came in. Even though he was not as tall as Jonathan, he had to duck beneath the low rafters. The vicar did it with the ease of practice as he removed his coat, hat and gloves, and hung them on pegs by the door.

"Thank you, Mr. Bradby, for getting the fire going." He held out his hands to the hearth. "Even the old-timers are saying they cannot remember a winter this cold this early in Sanctuary Bay." He faced Jonathan. "But you didn't come here to talk about the weather, or so I am assuming." He pulled up a chair and sat. "What can I help you with, Mr. Bradby?"

The words he had thought about saying so often withered on his tongue. It had been a mistake to approach Mr. Fenwick. He had known the Meriweathers for as long as he had been their vicar. Maybe Jonathan should have sought out advice from a clergyman who did not know either him or his friends.

Mr. Fenwick gave him an encouraging smile, and Jonathan realized the vicar had mistaken the cause for his hesitation when Mr. Fenwick said, "You need not worry about the chance of my sister overhearing our conversation. Vera is joining the Meriweathers and Lord Northbridge at Meriweather Hall for the afternoon." Another smile eased his stern face. "She gives me time alone on Sundays for prayer and contemplation and for conversations with my parishioners."

The vicar's words offered him the exactly the excuse he needed to leave. "I am not one of your parishioners, so I should not take up your time." He stood. "Thank you."

Mr. Fenwick got up and somehow blocked his way to the door without being obvious. Not that it was difficult in the cramped cottage where Jonathan felt as if he needed to bend double to avoid striking his head.

Motioning toward the chairs again, the vicar said, "Please sit, Mr. Bradby. I have never heard it said that the good Lord cares where we speak to Him as long as we speak from the heart."

How Jonathan longed to do exactly that! To bare his pain and accept the cost of his lies, so he could finally put the war and its pain behind him.

He sat and said, "I need your advice, Mr. Fenwick, on an issue that gnaws at me."

"Whatever you say will not leave this cottage other than rising to God's ears."

"Good." He had seen the trust the Meriweathers put in their vicar, so he must do the same. "My friends have one impression of me, and it is not exactly the truth. I know I should be honest with them." He looked down at his fingers that were clasped so tightly that his knuckles were bleached. "I should have been long ago."

"The truth does not become less important because time has passed."

"But speaking it does."

Mr. Fenwick nodded. "I understand."

"You do?" he asked, surprised.

"Mr. Bradby, in Psalms, it is written, *'Thou hast set our iniquities before Thee, our secret sins in the light of Thy countenance.'* That tells us that it is the most unusual person who doesn't have some secret. In fact, I have never met anyone, man or woman, who is completely forthright. All of us, and I'm including myself when I say that, have done things or said things or overlooked things that in retrospect makes us ashamed. Speaking of it later is often too difficult, so we carry that truth as a secret branded on our soul."

"That is what it feels like. Something burning on my soul."

The vicar smiled gently. "Never forget that verse from Psalms."

"That there is One from whom I never can keep a secret, for He sees into the deepest portions of our hearts?"

"Yes."

"I have spoken to Him, and I believe I know what He wishes me to do." His mouth twisted. "Which is why I am here."

"I will not query more deeply into what preoccupies you, Mr. Bradby, but I can tell you what the Apostle Paul wrote. *'We henceforth be no more children, tossed to and fro, and carried about with every wind of doctrine, by the sleight of men, and cunning craftiness, whereby they lie in wait to deceive; but speaking the truth in love, may grow up into Him in all things.'"*

"So you are suggesting that I should trust my friends?"

Mr. Fenwick hesitated as if trying to think of another quote to answer Jonathan's question. "Yes. Trust your friends. They are good men and women." A smile flitted across his lips. "I am assuming that you consider the Meriweather women your friends."

"I certainly do." There was a bit too much fervor in his voice, but he was ready to grasp onto any suggestion as a way to pull himself out of this morass he had let go on for too long. "And I want to keep them as friends."

"Perhaps through prayer, you can come to understand why you are withholding the truth from them. Shall we pray together?"

Jonathan nodded, even though he knew what God's answer would be: Jonathan must own to the truth. So he prayed for the courage to do God's will. He would need every bit that his friends believed he had.

Chapter Ten

When Jonathan arrived at Meriweather Hall shortly after the evening meal, Cat wondered where he had spent the day. Vera had told her that he had asked to speak with her brother. Cat had been glad to hear that.

But, as soon as she saw Jonathan's tense expression, she was certain that he had not found the answer he needed. She pushed back from the desk, away from the accounts he had straightened out for her and hurried out into the hall.

"Jonathan?" she called.

He paused but did not turn. His rigid shoulders told her that he had no interest in talking.

"Mrs. Porter said she would keep a plate warm for you." Cat squashed her curiosity about where he had been. The answer was right in front of her, because the polish on his boots had been scoured away by sand. He must have been walking along the shore. "I can have your supper sent to the dining room or your chamber, whichever you prefer."

"Thank you." He started to walk away.

She followed. "Where do you want to eat?"

"It doesn't matter. Whatever is simpler for your household."

His voice was gloomier than she had ever heard it, and his steps were as heavy as if he dragged a herd of elephants in his wake.

"Is there anything else I can do?" she asked, her face getting hot as she realized how her question sounded.

"No."

Knowing she should let the matter go, she could not keep herself from saying, "You have changed."

"Haven't you noticed that war changes a man?" He turned. His eyes were hollow with torment.

She longed to take his hands and draw him into the closest room where he could divulge what was making him heartsick. "Jonathan, I am worried about you. So please don't try to betwattle me with such a question. I didn't know you before the war."

"True, but—"

"You have changed since you were here last time."

"I didn't realize I was acting differently."

Pain shot through her heart. "Jonathan, please don't be false with me. I could not bear it."

"I am sorry, but…" He did not finish the apology as he walked away.

She watched him leave. She wanted to give chase and demand that he be honest with her. She stayed right where she was. How could she help him if he refused to tell her the truth of what caused him such pain?

Maybe he did not want her help.

The thought drew her up short. He had told her that there was nothing else she could do. Just tonight with supper or did he mean forever?

Her heart threatened to crack in two, and she could not ignore how deeply he had found a place in it.

Cat paced from one side of the small parlor to the other, as she told Sophia about the conversation with Jonathan. Candles flickered with her passage, making her shadow dance on the wall.

"Do you think his distress has to do with Charles or the children?" Sophia asked as she sat beside the window.

"Of course not. He adores the children, and we all know what he did for Charles."

"Miss Kightly could not be the cause. Her arrival has Cousin Edmund all on end. Not Mr. Bradby." Sophia frowned. "Not that it matters now that she's gone back to Sir Nigel's house."

"When did that happen?" asked Cat, shocked out of her dismay.

"When Sir Nigel left after the evening meal, she went with him. He became incensed when someone mentioned the effigy that you found in the woods. He made no secret that his great-niece must not remain where she has been threatened."

Cat took in the information, which was hardly surprising. Trust Sir Nigel to overreact.

"Be that as it may," she said, "Lillian isn't to blame. Jonathan has been acting oddly since he arrived. Haven't you noticed?"

"I noticed he was a bit more exacting than usual."

"A bit?" Cat laughed without humor. "Sometimes it is as if I am in the company of a complete stranger."

A knock came at the door, and it opened slightly. Charles looked around it to ask, "Am I intruding?"

"Of course not." Sophia came to her feet and held out her hands to her fiancé. As she took them, she said, "So cold! Have you been riding?"

"No, I took the children out for a walk before bed because Michael had to 'see the sea,' as he always says. They insisted on going all the way out to the end of the headland. Something about seeing a mermaid crying. I don't know where they got that idea."

Cat laughed. "You can blame me, Charles. I had them sorting sea glass with me this afternoon, and I told them how we call the pieces mermaid tears."

"Ah, a great mystery solved." He sat next to Sophia and put his arm around her shoulders.

"Now that we have solved one mystery, maybe you can solve another for me," Cat said as she sat facing them.

"Which mystery is that?" Charles asked.

"Jonathan. He isn't the same man he was when he first came here with you and Cousin Edmund."

Charles drew in a deep breath. "To be honest, Catherine, it puzzles me, too. Bradby had tongue enough for two sets of teeth. Before he saved my life, he never was without a quick answer or a brilliant suggestion."

"As a solicitor, he has to have an agile mind."

"So true."

"When did he change?"

Charles looked past her to the fire on the hearth. "The day after the battle when he saved my life, he was a different man. Instead of profound comments, he acted as if everything he said must be a jest."

"We saw that on your visit in the fall." Sophia blinked on tears that jeweled her eyes. "I saw how hurt he was when nobody laughed at his quips."

"Maybe," Cat said, "that is why he struggles to avoid funning now and is stern and grim." She picked up a cup of tea that had gone cold while she pondered why Jonathan had changed and then put it down when her fingers trembled with despair. "And if someone praises him for being a hero, he goes as silent as the world before the first dawn."

"He is still acting that way?" Charles gave a deep sigh. "I have prayed so often that whatever torments him will be banished from his soul."

"As I have," Sophia added. "And I will keep doing so."

"I'm glad you will." Cat hoped neither Charles nor her sister noticed that she had not spoken of praying for Jonathan, too. She could only hope that He would heed their prayers and help Jonathan.

Sunshine ran along the passage on the ground floor of Meriweather Hall. So did a youngster.

Jonathan skipped to one side to avoid a boy who raced past him. It could not be Michael, for the boy was twice Michael's height. Jonathan got out of the way as two more boys hurried after the first one. They were laughing and barely took note of him. A coterie of a half-dozen girls of various ages walked toward him. When he nodded a greeting, they giggled and followed the boys toward the back of the house.

"We aren't being invaded," said Cat as she came along the passage.

He stared, unable to deny himself the pleasure of her beauty. The sunlight glistened in her ebony hair and dark eyes. Her simple gown of a fresh pink that matched her cheeks suited her far better than any elegant confection of silk and lace worn at Almack's. Only belatedly did he notice Miss Fenwick standing behind Cat.

"It's a Christmas tradition to invite the village children here to make plum cakes," Cat continued with a smile as if they had not exchanged sharp words yesterday evening. "You know how important traditions are to us at Meriweather Hall."

"I have seen that."

"You are welcome to join us. Jobby is already the center of attention, though once Mrs. Porter brings out the minced fruit, all the children will be focused on sneaking bites when she isn't looking."

"The kitchen will be crowded. You don't need me there to get in the way."

"The more the merrier." With a laugh, she proffered her arm as he had to her so often.

He pushed aside his dismals and looped his arm through hers. When she linked arms with Miss Fenwick, the three of them walked together the short distance before a table narrowed the hallway.

Cat started to move away, but he caught her hand and pressed it back on her sleeve, as Miss Fenwick hurried forward to herd the youngsters toward the kitchen stairs. Cat looked up at him, wonderment in her eyes, and he knew she felt the same lightning pulse when his skin had brushed hers.

I sought the Lord, and He answered me, and delivered me from my fears. The line from Psalm 34 had been one he had prayed on last night. He still feared that his friends would despise him for his deception, but he continued to seek the Lord's direction. When the time was right, God's time not his own, the answer would come.

"Are you doing better today?" Cat asked beneath the excited voices of the children.

"I am." He had not yet found the answer to his quandary, but he believed that he would with God's help. Then, and only then, he might speak of the way the touch of her fingers set his heart to galloping like the village children.

"I am glad."

"I am, as well."

The smile she gave him would brighten the sky at midnight, and its warmth softened another layer of the ice around his heart.

The kitchen was in an uproar but a joyous uproar. Even Mrs. Porter was grinning broadly as she and her staff made sure each child had a place at the long wooden tables.

"You, too, Mr. Bradby," the cook gushed. "Everyone in the kitchen joins in today." She gestured toward the table.

Jonathan hesitated a moment, but Cat whispered, "You might as well comply. She won't let you escape without some flour on your apron."

"I don't have an apron."

With a laugh, she plucked two folded aprons off the pile one of the kitchen maids carried along the table. She handed one to him before looping the top of the other over her head.

He stared at the crisply pressed apron. "I will look like a fool."

"You will look more addlepated if you have flour all over your waistcoat."

Again he hesitated, then his gaze was caught by two boys on the other side of the table. They appeared around eleven or twelve years old, and they were watching him as they held aprons in their own hands. If he refused to wear the apron, the boys would, too. He did not see any youngsters older than the two, and he guessed that this might be their last year for coming to Meriweather Hall for this annual event. Ruining it for them would be cruel.

With a broad smile, he shrugged off his coat. He pulled the apron over his head and tied it behind his back, as if he wore an apron every day. The boys glanced at each other, shrugged and followed suit. He gave them a nod, but said nothing as Mrs. Porter's assistants began putting large earthenware bowls in front of each person. The aroma of candied fruit that had soaked in its juices and honey wafted up, and he could not keep from bending over to draw in a deeper breath.

"No samples," Cat teased as she followed the kitchen maids with a bucket of wooden spoons. She paused to let each volunteer select one. On the other side of the table, her sister was doing the same.

"Just enjoying the fragrance," he said.

"Be patient and you can enjoy the taste." She held out the bucket to him.

He pulled out a long-handled spoon. "I thought wooden spoons were used on Stir-up Sunday. To signify the wood of the Christmas manger."

"Mrs. Porter does use a wooden spoon when she invites the whole household to stir the mincemeat for the Christmas pies, but we also use a wooden spoon when we mix fruit for the villagers' pies."

He smiled. "Should I turn the spoon clockwise,

close my eyes and make a wish as one does on Stir-up Sunday?"

"You may, but I doubt it will gain you anything other than splashing fruit and honey onto the table." She laughed as she continued along the large table.

He watched her as she spoke kindly to each child. If one of the children was too short, she called for a chair to be brought so the little one could mix the fruit in his or her bowl. She worked with the children, helping those who needed it, praising those who were working hard and gently reminding those who were more interested in fun of the importance of their task. She easily handled each problem as it arose. How could she believe she was inept at overseeing an important event, when every child smiled more broadly after she spoke to him or her?

He noticed as well that the children were open and excited to talk with her. The lives of the Meriweathers were entwined with the villagers'. He had seen that during his previous visit.

Jonathan let himself get caught up in the holiday excitement as the children mixed the fruit. Half would stay at Meriweather Hall to be made into puddings and pies. The rest would be sent home with the children who would be taken back to the village in the big wagons the fishermen used to carry their catch to market.

The two boys across the table nudged one another with elbows, then the younger one asked, "Were you a soldier?"

"Yes." Jonathan kept stirring the thick mixture.

"Did you fight Boney's army?"

"Yes."

He steeled himself for another question as the boys grinned at him.

"Told you so," said the taller boy. "My dad said both of his lordships and Mr. Bradby were soldiers."

"Are you a hero like Admiral Lord Nelson?" asked the younger boy.

Before Jonathan could answer, Cat put her hands on the boys' shoulders. "How are you two coming along? Is your mixture ready?"

"Aye!" both boys crowed.

She hooked her finger. "Then come with me. I could use your help with the younger ones."

Their thin chests puffed out with pride. "Aye, Miss Catherine!" They bounced along behind her.

Oddly, irritation pricked Jonathan. Did Cat think he could not deal with two young boys? He silenced that thought, ashamed that it had come into his mind.

Crack!

He looked down to see his wooden spoon in two pieces. He must have been gripping it so hard it had broken. The children on both sides of him gazed at him with wide eyes.

"That happens," Miss Fenwick said as she handed him another spoon. "Every year."

He took the second spoon, then pulled out the broken spoon by what was left of its handle. Fortunately it was long enough so that only his knuckles brushed the gooey mix. Even so, the stickiness clung to his fingers, cementing them together each time they touched.

"Guess you don't know your own strength," a boy on the other side of the table joked.

"Guess not."

His answer gave the boys all the invitation they

needed to pepper him with questions about fighting Napoleon's army. He gave them short answers, not willing to ease their curiosity while so many other young children within earshot.

When Cat returned, she asked him to help pour the mixture into the pots for each family's share. She looked so pretty with her cheeks reddened by the heat and wisps of hair curling around her face. She laughed when she saw the broken spoon by his bowl, but her jesting made him smile, because he knew she wanted to put him at ease. And she could, as no one else did. So much so that he needed to be on guard that he did not blurt out the truth about the lie.

No, he would not think of that now. For this moment, he would enjoy her company and drink in the sight of her bright eyes and bright smile. He joined her and Mrs. Porter who oversaw the division of the fruit mixture, so each household would have plenty. Miss Fenwick helped count out the members of each family, because some of the youngest children considered their cousins the same as sisters and brothers. They hurried because the wagon drivers were anxious to be on their way. If the roads between Meriweather Hall and the village froze, they could be treacherous.

Suddenly shouts came from behind Jonathan. Something slammed into the back of his head, then another in the shoulder. Looking back, he jumped aside before another gob of fruit hit his head. A child shrieked, then Mrs. Porter did as sticky fruit hit her right on the chin. Soon the air was filled with flying fruit. Most of the children were joining in, except for a few of the smallest ones who hid under the table. Even they were giggling with excitement.

Jonathan let out a bellow that worked as well in the kitchen as it had on the battlefield. Some of the children froze, their hands filled with fruit. Others quickly dropped the fruit into the bowls beside them, but three older boys at the far end of the table kept throwing fruit at each other.

He walked past the children with guilty faces and reached for the arm the closest boy. As he grabbed him, the boy released his handful of fruit. It flew across the table and hit Cat on the cheek. She was holding the other two boys firmly by their collars. All the boys gasped, and their faces turned gray.

"Enough," she said as calmly as if they were having a comfortable coze in the parlor upstairs. "Clean up this mess. All three of you." She turned, giving Jonathan a good view of the fruit clinging to her face and hair. "The rest of you take what's left in your bowls to Mrs. Porter. Let's hope there will be enough for pies for everyone this year."

Silence clamped on the kitchen as the littlest ones crawled from beneath the table, and the others did as Cat ordered. Jonathan released the boy he held and went around the table to where Cat stood, her arms folded in front of her as she kept a close eye on the children.

"Are you all right?" he asked quietly.

"Annoyed, but all right."

"May I?"

"May you what?"

With a smile, he peeled the fruit off her face. His expression wavered when he saw the pink spot left behind. If a man had been the one to leave such a mark, Jonathan would have challenged him to grass before breakfast, but dueling a boy would be ridiculous. The boys had not considered that anyone could be injured.

"There are more bits in your hair," he said, keeping his voice light. "Hold still."

As soon as he ran his fingers through her loosened hair to sift out the fruit, he knew he was being foolish. Scents of some flowery perfume, mixed with the honey sweetness of the fruit, flavored every breath he took until his head spun.

Moments ago her soft skin against his fingertips had daydreams urging him to slide his fingers along her eyebrows, her cheek, her chin, her lips.

He pulled back before he could surrender to that fantasy. When she yelped, he realized he had pulled her hair because his fingers had become attached to the fruit in it. He started to apologize, but she waved him away and thanked him before going to help Mrs. Porter.

He should be grateful she showed more sense than he did, but all he felt was sad and empty...as if he had lost a precious gift before it had even been his.

Chapter Eleven

Cat stood in the middle of the great hall and tried not to shiver as she compared her sketches to the room. She had come here after bidding Vera a good trip back to the village. Sophia had another fitting today, and then the *modiste* was going up to the nursery to measure the children for costumes for the ball. They would not attend long but were excited about the chance to have costumes and to see what the adults wore. That and making sure the wedding decorations were in place gave Cat the perfect excuse to avoid Mme. Dupont.

On her sketch, she needed to move one of the great iron chandeliers closer to the hearth at the back of the hall. That meant she would need to reconsider how she would drape greenery from the rafters around it. The chandelier would be lit with great, thick candles, and she must take care that none of the flames came too close to the greens.

Something tickled Cat's nose. She turned to rub it away as she worked quickly to refine her sketch.

The itch continued. Oh, no! She hoped she was not getting a cold. She did not want to be sick for her sister's wedding. Then she drew in a deep breath and knew it was not a cold.

Smoke!

She raced across the great hall and out into the corridor.

"Fire!" she shouted. "There is a fire in the house!"

The alarm was taken up by a footman in the hallway, and he yelled up the stairs. Footsteps pounded down while Ogden appeared out of a nearby room.

Cat did not wait to hear his instructions to the footmen. She turned toward the kitchen stairwell. Smoke billowed up the steps and into the hallway. Ignoring the shouts behind her, she raced to the kitchen.

Her eyes burned as every breath she took felt as if it were on fire. Smoke hid the bottom of the stairs. She pushed forward at top speed. Such thick smoke could overcome anyone in the kitchen quickly. Grasping an apron from a nail by the door, she covered her mouth and nose as she reeled forward.

Then the smoke seemed to collapse toward the floor. She stared at Jonathan who stood by the hearth, something in his outstretched hand. A salt cellar, she realized, as he slowly lowered his arm.

Mrs. Porter rushed forward to thank him for putting out the fire as Ogden and his footmen burst through a door on the other side of the kitchen, buckets of water at the ready.

"What happened?" asked Cat as everyone looked at Jonathan who stared at the smoky remains of the fire.

"That is what I would like to know." He carefully reached in and pulled something from the embers. A piece of cotton. Even as he lifted it, oil dripped off it and sizzled as a smoky flame erupted. "I assume you recognize this, Mrs. Porter." His eyes flared as the fire had.

"It is one of our aprons," Mrs. Porter said, every word shaking with dismay. "But how did it get on the hearth?"

"Along with the lard container." The tip of his boot rolled a broken crock from the hearth.

The cook frowned. "I never keep the lard near the hearth. It is too dangerous. I learned that when I was at my mother's knee."

Cat put a gentle hand on the cook's arm. "No one is accusing you, Mrs. Porter. There were a lot of people in the kitchen today. Someone must have moved the container by accident."

"And it could have been bumped onto the fire," Ogden said as he motioned for the footmen to carry the water buckets back outside.

"Though why it would take so long to melt and catch fire baffles me." Jonathan squatted by the hearth. "I would like to blame this on the children's fruit battle, but we would have smelled the smoke once we got them in the wagons and on their way. This must have happened later."

"Which still means it could be an accident." Cat saw the kitchen maids exchanging anxious glances. None of them wore a guilty expression, so she doubted one had bumped the lard onto the hearth by mistake. They were too well trained. So who had? "Jonathan, when did you smell the smoke? That might give us some idea when it started."

Standing, he turned to her. His face was sooty, but the fury in his eyes was even more powerful. "I realized I forgot my coat, so I came to retrieve it. When I got here, the kitchen was empty, and the fire was blazing out of the hearth."

"Mrs. Porter, isn't there usually someone in this part of the kitchen?"

She nodded. "But several of the girls had gone to deliver meals to the stable, and the rest were working with the footmen to make sure the dining room was ready. I was in the stillroom, checking that the fruit had been stored properly so it would not ferment before we made pies." She pressed her apron to her stomach and blubbered, "Oh, Miss Catherine, I am sorry."

Cat put her arm around the cook's shoulders and gave them a gentle squeeze. "No damage has been done other than a burned apron, a broken crock and our rattled nerves."

Boots resounded on the steps, and her cousin came into the kitchen followed by Charles and Sir Nigel. She wondered what her neighbor was doing back at Meriweather Hall so soon, but now was not the time to satisfy her curiosity.

Not that she had a chance because Cousin Edmund asked what had happened. He nodded when Jonathan gave him a quick explanation. His smile returned as he clapped Jonathan in the back. "Well done, Bradby. You saved us again."

As her cousin continued to congratulate Jonathan, Cat saw dismay battling with relief on his smoke-stained face. It was the same expression he had worn the day he had dived into the waves to save the child being washed out to sea. He had looked exactly like that when they went ice skating, and he had thought Gemma was in danger.

What was it about being lauded as a hero that unsettled him?

Sir Nigel paused by Cat and asked if she was all right.

"I am fine, thank you. Did Lillian come with you?"

His smile became a caricature of his usual jolly one. Lines she had never noticed cut deeply into his cheeks. "I won't have her here while someone feels free to leave such a hideous message in your wood. Actually that is why I came today. I thought your cousin might wish to have you and Miss Meriweather and the children come to my estate until the perpetrator is hunted down."

"That is kind of you, Sir Nigel." The words tasted bitter on her tongue. "Did Lord Meriweather agree?" She could not imagine her cousin would have, because decisions remained impossible for him.

"He acquiesced to Lord Northbridge who prefers to keep his family beneath this roof. I hope they don't come to rue that."

"Thank you for offering," she was able to say more sincerely now that she knew they would not have to stay at Sir Nigel's house which was filled with his absurd artwork.

Walking away, Sir Nigel said, "Ah, Bradby, you are ever the right man to have around in an emergency. Good for you for stepping up and saving the day."

Jonathan muttered something, then headed toward the stairs. He left without another word to anyone.

Cat snatched his bright green coat from a nearby chair and followed. By the time she caught up with him, he was almost to the stairs leading to the upper floors.

"Jonathan!" she called.

He paused, surprising her because she had been un- sure if he would. "Yes?"

"You forgot this." She walked around him and then faced him as she held out his coat.

"Thank you." He bit off each word but took his coat, draping it over his arm.

"And thank you for what you did down in the kitchen."

"No need." He looked at a point over her head. "It doesn't take a hero to put out a grease fire with salt."

"I didn't say anything about you being a hero. I sim- ply thanked you for keeping it from spreading." She folded her arms in front of her and gazed up at him. "Why is it so important to be a hero again? Haven't you proven your courage by saving Charles?"

"You don't understand." He moved to pass her.

She stepped in front of him again. "How can I un- derstand when you don't explain?"

"Ask anything you want of me. Just not that."

"Why not?"

He scowled at her. "Cat, I asked you—"

"You said I could ask anything except why you feel the need to go on proving yourself a hero. I asked why you don't want to talk of it." She closed her mouth be- fore she could tell him that she did not want him to die as Roland had in an attempt to show everyone that he deserved their respect.

A faint smile drifted across his lips, but his expres- sion grew sad. "Don't try to trip up a solicitor with words, Cat. You won't get anywhere."

"I don't want to 'get anywhere.' I want to know what I can do to help you."

He stared at her as if memorizing every inch of her

face. He sighed and shook his head. "There's nothing you can do."

"There must be something."

He put heavy hands on her shoulders and shook his head. "No, Cat, you must accept that even you can't cure everything. This is between God and me. The only thing you can do is pray for me."

She pulled back as her tears made him blur in front of her. The one thing he had asked was the one thing she had tried to do over and over and had failed. She stared at the floor, wishing she knew how to fix her connection with God. By the time she raised her eyes, still having no answer, Jonathan had walked away.

The wind was icy cold when Jonathan stepped from his carriage at the top of the steepest street in the village. The ride from Meriweather Hall had been even more frigid because Cat had not spoken to him other than to thank him for letting her join him as far as the vicarage. She planned to help decorate the sanctuary for Christmas with Miss Fenwick and some of the other women from the church.

He should have been grateful. If Cat had asked why he had behaved so strangely after the fire in the kitchen, he could not be honest with her. The idea of lying to her further was repugnant, but Sir Nigel's words had been like a fist to his gut. A painful accusation that he was not the man that they believed him to be. Though the cloak of hero had never fit comfortably on his shoulders, now it seemed to be grinding down upon him, a constant reminder that he had been false with the people who mattered the most to him.

Just as his parents had.

After all his efforts to be unlike his parents, to live a life filled with honesty and no delusion, he had fallen into the trap of being too exactly the same. Sir Nigel's words had proven that.

Maybe he should take his leave of Meriweather Hall. *A coward's choice,* came the taunting whisper in his mind. He wanted to shout back that he *was* a coward. He did not dare to tell the truth and lose his friends' esteem. Or, even more important, to lose Cat's esteem. Thinking of her regarding him with disappointment and disgust made his stomach twist like a damp washrag.

Even so, he had hidden his thoughts behind an unemotional mask when Miss Fenwick had emerged from the vicarage. The vicar's sister had worn a broad smile, but it disappeared the instant Cat stepped from the carriage. Though no words had been spoken, the vicar's sister must have discerned the truth from Cat's face.

He wished he knew why she had raised a wall between them after he had said there was nothing she could do but pray for God to help him. He had thought it was a good solution, when Cat could not help him otherwise, because she did not know the truth. Instead, his request had driven her away, and he could not guess why.

As he had left her and Miss Fenwick in the vicarage's garden, he said only that he would return to the church when his business was completed. If the ladies were not finished, he would wait or assist them as they wished. He had received a perfunctory "Thank you" from Cat.

Watching his step because the cobbles on the steep street were slick with ice in places, Jonathan descended toward the sea. He planned to talk with the fisher-men. His comment to Cat yesterday about trying not to trip up a solicitor with words had gotten him thinking. Maybe *he* could trick the fishermen into telling him something about the smugglers that was not known at Meriweather Hall.

He caught the movement of draperies, and he guessed someone had taken a glimpse to see who was skimble-skamble enough to be out on such a cold day. He would have to choose his words with utmost care, because the villagers already were suspicious of out-siders.

A door was open into the street just past where the beck disappeared under the buildings. Was the smug-glers' tunnel connected to the building with the open door? Deciding he would take a peek inside as he passed, he slowed. His feet almost went out beneath him, but he caught the rail beside nearby steps. He inched forward and looked in.

It was a store. He edged inside and away from the door to a spot where he might not be noticed. He could not imagine a better place to *listen* to what the locals had to say about the smugglers. He doubted they would speak openly, but he might gain some insight into the criminals who lived among the villagers.

Wares were stacked everywhere with no order he could discern. Fishing gear mixed in with bolts of fabric. Foodstuffs filled shelves along with cutlery. The wooden floor was filthy, and the boards had been eroded by many sand-caked boots.

Even so, more than a dozen people were crammed into the tight space. Two stood behind a low wooden counter, and he guessed they were the shopkeeper and his wife. Both were bent from long hours of work, but their clothing was clean and unpatched, though of an odd collection of colors and patterns that even he would disdain. He suspected the wife had stitched their clothing from fabric that did not sell.

Drawing his hat lower over his brow, Jonathan leaned back against a barrel that had a fishy smell. It was not marked in any manner, and he could not help wondering if it had been brought ashore by the smugglers. He pushed that out of his head and concentrated on the hushed conversation by the counter.

A woman facing the storekeeper said, "It will be strange to have Miss Sophia move away from Sanctuary Bay. The old lord is gone, and soon she will be."

"The new lord has shown a lot of interest in the village."

"Too much sometimes," said a man's voice from beyond the women.

Jonathan fought the urge to spin around and see who had spoken. He was certain the man was grumbling about Meriweather's interest in halting the smugglers. He hunched more into the shadows, so nobody would pay any attention to him. That had worked when he was in public places in Spain and France, and he hoped it would now.

He refocused on the conversation by the counter. The woman had placed several items on the counter, and the shopkeeper's wife was adding up the prices on a slip of paper.

"We shall have to wait and see if the new lord comes back once he goes to London," the storekeeper said.

"I have heard," another man piped up, "that the new lord came here for the peace and quiet after the war."

"But the war is over, and now he will assume his seat in Parliament and get involved with politics."

"Which always causes more trouble for us." An elderly man to Jonathan's left pulled out his pipe, and a ring of smoke curled around his head. "That is all the milords do in Parliament. Meddle in our business and raise taxes, so we can pay for theirs."

Jonathan chuckled to himself. One thing never changed: people complaining about government and taxes. Maybe that would turn the conversation to avoiding taxes with smuggling.

"We need more men like Utting," someone said.

"Now there was a hero of the first degree," the storekeeper said with a sigh. "But his mother's grief will never be over, because he died far off in America, and his body isn't in the churchyard. Never will be."

"It was good of the Meriweathers to pay for a memorial stone for him." The woman put her purchases into the cloth bag she wore over her wrist. "We were lucky we had such a generous lord in the old Lord Meriweather."

The shopkeeper leaned over the counter. "Heard he did it because Miss Catherine was so distraught with the news of young Utting's death."

"Aye. After Sunday services, she and young Roland always spent time together."

Jonathan stiffened at the name. Meriweather had mentioned a man named Roland. He had said that Cat had been in love with the man who had joined the navy. Now these people were saying Roland Utting had been a hero.

A real hero. Not a fake one like Jonathan. He should have guessed a woman like Catherine Meriweather, loyal and dedicated to her family and community, would fall in love with a true hero.

As if to second his thoughts, the woman said, "Miss Catherine must miss him as much as his mother does."

"Maybe more," agreed someone else.

The storekeeper nodded vehemently along with the others, then his eyes locked with Jonathan's.

"Sir!" The shopkeeper's face blanched. "I didn't see you there. Is there anything I can do for you?"

Everyone looked at Jonathan. As a stranger, he was not welcome in the shop, he knew. But the stares threatened to strip away his deception and reveal him for the liar he was, a man who never would be worthy of Cat's love.

"Just came in to get out of the cold," he mumbled before he turned to go out the door.

The villagers stepped aside to let him leave, but he knew how a leper must feel. The door closed behind him, leaving him out in yet another snow shower.

God, I need Your help. I am lost in my lies, and I don't know how to escape the maze I have built for myself. Lead me, I pray.

He continued to pray as he went down to the beach. There, in the silence broken only by the waves and the wind, he hoped God's reply would help him ease his aching heart without losing Cat, who had become part of it.

"I think that is everything." Cat looked around the church. The air was damp and chilly because the wood stove at the back was not lit. Yet the sanctuary looked warm and festive with greenery festooning the doors of the pews. The rail in front of the altar was wrapped with ivy, and shiny holly caught every bit of gray light coming through the windows. Evergreens edged the deep windowsills.

"It looks beautiful," Vera said. "Even better than last year."

"When we thought we might have a new church by Christmastide this year."

Vera grinned wryly. "Don't mention that in Gregory's hearing. I have never seen him so frustrated. Everyone knows the roof will come down on our heads one of these days, but nobody wants to decide whether we should put on a new roof or simply build a new church closer to the village. Half the doors here don't work. The hinges and lock on one to the cellar rusted shut. I don't think Gregory has been down in the cellar in years. He often turned to your father in matters like this."

"But now Cousin Edmund cannot help him."

"That is so sad." Vera scooped up the remnants of the greens and dumped them in a basket. "I see Lord Meriweather struggling, and I wish I could tell him that I am praying for decisions to become easier for him."

"He would appreciate that, but he would be embarrassed as well, because he hopes no one notices that he can't make even the simplest decision."

"Which is why I have said nothing." She sighed as she bent to pick up the basket. "I had hoped having Lord Northbridge and Mr. Bradby here would help him, but I guess there is nothing we can do but pray for him and have patience."

"We try to have patience," Cat said, skirting the issue of prayer again. "Where we can, we offer to make decisions for him, but certain matters—"

"Like a new roof on the church or a new church."

Cat nodded. "Those matters require him to decide, because the majority of the cost is the responsibility of Meriweather Hall." She held the door so Vera could walk out onto the covered porch.

A dull thud sounded.

Looking back into the sanctuary, Cat half expected to see some of the heavier branches lying on the floor. All were exactly where they should be.

"Did you drop something?" she asked her friend.

Vera shook her head. "I think the sound came from outside."

"Just in case, maybe we should check the sanctuary."

"Everything is fine. You fret too much about everything, Catherine." Her eyes twinkled as they walked out into the cold afternoon and closed the door behind them. "Or should I call you Cat, as Mr. Bradby did, when he brought you to the vicarage today?"

The day's chill vanished as heat climbed up Cat's face. "Of course you can call me Cat. I thought I was rid of the name, but it has returned."

"As Mr. Bradby has returned." Vera shifted the basket to rest on her hip. "Do you think you will see him when you go to London?"

"No. He lives in Norwich."

"Which is not that far from London."

"Vera, he has pushed me away over and over. He is concealing something that gives him a great deal of anguish."

"About the war?"

"I assume so, because Charles tells me that he changed after the battle where he saved Charles's life." She looked up through the flakes lazily drifting from the sky. "I have tried every way I can to get him to open up to me, but I have failed."

"Maybe it is God's will that Jonathan seeks someone else to be honest with first." Vera smiled. "I will pray for him to find peace. You must pray, too, Catherine, even though I know you avoid it since your father died."

Cat stopped and stared at her friend. "How did you know that? I mean…" No, she would not be false with her bosom-bow. Closing her eyes, she took a deep breath before she opened them. "How long have you known?"

"Since Lord Meriweather's funeral. I chanced to overhear you speak angrily to God."

"And yet you have stayed my friend."

Vera set the basket on the vicarage's front step. Facing Cat, she gave her a quick hug. "My dear, dear friend, it isn't my place to judge. God should be the only one judging us."

"And He must find me faithless."

"You?" Tears filled Vera's eyes. "I don't believe you could be faithless if you tried. God has broad shoulders, and He understands when His children question His love. You said by your father's grave that God hadn't heard your prayers. Look into your heart, Catherine. Into that place where God speaks to you. Look and listen. You can be angry with Him, but He is patient. It says so right in the Bible." She closed her eyes and recited, *"'Love is patient, love is kind. It does not envy, it does not boast, it is not proud. It does not dishonor others, it is not self-seeking, it is not easily angered, it keeps no record of wrongs. Love does not delight in evil but rejoices with the truth. It always protects, always trusts, always hopes, always perseveres. Love never fails.'"* Opening her eyes, she smiled. "That's from the thirteenth chapter of First Corinthians, and those are my favorite verses."

"But that is love."

"God is love, Cat. He is patient and kind, and He rejoices in truth. Our truth, when we come to Him and open our hearts and pour out what is hidden within."

Cat was at a loss for what to say.

Vera reached to open the vicarage door. "Find a way to open your heart to God, Cat, and maybe you can find a way to help Mr. Bradby open his." She squeezed Cat's hand. "I know you can."

With a gasp at the touch of Vera's wool gloves on her skin, Cat said, "Oh, I forgot my gloves."

"Let's go back and—"

"Nonsense. I will get them."

"Where did you leave them? On a pew?"

Cat nodded. "My family's pew, or I think I did." She gave her friend a hug. "Go and get your brother's supper started while I get my gloves."

"Think about what I said."

"I will."

Hurrying to the church, Cat grimaced at the snow. It was nice to have snow for Christmas, but if it had not started falling until Christmas Eve, she would have been happier. She shook her head as she stepped into the porch. Flakes flew in every direction, including one down her back. She winced as she went into the sanctuary.

The storm left the windows dull as she walked along the aisle. She opened the door to her family's pew and stepped inside. Picking up her gloves, she held them as she sat and leaned back against the gray boards that needed another coat of paint. The walls of the pew were almost as tall as she was. With the door closed, she felt cut off from the world. She wished she could feel closer to God here.

As she closed her eyes to pray, Jonathan's face appeared in her mind. His smile, his frown, his eagerness to help when he had been with the children in the kitchen or searching for mermaid tears, his closed-up expression when he had tried to let no one know how being called a hero upset him. Those flashed by, then came the image of his pale blue eyes with the navy edges that displayed every emotion, even the ones he tried to hide. Even the ones he did not try to hide, especially when they stood face-to-face, and every breath she took was filled with his essence.

No other man, not even Roland, had ever made her laugh as he did or filled her dreams as he did. He wanted to kiss her. She saw that in his eyes. She felt it in his tender touch. If he wanted to kiss her and she longed for his kiss, why did he pull away?

Why? she prayed. *God, can You help me understand? I miss You.* Those words came from her heart. She held her breath, hoping for God's answer.

Instead of the soft voice she once heard within her heart, she heard something else. She was unsure what, because the boards surrounding the pew distorted the sound. Then she heard another thud. It was not unlike the thud that had startled her and Vera earlier, something that seemed to come from outside the sanctuary, but still sounded like it was inside the church.

She stood and saw two men by the altar. "Sir Nigel! Lord Ashland!"

They spun to face her. Shock emblazoned their features for only a moment. Both regained their composure at exactly the same time.

Lord Ashland stepped forward, giving her his cool smile. He was not much older than her cousin, but he had the superior air of a man born to privilege. Others might call his dark looks handsome. Cat always felt uncomfortable in his company. Not that she had seen him often, because he kept to his estate. She wondered what he was doing in the village church on a snowy afternoon.

"Miss Catherine," the viscount said in his smooth voice, "I hope we aren't intruding on your worship."

"You have not. I hope I have not intruded on you gentlemen. I didn't see you when I came in, and Vera and I just left a few moments ago."

Sir Nigel opened his mouth to answer, but Lord Ashland halted him by asking, "Was that you and Miss Fenwick we heard down here?" He hooked a thumb toward the balcony. "We glanced over the rail, but didn't see anyone." Brushing a fastidious hand against his coat sleeves that were fuzzy with dust webs, he added, "Please don't mention this to either Miss Fenwick or the vicar. We want the installation of an organ to be a pleasant surprise for them."

"An organ in *this* church? But why? The parish is discussing building a newer building closer to the village so it is more convenient for the congregation."

"I hadn't heard that." Lord Ashland scowled at Sir Nigel. "Didn't you deem that something I should know before I made such an investment?"

The baronet shrugged his shoulders as if the matter was of no importance, but his gaze darted between Cat and the viscount like a quick-moving insect. "Nothing has been decided, Ashland. Such matters move with a turtle's pace in Sanctuary Bay." He smiled at Cat. "I mean no insult to your cousin, Miss Catherine."

"Of course not," she replied, even though his apology suggested just the opposite. "I am astonished you are so interested in our church."

"I always want the best for my great-niece." His smile grew even wider before he added, "She enjoyed meeting your vicar so much during her short visit here that she asked that I bring her to services on occasion."

Cat mumbled something about Lillian visiting would be nice, but again she suspected Sir Nigel's words had a double meaning. If Cousin Edmund and Lillian married, the Sanctuary Bay parish church would be where they worshipped. Should she warn her cousin of Sir Nigel's plans? No, that would be silly. Sir Nigel's plans would come to naught if Cousin Edmund did not fall in love with Lillian.

Lord Ashland glanced at Cat, and his smile returned even though his eyes remained icy, growing colder each time he looked in the baronet's direction. "If you will excuse us, Miss Catherine, I believe Sir Nigel and I should continue this discussion elsewhere. Again, accept my apologies if we have intruded on your worship here."

Sir Nigel did not protest when the viscount herded him down the aisle and out of the church. The door to the porch loudly shut in their wake.

That had been weird. Holding her gloves, she drew on one and then the other, as she stared at the closed door. Then she turned to look at the altar and thought about Vera's advice.

Find a way to open your heart to God, Cat, and maybe you can find a way to help Mr. Bradby open his.

She was not sure where to begin, but she intended to learn.

Right away.

Chapter Twelve

The banns were read for a second time, Michael once again sitting next to Jonathan. The little boy wiggled and grinned when his father's name and Sophia's were mentioned. Cat was not the only one smiling at the child's delight with the upcoming wedding.

Next week, the banns would be read again, and then Sophia and Charles could exchange their vows. Her sister would leave Sanctuary Bay for the south of England to live with her new family. Soon after that, Cat would go with Cousin Edmund to London. She would have to show some passing interest in the *ton,* because she did not want to hurt her cousin's feelings. Once she had visited the British Museum and the Royal Academy of Art and maybe a few other important sites, she could devise an excuse to return to North Yorkshire. She suspected her cousin would be agreeable, as he must focus on his duties as the new baron, including finding a wife to give him an heir.

Cat struggled to concentrate on Mr. Fenwick's sermon. Each time she looked toward the altar, she could not help thinking about Lord Ashland and Sir Nigel's peculiar behavior. She had tried to tell both Jonathan and her cousin about it. She had no chance. While she was at the church, Jonathan had returned to Meriweather Hall and sent the carriage for her. The men were closeted in the billiards room when she got back to the house, and they did not come out even for the evening meal.

This morning had been as frustrating because the men took one carriage, while she and Sophia and the children were relegated to the other. She knew they were plotting a way to end smuggling in Sanctuary Bay, but she wished they would include her and her sister. Not only had they lived here the longest and knew the local residents best, but Meriweather Hall was their home, too. At least for now.

She would ask Sophia after church to speak with Charles. Surely he would listen to her and invite them to the discussions.

Rising when the rest of the congregation did for the final hymn and the benediction, Cat could not keep herself from glancing at Jonathan. He was busy with Michael and Gemma. The children called him uncle and adored him as much as he did them. Before the service began, they had chattered about the games they had played in the nursery with Alice, the nursery maid, and asked Jonathan to join them. He agreed. What a good father he would be!

She sighed. A good father would expect his wife to run an excellent household, overseeing small details, so he was not burdened with them. That was not her. She could not even plan a wedding breakfast without Jonathan's assistance. If she became immersed in her sketching, a whole day could go by without her noticing. That was fine for a younger sister with limited responsibilities, but not for a wife in charge of the household.

Cat hung back as the others went out. She thanked Mr. Fenwick for an excellent sermon, though she had scarcely heard two words. He held her hand a second longer than usual, and she looked up at his kind face. He said nothing, and she guessed he was waiting for her to speak. She simply wished him a good morning and walked toward where the carriages had been parked.

One had already left, and the coachee was on his back beneath the other one. Beside it, Jonathan squatted with Michael copying his motion.

"What is wrong?" Cat asked as she came to stand beside them.

"Something with the brake," Jonathan replied. "It seems to be sticking. With the steep hills around the bay, we don't want to risk it."

"How long will it take?"

The coachee shrugged as he kept toying with the brake on the front wheel.

"Maybe you should go over to the vicarage," Jonathan said. "It's bone-chewing cold today."

"I don't want to intrude on a Sunday because the Fenwicks often have parishioners in."

He lowered his eyes and nodded.

She wondered if he was thinking of his own conversation with the vicar. "We could walk."

"It's a long one."

"Not if we go down to the shore and around the bay. It's much shorter than the road."

Michael popped up and grinned. "See the sea?"

"Most definitely." She held out her hand, and the

little boy took it. "Do you want to come with us, Jonathan?"

She made her invitation sound casual, but she held her breath as she waited for his answer. He had a good reason to excuse himself from the long walk to Meriweather Hall…and to avoid spending time with her.

When he nodded, she longed to jump up and down with excitement as Michael did. She simply smiled.

Jonathan paused only long enough to ask the coachee to let Lord Meriweather know their plans. If they reached Meriweather Hall before the carriage did, Jonathan would send someone to help the coachee with the repairs.

The road leading to the village was empty, because the villagers had sought their comfortable homes. Cat swung Michael's hand in rhythm with their steps. When the little boy wanted to run ahead to the top of the steep street, she agreed after he promised to wait there for them.

As soon as Michael was out of earshot, Cat wasted no time telling Jonathan about the odd incident with Sir Nigel and Lord Ashland in the church.

"An organ for the church?" Jonathan buttoned his greatcoat under his chin as the cold wind swirled around them. "I could have sworn I heard Meriweather say something about a new building because the old one's roof will not be safe much longer."

"That was what I thought, too, but…" She shrugged. "I should know by now not to listen to Sir Nigel. He views the world as he thinks it should be, whether it is that way or not."

"I wouldn't want to live like that. I like to see things as they truly are." He gazed across the headland beyond the village. It mirrored the one near Meriweather Hall. "The problem with insisting that the world conform to one's view is to believe that anyone who disagrees with that delusion is wrong. God created this world, and we should appreciate it as He made it and us." He looked at her and smiled. "Sorry. I didn't mean to give you a sermon."

"You speak with the same fervor as Mr. Fenwick."

"But not with his eloquence." He laughed. "A solicitor is not called to the bar for court trials, so I don't need to be so well-spoken."

She gladly put her hand on the arm he offered. Only now when she stood beside him again did she realize what a void his absence had created. A rush of tears burned in her eyes. Once the Christmas Eve ball was over, he would leave. When would she see him again? Surely he planned to come back to Meriweather Hall to visit his friend, but seeing him on rare occasions would not be often enough.

Michael ran to meet them when Cat and Jonathan reached the sheer drop through the village. Snow drifted from the dim sky, wafting on the wind that curled around the buildings. A few village children ran around, holding out their tongues to catch snowflakes. Michael joined them, as eager as if the snow were made of spun sugar. When a woman called for the children to be careful on the steep street, they went more slowly, but only for a moment or two. Then they began chasing snowflakes along one of the comparatively flat streets that broke off from the main one.

Cat called Michael back. He reluctantly obeyed, though he kept looking at the children playing along the side streets. With a smile, she told him that he could go back with them if he promised to come as soon as she called him. With a cheer, he ran to join the other youngsters.

"I hope Charles won't be upset with me that I'm letting him catch snowflakes with the other children," Cat said.

"He wants them to be adventurous."

"Even after we had to hunt them down after they decided to play hide-and-seek?"

He chuckled. "Adventurous but within sight."

She tightened her hold on his arm as they walked carefully down the most precipitous section of the street. "It is so delightful to see the children playing."

"It is nothing but an illusion of happy families." His smile vanished.

"No, you are wrong."

"Am I?" He pointed through the snow at the houses higher along the cliff. "All these people act as if they are busy earning a living by fishing when you know as well as I that—"

"We cannot talk about *that* here." She pulled away from him and called up the street to Michael.

Jonathan clamped his lips closed, stung by Cat's reminder that he and his friends were not the only ones listening. The smugglers would be glad to gather any information that they could use in their deceptions.

When Michael slid down the street to where they stood, Cat took Michael's hand and kept going. She did not look back to see if Jonathan had followed. That, as much as anything, showed her vexation with him.

He trotted behind them down the street. Fresh snow covered the dirty cobbles, but could not diminish the odor of gutted fish. As he crossed the stream, he looked at where the water disappeared beneath the houses. That tunnel led down the cliff, but where did it come out? Was it the trickle down by the fishermen's cobles, or did the smugglers' tunnel branch off from this one? He wished he could look for it but not when he was accompanying Cat and Northbridge's boy. He could not put them in danger.

At the foot of the street where the boats were pulled up on the sand, Cat steered Michael along the beach. She paused and pointed at the beach. Was she searching for mermaid tears in a snow flurry?

"Look out," she called as Michael picked up something and flung it toward the sea.

Or Jonathan assumed that was its intended direction, but the rock curved and landed only a few feet to his left.

Going to the little boy, Jonathan said, "Let's find something softer to throw. Like some driftwood." He picked up a piece and held it out to Michael. When the little boy hauled back his arm, Jonathan gave him a gentle push toward the edge of the wet sand. "If you get a little closer, you'll have better luck hitting the water."

Michael chortled and took several steps toward the sea. He flung the wood and cheered when it hit the water. Before it had sunk, the little boy was already looking for another chunk to throw.

"Keep up with us, Michael," Cat called. "I want to be able to see you at all times."

Excited with his chance to play on the beach, the little boy obeyed. He did not let them get more than a few feet ahead of him before he raced forward to a spot where he found something else to throw.

"I owe you an apology," Cat said suddenly.

"No. I owe you one," Jonathan replied. "I know better than to speak so unthinkingly in the village."

"And I should not have walked away in a huff."

"It sounds as if we are even in being mutton-heads."

She laughed as she put her hand on his arm again. "I shall endeavor to do better, especially when I get to Town. I know that if I get into a peal in London, I will embarrass my whole family by being labeled a termagant."

London? Why was she talking about Town now? Each time she spoke of the Season, anger roiled in Jonathan. To have this sweet young woman altered as others had been seemed like a crime.

"You may find the Season isn't what you anticipate," he said.

"I am sure it is quite different from what a girl from the country could imagine." She bent and brushed away some sand, but found only a broken shell, and he realized she had been looking for mermaid tears all along. "But I am eager to see things I have not had a chance to see here."

"Oh, I am sure you will." He chided himself for the bitterness in his voice, but that vexation became shock when Cat looked up at him and nodded her agreement.

Maybe, a small voice within him whispered, *you should go to London, too. You could protect her, if you have already proved that you are really a hero.*

That thought brought him to a complete stop. Cat stared at him as if he had lost his mind.

If he listened to that small voice, then he would be insane. To chase after her to Town would be an announcement of his intentions to marry her, and she would be humiliated in front of the Polite World when he did not offer for her. He could not entangle his life with another young woman who was eager to participate in a London Season. He had endured a harsh lesson from Augusta Williams. He had hoped to give her his heart, and she had thrown his affections in his face. He could not imagine Cat treating him the same way, but neither had he anticipated Augusta changing so much.

Michael rushed to them to show off a shell he had found, and Jonathan watched as Cat spoke with the little boy, her voice as excited as his. Had she and her late hero Roland talked about having children? Did she still mourn him as deeply as she had when the news of his death had arrived at Meriweather Hall?

Lord, I need Your guidance. There must have been a reason for You to bring me to Sanctuary Bay and to Cat. Is it so that I may become the hero everyone believes me to be? Am I supposed to prove that so I can help her when she embarks upon the Season in London? Help me see why You brought me here, I pray.

Jonathan murmured a fervent "Amen" as Michael ran to the water's edge again. They had almost reached the middle of the great arc of Sanctuary Bay. Ahead of them, the cliff was broken by a wide stream. Was this the same one as in the village? If the stream had been routed so far from the village, it would allow the smugglers to do their illicit deeds without even their neighbors seeing.

Excitement bubbled up within him. He might, even today, strike a blow against the smugglers. If he discovered where they stashed their goods, he could cripple them. At least temporarily.

"I want to look in here," he said, as he came around

the edge of the cliff. He was amazed how wide the opening was. It was large enough to hold the stables at Meriweather Hall.

Or a ship and smugglers and their cargo of contraband.

"Why?" Cat asked as she motioned to Michael to catch up with them.

"This would be an excellent place for the smugglers to hide."

"All the more reason to stay away."

He continued to scan the cliffs. "Are there caves back there?"

"Probably. There are several caves along the shore. Some are natural, and others were built to channel water down from the meadows."

He put his hand on the rough stone. "This is so different from the shore in Norfolk. The land is as flat as a table and barely above the sea. The water is drained there by the levels."

"Levels?"

"A series of canals and ditches used to drain The Fens. When they were built in the seventeenth century, more farmland became available, and mills were built to grind corn. Some of the mills have been converted to wind pumps to control the water in the canals and sluices." He gave her a wry grin. "Forgive me. A solicitor must learn a lot about property and its history in order to better serve his clients."

"You like your work, don't you?"

"Very much. I enjoy bringing structure out of the chaos of old land records, some that go back to William the Conqueror's *Domesday Book*."

"That must make the land in The Fens much easier

to deal with, because it appeared less than two hundred years ago."

He laughed. "So one would think, but someone has always owned that land since before the Romans. Even if it was submerged for eons."

"But you enjoy the challenge."

"That I do."

"Was that why you decided to live in East Anglia?"

"No, but it was the reason I stayed after my father arranged for me to read the law with a friend of his, after I finished my studies at Cambridge."

She looked across the waves. The breeze lifted the wisps of hair around her face and set them to dancing. "Look at the sun. We need to hurry if we wish to get home in time for the midday meal."

"But if there are smugglers here—"

"There are smugglers, Jonathan, in every seaside town around England. Even in East Anglia, I am sure. If the people here stop smuggling, someone else will begin."

"So that's it? You are going to give up?"

"I think we should," she said, startling him. "The message from that effigy was clear, and Sir Nigel is worried enough to insist Lillian return to his house."

He grimaced. "So now you are going to base your decisions on what Sir Nigel does?"

"Don't be absurd, but we would be foolish to ignore the warning."

"I have not ignored it, and I can assure you that neither your cousin nor Northbridge has."

"I know that, Jonathan." She walked to the stream that had dug grooves in the sand. "Charles told my sister that you are gathering information, and you will put it to good use as soon as you can."

"That is what I want to do here. Gather information. I would appreciate your help, but if you want to continue to Meriweather Hall, go ahead."

Cat found Jonathan's zeal unsettling, and she was tempted to tell him so. Angry words would gain her nothing, because it was clear that he had made up his mind. So had she. Holding out her hand out to Michael, she drew the little boy close.

Michael looked up at her. "Are we staying or going?"

She forced a smile and said loud enough for Jonathan to hear her, "Let's keep going. Your father will be worried if we take longer than we should getting home."

As Jonathan waded through the water that was only a few inches deep, he said, "This will take only a moment." The beach was wide and low enough for a ship to sail up it at high tide. He squatted to seek any signs of such activity.

"We are leaving," Cat said. "Right now."

"If that is what you wish, then go. I will be there as soon as I look around a little bit." His voice echoed oddly against the cliff walls.

Cat started to walk away and then paused. Jonathan could be stepping into a wasp's nest. If the smugglers really used this area, they might have posted someone to guard their stolen goods. She could not risk the child, but the thought of leaving Jonathan here alone twisted her stomach into knots.

"Cat!"

At the shout, she ran across the shallow stream as

fast as Michael could go. Jonathan pointed to a pile of wood.

Michael pulled away from Cat. Racing over to it, he picked up a long piece of wood and threw it into the waves. He giggled as it was swept by the current out to sea.

Saying nothing, Jonathan pulled a square piece out and held it up to her. Stenciled words identified it as a part of a crate of brandy.

"No sign of stamps to show that British tax was paid," he said as he tossed the wood on the other pieces. "So we know that the smugglers have been here."

Cat looked at the narrow path leading directly up the cliff. Walking it would be difficult. To do so carrying a heavy crate would be almost impossible.

"They wouldn't have gone that way," Jonathan said. "One of the caves in these cliffs must be connected to a way to take the goods from here to the top of the cliff. We are not that far from Meriweather Hall's dower cottage which they used for storage until your sister discovered it."

Every instinct told her to leave this place as fast as they could. "Let's go! Now!"

"All right." He took a single step, then halted with a frown. "Look up there!" He pointed to the southern rim of the cliffs.

"That is Meriweather Hall." She gasped and stared at the roof and the chimneys. "I can see the highest floors. Doesn't that prove the smugglers would not come here? If someone looked out and saw them—"

"The only ones who might look out of those windows are children or your servants. The children wouldn't know what they were seeing, and none of your servants would be foolish enough to speak of their suspicions. Especially after the threats to your gamekeeper and his mother."

An icy chill raced down Cat's back and then up to settle its cold fist around her heart. "Papa had feared for Sophia when he had thought she was getting too close to learning the identity of the smugglers' leader. He was so worried that he took her to London on the pretense of giving her a Season. He feared for Sophia's life if she unmasked the smugglers' leader."

Jonathan stared at her. "Why didn't you tell Meriweather that?"

"I assumed he knew."

"I doubt he does, because he is eager to unmask the smugglers' leader."

Cat leaned her shoulder against his chest, knowing she was being brazen, but needing his strength to comfort her. She closed her eyes and wished she could melt into him. Even with the tang of the sea air and the cool freshness of the winter wind, she breathed in his scent that was a mixture of wool and leather and soap. She did not want to move. Not ever, because she knew he would allow nothing to happen to her, if he could prevent it.

"Do you think that is why Cousin Edmund wants *me* to go to London for the Season?" she whispered.

"Possibly." His arm came up to encircle her shoulders, and her breath caught. She could not remember ever being so safe and in so much danger at the same time. She dared not raise her head because, if she looked into his eyes, she might not be able to fight her longing to draw his head down to hers for a kiss.

Jonathan's next words shattered her fantasy. "You

may be right about why he wants you to go to Town. With his duties and obligations there, Meriweather would not be here to protect you. Let's get out of here."

He held out his hand to Michael, but kept his arm around her shoulders. As they walked away, she saw him glance back. He sighed, and she guessed he was disappointed not to be able to subdue the smugglers in their den. She was certain he planned to come back with Cousin Edmund and Charles.

As soon as she returned to Meriweather Hall, she would ask Sophia to pray for their safety. She did not know what else to do, because she no longer trusted her own prayers would be heard. A soul-deep ache riveted her as she realized how much she had lost the day her father had died. Even more than the day she was told that her sweet Roland had been killed. She did not want to lose anything—or anyone—else.

Chapter Thirteen

Cat looked from her sketchbook to the tables and then up at the rafters. The tables were where they should be, and the footmen were stringing the greenery according to her instructions. She drew in a deep breath of the fresh scent. Soon the great hall would look as she had imagined. Snow had piled up overnight on the windowsills, and the stained glass sent colors across the tables that were already draped with tablecloths, sparkling off mermaid tears scattered there.

One of the maids laying out the rest of the white tablecloths began to sing an old hymn. Her voice was pure and dulcet, each note rising to spin about the rafters.

"The holly and the ivy, when
they are both full grown. Of
all the trees that are in the wood,
the holly wears the crown."

Cat joined the others in singing the refrain. Deep voices blended with high-pitched ones, and nobody cared if a note was flat or sharp, for they sang from the heart.

"Oh, the rising of the sun, and the running of the deer, the playing of the merry organ, sweet singing in the choir."

As the second verse began, all the voices faded into silence except the maid who had begun singing.

"The holly bears a blossom as white as lily flower, and Mary bore sweet Jesus Christ, to be our sweet Savior."

Everyone sang the refrain, pausing in their work as they created a harmony that grew more complex with each repetition of the refrain. When the last verse was finished, silence filled the great hall. Then Cat applauded. The servants began to cheer as they returned to their work.

How she would miss her home while in London! If all went as she hoped, she would return right after visiting the Elgin Marbles. She held the sketchbook over her heart as she walked to look out a window. The trees rocked in the wind that never seemed to die so close to the sea.

Roland, when I stand in front of those sculptures, I know some part of you will be there with me. I know we will see them together.

Tears welled up in her eyes. When had she last thought about him, the only man who had ever understood her love of the beauty of a line drawn by a master artist? What other man would ever understand her as Roland had?

Jonathan's face appeared, unbidden, in her mind. She shook her head, trying to clear it. Jonathan Bradby was a practical man, interested in facts and figures. The only lines that concerned him were property lines and assuring his clients that they were in the right place.

Even as she thought that, she knew she was not being honest with herself. He had helped find mermaid tears, which certainly was not a practical pursuit. And what pragmatic man would call her Cat?

She was looking for excuses to push him away, because she was shaken by how much she longed to be with him, to have him hold her as he had by the sea last Sunday. Even almost a week later, she still resonated with the sweet sensation of his arm around her shoulders while they had walked to Meriweather Hall. She had been so busy since then that she had scarcely seen him, but he never was far from her thoughts.

That had to stop. To fall in love with another warrior hero could mean facing the same pain all over again. She had barely endured it once. To go through that one more time was too devastating to imagine.

It would be better if she thought about Jonathan as the friend she had vowed he would be. As his friend, she had to wonder why he was so determined to stop the smugglers. Did that have something to do with the pain that billowed into his eyes when he thought nobody would notice?

Find a way to open your heart to God, Cat, and maybe you can find a way to help Mr. Bradby open his. Vera's advice was good, but, in spite of praying each night and morning for the past week, Cat still waited to feel God in her life.

Time was growing short. Once the wedding and the masquerade were over, Jonathan would go home to Norwich, and she would travel to London. Her heart cramped each time she wondered if their paths would ever cross again. It was almost too unbearable to think about.

"How lovely! I should have guessed, Catherine, that you would be in the midst of everything." Lady Meriweather's cheerful voice was brightened with a laugh as she walked into the great hall.

Cat ran to greet their mother. Lady Meriweather's fur muff hung from one sleeve, and a jaunty green hat was perched on her black hair. Of a similar height as Cat, she wore her years well.

"Mother!" Cat cried as she hugged her mother. "Why didn't you let us know you were coming back?"

Lady Meriweather kissed Cat on the cheek. "I got here as quickly as any message would."

"How is Aunt Electra?" Cat asked, her smile so broad that her cheeks ached.

"Her leg is healed, and she is learning to get around again. She insisted that I come home. She was concerned with the storms we have had that, if I waited even a day longer, another one might arrive, and I would end up missing my own daughter's wedding." She laughed. "To be honest, I believe she was eager for me to leave, so I am not there to insist that she exercise her leg more. She would prefer to sit in her parlor, receive callers and their sympathy, and tell the story of her tumble over and over."

"Mother, Aunt Electra was gravely hurt!" Cat tried to make it a scold, but ended up laughing.

"Ah, *gravely*. That was a description she did not use herself." Mother chuckled. "Maybe the only one."

Her aunt had been named well, because she yearned to be the center of attention, as if she were the heroine in a Greek tragedy. The slightest incident could become, in her telling, a disaster of titanic proportions. Cat had a tender spot in her heart for her outrageous aunt who had married a baronet, then a viscount and most recently another baronet. Her first two husbands had left her a wealthy widow, and her new husband was happy to help her enjoy that fortune. They had been planning a yearlong tour of the world when Aunt Electra had had the misfortune to trip over her lapdog and break her leg.

Lady Meriweather vowed to save the best stories about her visit to York for dinner and then hurried away to see the children who would soon be her grandchildren. From the first time they had met, she had developed a special relationship with Gemma and Michael who adored her.

Cat turned her attention back to the decorating. She explained her ideas, and the servants gleefully arranged the greenery as she asked. While they worked, one of the footmen began singing the haunting "Coventry Carol."

"Lully, lullay, thou little tiny child, by, by, lully, lullay."

She sang, too, determined that she would enjoy this Christmas and her sister's wedding instead of thinking about how the New Year would mean Jonathan leaving.

Jonathan watched as Meriweather signed the bottom of the final page in the stack. When his friend looked up, Jonathan smiled.

"That is it?" Meriweather asked.

"Yes. That is all you need to do. You have the lease on the house in Bedford Square for the next three years." He dusted the page to guarantee the ink would not run and then set it atop the others. "Such a simple matter could have waited until after the holidays. You aren't leaving for Town until the latter part of January, and you had a gentlemen's agreement with Forsythe. You didn't need to worry about someone else renting the house out from under you."

Meriweather leaned back from his desk and folded his arms over his chest. With a triumphant smile, he said, "But, if I had listened to you and waited until after the New Year, then you would have had no reason to rethink accepting our invitation to the wedding and the Christmas Eve ball."

"That is true, but I cannot believe that you would have missed me if I didn't attend an absurd masquerade ball. What is the real reason you were so insistent that I return to Meriweather Hall?"

"I thought that was quite obvious."

Jonathan put the signed papers in the box that would convey them to London. "It might be obvious to you, Meriweather, but not to me."

"I am outnumbered."

"By?"

"The women in this family. Three of them. One of me."

His brow furrowed. "You can't be suggesting that the Meriweather women did anything to make you feel unwelcome."

"Just the opposite." His friend stood and turned to look out the window at the somnolent garden. He put one hand on the molding. "Lady Meriweather is always gracious, and she is as concerned about my welfare as my own mother was."

Jonathan said nothing, but he was starting to understand. Unlike his mother, who had as little to do with her children as possible once they were born, Meriweather's mother had been a vital part of his life. She had died when he was barely eleven years old, so having a mother again must seem odd.

Just as having a loving mother would be strange for Jonathan. He could never remember his mother hugging him or praising him, unless she had guests and wanted to show off what an excellent mother she was.

His father had been the same. A feigned interest in his children when it would reflect well on him, but the rest of the time, he offered only indifference.

Growing up, seeing his parents treat each other with the same lack of affection as they did their children, he had thought every family was like that. He had learned the truth that other children were embraced, their tears dried when they scraped a knee, applauded when they achieved some goal…but by the time Jonathan had discovered that, he had been an adult.

What made a couple who had at least appeared to be in love change so completely? Maybe his father had been right when he had told Jonathan and his brothers that love was just foolishness invented by women to get men to do their bidding. He had wanted to discount that as another lie, but then Augusta had treated him exactly as his father had warned she would. She had used him until she could find someone else with more wealth and a title who would do as she wished. Every ounce of him wanted to argue that Cat would be different, but was he ready to test that possibility? No, and maybe that was the greatest proof that he did not deserve to be called a hero.

"And Sophia and Catherine…" Meriweather's hand slowly closed into a fist as Jonathan looked at him again. "I know they are frustrated with my inability to step into their father's shoes. Maybe if I had been raised to the life of a peer, it would be different."

"I can't help you with that. I am the youngest son of a youngest son."

"And be grateful that won't change."

As Meriweather went on, Jonathan listened with one ear and prayed silently for God to help his friend. *Guide him, Lord. Let him return to being the man he was before his experiences in the war made him question every decision. Help him see how truly special is the welcome he has received from Cat and her family. If I can be of use, Lord, use me.*

A sense of comfort settled on him, and he welcomed it. He was confident that God would show him how to help Meriweather.

"Can I ask you something, Meriweather?"

"Of course."

"Are you taking Cat to London to protect her from the smugglers?"

His friend stiffened as his eyes narrowed. Suddenly Jonathan was facing the man he had known on the battlefield: loyal, filled with resolve, and ready to do whatever was needed to serve his country and protect his fellow soldiers. The transformation was startling, and relief flooded Jonathan. Until now, he had not realized how much he had feared that Meriweather would never be more than a faint shadow of the man he once had been.

"What gave you such a bizarre idea?" Meriweather asked.

Jonathan quickly explained what Cat had told him last Sunday on the shore, about her sister being sent to keep her away from the smugglers who believed she was getting too close to the truth. Shock stripped color from his friend's face.

"I assume," Jonathan said, "that no one mentioned this to you."

"Not a whisper." He walked to the hearth. Clasping his hands behind in his back, he stared at the flames. "Why would they keep something so important from me? Do they believe me to be utterly inept?"

"I don't think the omission was intentional. Cat believed that you already knew."

"Why didn't you tell me before now?"

Jonathan shrugged. "Each time I wanted to speak to you about it, one of the Meriweather women or another would appear. I did not want to distress them further."

"This changes everything."

"Does it?" Jonathan got up as his friend turned to look at him. "Miss Meriweather will be gone from here once she and Northbridge are wed. Cat is going with you to London along with Lady Meriweather, I assume."

"While I simply leave my estate to the smugglers?" He held his head in his hands. "What to do? What to do?"

Sorry to upset his friend, Jonathan put a hand on his shoulder. "It is almost a month before you have to make that decision."

"True." Meriweather's head popped up like a puppet's.

"Who knows? We may have had our victory over the smugglers before you leave, and then the decision is made for you."

"True." A smile eased across his friend's lips. "Any ideas how to do that?"

Jonathan grinned. "I might have a good one."

"Let me send for Northbridge, and we'll talk it over." Meriweather, his good nature resurrected, clapped him on the shoulder. "We will beat them yet."

"I hope you are right." Jonathan walked to his chair so he could make sure his face did not betray him. He still wished he could keep Cat from going to London, but he would rather have her changed by the *ton* than to imagine her cowering in Meriweather Hall, at the mercy of outlaws.

The great hall was hushed. Dusk had invited the shadows to emerge from the corners, and the light from the few candles burning on the tables could not reach the rafters. The holly that had gleamed in the sunlight was dull and lifeless. Even its bright berries were swallowed by the darkness.

Cat stood in the middle of the room and turned to take it all in. While there were still sections of the room that needed to be finished, everything should be ready by the wedding breakfast. She had almost made a muddle of everything, but, with Jonathan's help, everything should be perfect for the celebration.

"Beautiful," Jonathan said from by the doorway.

As she faced him, her breath caught. In his bright green coat and crimson waistcoat, he brought the colors of the holly back to life. But she hardly noticed his clothing, as she was captured by the smile that tilted his lips and glittered in his pale blue eyes. Its warmth uncurled in her center, sending a tremor outward to her fingertips and toes.

He walked toward her. She was unable to move, held in place by his gaze and her own longing to be in his arms. He held his hand out to her. She put her fingers on his palm, and he raised them smoothly to his lips. Her own lips parted with a soft sound that was both a gasp and a sigh, as she surrendered to the sweet pleasure of his lips on her skin.

Raising his head, he whispered, "So beautiful."

"Yes, the great hall—"

"You, Cat. You are so beautiful."

She pulled her gaze from his and looked at her dirty gown that was sticky with pitch from pine branches. Patches of dirt showed where she had carried other greens to the footmen hanging them on the rafters.

"You are hoaxing me," she said with a laugh. "I am a complete rump."

His face remained somber. "No, Cat, I am not teasing you. I think you look beautiful." He brushed a strand of hair back from her face, his fingers lingering lightly against her cheek. "I always think you look beautiful."

Overmastered by the undisguised honesty in his eyes, Cat glanced away.

"And the great hall looks wonderful, too," he said when she did not reply. "I can see why you wanted the mermaid tears."

She walked with him to one of the tables where she had scattered the sea glass between where each guest would sit. "You helped make it possible, Jonathan."

"It was your idea. I am astounded you found all these mermaid tears in such a short time."

"For the past few months, rain or snow or sunshine, I've looked. Sometimes Vera helped me, and I was so glad when you offered to come along, too. It was great fun, wasn't it?"

"Everything is more fun when it is with you, Cat."

Warmth spread through her at his words, but she tried to ignore it. That was impossible.

Did he realize how his words unsettled her? Maybe that was why he continued past the table and gazed at the rafters. When he reached the section that had not yet been decorated, he turned and smiled.

"If you need more greens, I will be glad to drive you to the wood to collect them." His grin broadened. "You need not fear for your life. I am quite skilled in the box. After all, I drove often on the Continent."

"You did? I thought you were an officer."

"I was, but when some of the drivers got sick, I ended up taking the reins on a ration wagon. We learned to do whatever was necessary, no matter what rank we held." He chuckled. "Sort of like when you bring the village children here to stir the fruit. Everyone here pitched in to help."

Cat swallowed her gasp when she saw her sketchbook on a table just past where he stood. She edged around him, talking about how the rest of the greenery would look. She picked up the book.

"What is that?" he asked.

She closed it to keep the drawings hidden. "Just some notes I made for the staff, so they knew what I wanted where."

"Clearly they followed your directions well." He continued along the tables.

Cat wanted to call him back, so she could show him the sketches she had made. Certainly he would not laugh or look annoyed as other men had. He had believed she could learn to handle the paperwork for these events, and then he had taken the time to teach her. If he had patience with her cousin's inability to make a decision, surely he would have the same with her art.

But the moment had passed, and she stuck the book in a pocket beneath her apron. She strolled through the great hall with him and pointed out some of her favorite ways the greenery had been draped over the windows and across the rafters.

"This is remarkable," Jonathan said, smiling. "Elegant and grand, yet charming."

"I am sure I will see sights even grander when I get to London."

"Maybe grander, but none as heartfelt."

Again she was delighted with his praise. "I hope Sophia and Charles will like it, too."

"They will."

"There are still more greens to be hung, but everything else is ready."

He pointed toward the corner to the right of the entry. "Certainly over there. It looks rather bare." He walked to the corner beneath where the rafter had yet to be trimmed.

"I planned to hang a kissing bough here," she said as she followed him. "Don't you think this would be a good location for the kissing bough? Close enough to the tables to give anyone an easy excuse to stop here, but still in the shadows, so if someone wishes to steal a kiss, it will be convenient."

"Someone else must have thought so, too." He cupped her face gently in his strong hands as he whispered, "Look up, Cat."

She did. Overhead, concealed until now by the thick shadows, was the round ball of holly and ivy and mistletoe. When he whispered her name, she lowered her gaze to lose herself in his. Along her cheeks, his hands opened as if he cupped a gentle flower. She let the glow of his eyes draw her even closer.

His arm slid around her waist, and his mouth began to descend toward hers. In that moment, time seemed to halt. She was aware of everything. The buttons on his waistcoat pressing against her. The faint mat of whiskers on his cheek. The wool of his coat's sleeve beneath her fingers as her hands rose toward his shoulders. His breath on her face in the moment before his mouth found hers.

His lips were gentle, offering the chance to respond. She did. She put her heart into the kiss, needing for him to understand what she did not dare to say. Not yet. Not when she feared if she spoke, the wondrous moment would end.

Too soon, he raised his head and smiled at her. "And to follow tradition, I should now say 'Happy Christmas, Cat,' right?"

Was that all he intended the amazing kiss to be? Just a buss as any gentleman might give her beneath the kissing bough? An ache stripped away her happiness. She had thought the kiss was special for him, too. It was just another jest.

Somehow she managed to choke out, "The same to you, Jonathan." She wanted to give him an excuse that would make her leaving appear natural, but the words would not come. Whirling, she rushed out of the great hall. She had no idea what expression he wore as she fled, because she did not look back.

Chapter Fourteen

"You look lovely." Cat embraced her sister, then stepped aside so Mother could pick a thread off Sophia's sleeve.

Her sister was a diamond of the first water, a gem without equal. Charles's love had persuaded Sophia to be proud of her height, and, with her golden hair swept up with pearl combs in a Grecian style, a few curls framing her face, she could have been one of the female caryatids Lord Elgin had brought from Athens.

"Even lovelier than any other day." Mother dabbed at her eyes with a handkerchief edged with the same Brussels point lace as Sophia's gown.

"Mme. Dupont outdid herself." Sophia turned in front of the cheval glass.

Even though the day was gray, the white silk of her gown shimmered and rippled as if a faint zephyr played along it. Above the hem, two rows of vandyking were edged with lace that matched what had been sewn along the modest décolletage. Unblemished white gloves waited on her dressing table, but she would not don them until she reached the church. The day was so cold that she must wear heavier gloves on the way to the village.

Cat's own gown was pink and with less decoration, but Mme. Dupont had paid attention to every detail. With her hair held back with a single pink ribbon, she would not have been out of place at a Town soiree.

Unwanted tears seeped into her eyes as she thought of London. Once she did as she and Roland had pledged, what then? She had always assumed she would come back to Meriweather Hall, but nothing awaited her here. She had no idea what she wanted any longer.

"Catherine?" asked her mother with enough impatience that Cat knew Mother had called more than once.

Sophia laughed. "She might answer more quickly if you call her Cat."

"Cat?" Lady Meriweather laughed. "I thought you hated that name."

Sophia gave Cat a playful grin. "She did until Mr. Bradby began using it, and now everyone calls her Cat."

"I am glad." Her mother gave her a quick hug. "I always thought it was the perfect name for you because you are as inquisitive as a kitten and look at the world in a different way than the rest of us. I remember when you were young, and you gave me a picture you had drawn. It was a scene I had viewed every day since I had married your father, but you caught the light in a unique way and made it seem new."

"You still remember that?" asked Cat, astonished. She had not shared her sketches with her mother in several years.

"Memories are pouring down on me like a rainstorm." Her mother shook herself and smiled. "Weddings tend to do that, especially for the mother of the bride."

The door burst open, and Gemma and Michael rushed in followed by Alice, the nursery maid. Gemma was dressed in a miniature copy of Sophia's gown, and Michael wore a black coat and breeches that were already speckled with whatever he had been drinking. Alice reached out to slow them, but they both eluded her grip.

Cat grabbed Gemma, and Lady Meriweather kept Michael from giving Sophia a big hug and getting what was on his clothes onto her gown. Both children protested until Lady Meriweather asked them to ride to the church with her.

"And Sophia will go with Cat," her mother finished with a glance at Sophia who nodded gratefully.

"What about Papa?" asked Gemma, her auburn curls bouncing on her shoulders with her excitement.

"Papa will go with the gentlemen." Sophia bent to smile at the children who, Cat knew, were already her own in her heart. "The groom isn't supposed to see the bride before the wedding ceremony. You will make sure of that, won't you?"

Michael puffed out his thin chest. "I will!"

Gemma quickly echoed his words.

"You look grand," Sophia said, then smiled at Alice. "I appreciate you keeping them busy and clean."

"I did my best, Miss Meriweather." The nursery maid grinned.

Sophia gave her a quick hug. Cat and her sister had grown up with Alice when her own mother oversaw the nursery during their childhoods. The bond remained strong.

When Cat answered a knock on the door, Ogden announced the carriages were waiting to take them to the church. He stepped back as Sophia gave both her mother and sister big hugs. The faint smile he wore was so unusual that Cat could not resist winking at him. He winked back, and she laughed.

"What is it?" Sophia asked as she drew her pelisse over her gown and then helped the children into their wraps.

"Just happy." She would not embarrass their butler by revealing that he had shown a side of himself she seldom saw. Yet his delight with the wedding was a sign that the whole staff would do their best for the events over the next few days. Not that Cat expected anything less.

While she donned her own pelisse and bright pink bonnet, Cat hid her sketchbook in a pocket she had Mme. Dupont add to her coat. That would allow her to smuggle her sketchbook into the British Museum when she went to London. Today, she wanted to sketch the moment when her sister took her vows with Charles. She would work on it and give the final picture to them for their first anniversary.

She took Gemma by the hand. They followed Sophia and their mother—who had a secure hold on Michael—down the stairs. Sophia dabbed away happy tears at the sight of the whole household staff lined up in the entry hall to see her off to her new life as Lady Charles Northbridge. Each bowed or curtseyed as Sophia walked past, and tears brightened the cheeks of more than one of the women.

Sophia paused in the doorway and said to the staff, "Thank you."

Her simple words conveyed what a long speech could not have. It was "Goodbye" and "Thank you" and "I will miss you" compressed into two words. She nodded to the footmen holding the door, then stepped through. When she returned, she would be a countess, and her home would be a grand estate far to the south.

Cat heard sniffling behind her as she hurried Gemma out before the little girl asked the questions displayed in her wide eyes.

The cold air struck Cat like a vicious blow. Even with her heavy pelisse, the frigid breeze found every possible way to sneak beneath the long fur-lined coat. Almost instantly her eyes began to water, and she blinked rapidly so her lashes did not freeze to her face.

"Brr," she said. "Maybe you should have waited until spring to wed."

Sophia smiled. "Why don't you suggest that to Charles? He wanted to have the banns read as soon as he asked me to marry him. I did convince him to wait until now so Mother could be here, but I doubt anything short of Napoleon escaping exile again and invading England would persuade him to postpone the wedding any longer."

"And you would be as averse to the delay."

"I would." Sophia's smile softened. "I am eager to hear Gemma and Michael call me Mama and to hear Charles call me his wife."

Cat kissed her sister's cheek. "You deserve every happiness."

"And I want you to be as happy."

"I have adventures ahead of me when I go to London with Cousin Edmund." She tried to put enthusiasm into her words. "You will come to London to see us, won't you?"

"Of course. Do you think I will allow my little sister to be fired off without being there?"

Lady Meriweather came to collect Gemma and took both children to the carriage in front of the house. She made sure each was sitting before she allowed the footman to hand her into the carriage. A snap of the whip and the carriage headed toward the gate.

A second carriage pulled up, and Cat smiled when Sophia took her hand. For her sister, there was nothing she wanted more than to marry Charles, but that did not mean she was impervious to nerves. Sophia's fingers trembled as they waited for the footman to step forward to open the carriage door.

"All ready?" called Jonathan.

Cat's breath caught as he stepped down from the box and bowed. For once, his clothing was understated, and the black coat and waistcoat he wore beneath his greatcoat were the perfect foil for his ruddy hair that was topped by his tall beaver hat. She could not help but wonder if that staid waistcoat was the one Mme. Dupont had made for his costume for the Christmas Eve ball. As he walked toward them, his boots were polished to a sheen that would have been eye-searing if the sun had been out.

"Ladies, your chariot awaits." He bowed again and opened the door.

Sophia placed her hand on his, and he gracefully handed her into the carriage. She drew her skirt and the thick pelisse in and away from the door, so Cat would not step on them when she climbed in.

Jonathan held up his hand again and bowed as if he were a footman. "Miss Catherine? May I assist you, too?"

"Yes." That single word was alive with the breathless anticipation of touching him again, even though their leather gloves would be between them. She bit her lower lip. The leather was not the only thing separating them. That she loved him, and he considered her no more than a friend, divided them.

"Let's hurry, Cat," he said, still holding out his hand. "The sooner we get started, the less snow I'll have on me by the time we get to the church."

"On you? Aren't you riding in the carriage with us?"

He shook his head. "Not exactly. I am driving you."

"What? Where is our coachman?"

"Randolph is so sick with an ague that he cannot rise from bed." He smiled. "I arranged with Mrs. Porter for some soup to be delivered out to the stables."

"Thank you, Jonathan," Sophia said from inside the carriage. "Kip can drive, if you wish."

He shook his head. "He is driving Lady Meriweather and the children, and your soon-to-be husband and Meriweather have my carriage. Don't worry, ladies. I do have a bit of experience with the reins, you know."

"Army wagons, as I recall," Cat said with a grin in spite of herself.

"I must own that my cargo today is a bit more precious than cans of wormy rations."

Cat laughed. "Such a compliment, Mr. Bradby."

"I believe in giving credit where it's due, Miss Catherine." He offered his hand again.

Before she put her hand on his, snow covered his

palm. It was falling even faster. He gave her a grim smile as he handed her in and closed the door behind her.

His expression told her all she needed to know. He believed the storm was going to strengthen. She looked at the sky. Clouds hung low over the sea, and the wind came in frequent gusts that rocked the carriage.

When the carriage began to move toward the gate, Cat put her feet close to the heated stones that had been wrapped and placed in a metal box on the floor between the seats. She loosened the curtains over the smaller windows on her side and let them fall. She lashed them to the lower part of the window.

Sophia did the same with the other small windows. "I know it is silly to leave the ones open on the doors, but I want to watch our journey to the church."

"That isn't silly." Cat patted her sister's arm and smiled. "You should savor every minute of this day."

"I never thought I would find a man who wanted to marry a duchess of limbs like me."

"Now *that* is silly. You are tall, but there is nothing awkward about you." She leaned back against the leather seat. "And isn't it perfect that the man who wants to marry you is the one you want to marry?"

"You know what would make it more perfect?" She wrapped her arms around herself, but smiled broadly. "If you and Mr. Bradby would plan a wedding, too."

Cat longed to agree. It would be easy to fall in love with Jonathan, but, even if she would not allow herself to make the same mistake again, he refused to let anyone too near. She was no closer to discerning the secret he kept from everyone. The secret of what had changed him during the battle when he had saved Charles's life.

"Let's talk about *your* wedding today," she said to curb her sister's conversation in that direction. "You picked the best weather for it."

Sophia gave her a faint smile as she looked out at the thickly falling snow. "Charles is sure to remind me that we could have married in the fall."

"Who would have guessed it would snow like this before Christmas? The weather has been odd all year."

"Is it snowing harder?" She leaned forward to peer out the window. "I hope Jonathan can see through the snow."

Cat laughed as she shifted her feet even closer to the heat box. "You are an anxious bride, Sophia!"

"I guess I am." She relaxed against the seat. "Not about marrying Charles, though. I have never been so sure of anything in my life."

Squeezing her sister's hand, Cat said, "You have no idea how happy it makes me to hear you say that."

"I am glad that—" She grabbed the leather strap hanging from the ceiling as the carriage rocked. "What…?" Her words ended in a scream.

Cat grabbed the other loop and held on as the carriage teetered wildly to the right. She looked out the window. She saw only sky and falling snow. They must be up on two wheels. Was the carriage going over?

"Jonathan!" she moaned. Could he hold on in the box when the carriage was tilting so far to one side?

Sophia gasped out a prayer.

Oh, how she hoped God would hear Sophia! *Lord, please listen to her!*

For a moment, she thought Sophia's prayer had been answered. The carriage righted itself, the wood screeching a protest as the vehicle was twisted in ways it should not go. Then the carriage leaned in the other direction. Branches thrust through the window. They must be falling into the hedgerow.

Cat ducked beneath the greenery. She clutched her sister's arm and pulled Sophia down as a thicker branch slammed into the window frame. Splinters and icy snow ricocheted through the carriage. Covering her head with her arms, she winced when the corner of her sketchbook struck her ribs.

She shrieked as the carriage righted again. How was Jonathan keeping it from flipping over completely?

They hit the hedgerow again. The sharp crunch of a broken wheel came seconds before the back right side of the carriage dropped to the ground. Sparks burst up as the metal axle struck rocks beneath the hedge.

The front of the carriage struck something in the hedgerow and slammed to a stop. Cat flew forward, banging into the other seat. The heat box careened toward the door, but did not break open. Sophia fell to the floor and moaned.

Cat pushed herself up by grasping a window. The carriage slanted toward the hedgerow but not so much that they would not be able to get out.

"Sophia?" she whispered, unable to speak louder.

Her sister slowly raised her head. A bruise was already darkening along her left cheek. "Are you all right, Cat?"

"Yes." Every muscle ached, and she guessed she had bruises of her own.

A horse screeched in pain and terror.

Cat exchanged a glance with her sister and then reached for the door.

It opened before she could touch it. Jonathan called, "Are you all right? Are either of you hurt?"

"We are fine," Cat replied. "What about you?"

"Nothing that time won't heal." He pulled his hat lower as a line of blood seeped out of his hair.

"You are bleeding!" She pushed the door farther open and grabbed the sides to pull herself out. She ignored his caution about her thin slippers being useless in the rapidly accumulating snow. Jumping down, she cringed when she heard the horse scream again.

"I am fine." He pulled a handkerchief out of the pocket of his greatcoat. Jamming it beneath his hat, he flinched as the cotton brushed against his wound. "One thing you learn in battle is that even the most minor injury to the skull causes a lot of bleeding."

"What happened?"

"Something burst out of the hedgerow and onto the road in front of us. The horses panicked." He looked down at his gloves that were torn from where he had held the reins so tightly that the leather had cut through them. "I need to check the horses."

Cat put her hand on his arm to steady him as he reeled forward. How badly *was* he hurt?

As if she had asked that question aloud, he shrugged off her hand. He walked stiffly through the snow toward the front of the carriage, and she followed. She gasped when she saw both horses down, tangled in the straps connecting them to the carriage. Jonathan motioned for her to stay where she was. Biting her lower lip, she watched, hoping that he would not be kicked by one of the panicked horse's hooves.

He sliced the straps from the traces. One horse scrambled up. It turned and raced toward Meriweather

Hall. He leaped forward to grasp the leather flapping from the other horse as it came to its hooves. The horse screamed and rose on its back legs. He stumbled back, pushing Cat out of the way.

When the horse came down on all four hooves, he jumped toward it. His fingers closed on nothing as the horse sped after the other one.

Cat stared after it, too shocked to move.

When Jonathan put his hand on her arm, he said, "You should get back inside the carriage. You are going to freeze your feet. My toes are cold, and I have boots. Get inside while I see what the damage is to the carriage."

She started to protest, then became silent as he walked away. She went to where Sophia called to her from the open doorway. Her sister gently probed the bruise on her cheek. Scooping up some snow, Cat handed it to Sophia who held it against her cheek.

"Thank you, Cat. That eases the throbbing."

"Use it only for a few seconds. Otherwise it will give you frostbite."

Sophia nodded. "Where is Mr. Bradby?"

"Checking the damage to the carriage. He needs to get in out of the storm, too. I will be right back. I want—I should—" Cat was startled to realize she had no idea what she wanted. That was not quite true. She wanted Jonathan to love her as she loved him. That did not seem likely, because she was adrift as she never had been, not even after Roland died.

Sophia gave her a gentle shove. "Go. With that wound on his head, he must feel even worse than we do."

She wondered if that was possible.

* * *

Jonathan was not surprised to see Cat had not gotten back into the carriage. He had hoped that—for once—she would heed his request. Trying to make his eyes focus, he strode to her. He was determined not to show any sign of how much his head swam with each step.

He was not very successful, because she rushed forward to put her arm around his waist and steer him into the lee of the carriage where the wind was less biting.

"How are you?" she asked.

Instead of answering her, he checked under the coachee's seat. He found a gun, but if there had been more balls and powder, they must have fallen out when he lost control of the carriage. By now, the snow would have buried them.

"You need to get in the carriage and stay warm as long as you can," he said.

When she began to protest, he scooped her up in his arms and slogged through the snow. There must be more than two inches of new snow on the ground, and, if possible, it was falling even faster. He had never seen snow pile up so fast. Maybe the wind was making it drift, but he knew better than to expect the weather to change because he wished it to. He had learned that during his months of living through blistering heat on the Iberian Peninsula.

Cat put her arm around his shoulders and nestled her head against his neck. He savored her slight weight in his arms, as he turned her so her heart beat against his. Holding her strengthened him and made his steps more sure, even as he struggled to keep his mind on getting her into the carriage, when all he wanted to do was kiss her again.

When he placed her on her feet in the sloping carriage, his arms felt too empty. He climbed up behind her and closed the door.

"Sit here," Miss Meriweather ordered, shifting on the seat so Cat could sit facing her. "You both need to be close to the heat box." She frowned when Jonathan opened his mouth. "Do not resort to gallantry, Mr. Bradby. I have been sitting by it the whole time. If you don't get warm and dry out a bit, then both of you will be sick. I shall not have you sneezing during my wedding."

Cat chuckled as he sat beside her. Sophia edged closer to the heat box, and they took care that their knees did not bump.

He looked from Cat to her sister and back. "Miss Meriweather, we are stuck here. We have no horses, and the weather is getting even worse. You and Cat are not dressed for walking any distance."

"Then we shall wait," Cat said with a courage that he had to envy. "Someone will be along soon when we fail to show up at the church."

He shook his head.

"Of course they will," Cat insisted. "They will come looking for us."

"Not here." The carriage door blew open. He pulled it closed and latched it. "I took a different route than the other carriages."

"What?" gasped Miss Meriweather.

"Randolph told me the road closer to the cliffs is quicker. I saw the storm coming, and I thought we had a chance of beating it if we came this way."

"So he knows where we are?" Cat hunched into her pelisse as an icy wind chased snow into the carriage.

"No. He mentioned that to me days ago, so, if anyone asks him, he most likely will assume that we took the usual road into the village."

Cat flinched along with her sister. "So nobody knows where we are?"

"The first horse was headed in the direction of Meriweather Hall. When it gets there, the stablemen will know something is amiss. They can track its hoof prints back to us."

"See?" Cat said to her sister. "All is not lost."

But Jonathan's eyes were shadowed with worry. He was trying to give them hope, when he had little. The snow was piling up, and any sign of the horse's route would quickly disappear.

He stretched past Cat and began rolling down the curtain on the window in the one door they could still open. He looked to tie it down, but the hooks were broken off. He tried tying it to the small piece left. It was futile.

"Can I help?" Cat asked.

"Do you see any way to keep this from flapping in the wind?"

She moved to sit on the other seat and ran her fingers along the side of the carriage. "No, there is nothing close enough." Suddenly she smiled. "Wait a minute." She took off her bonnet and undid the ribbon holding up her hair.

As the dark waves washed down over her shoulders, Jonathan stared. Her lush curls teased his fingers to comb through them as he brought her mouth to his. Even from where he sat, the light fragrance of cinnamon drifted from her hair. It was intoxicating, and he fought to keep a new wave of dizziness from sending him into oblivion.

He forced his eyes to focus and discovered that she had tied her ribbon to a curtain cord. She was able to lash it around a hook beneath the window beside her. The curtain still flapped, but only on one side.

"Excellent," he said. "We need to conserve what little heat we have in here. We might be here for a while."

Miss Meriweather collapsed into sobs, startling Jonathan. He had never seen Cat's sister lose control of her emotions.

Cat put her arms around her sister. "We will be fine," she said, giving Jonathan a silent plea to help her console her sister.

He took Miss Meriweather's hands in his and waited until she looked at him. Pulling a second handkerchief from beneath his coat, he handed it to her.

"You don't want those tears to freeze to your face, do you?" he asked.

He was rewarded by Miss Meriweather's smile and Cat's quick nod. He was glad he had chosen the right way to bring Miss Meriweather out of the dolefuls.

"You always carry two handkerchiefs?" Miss Meriweather asked.

"Any wedding I have ever attended has more tears than handkerchiefs, so I thought to be prepared."

"But now there isn't going to be any wedding," groaned Miss Meriweather.

"Nonsense," Cat said. "Whether it is today or another day, you and Charles will get married. Think how you will laugh in the years to come as you tell the story of our misadventures."

Jonathan listened as Cat continued to bolster her sister. He remained silent, while he tried to decide what they should do. He was not exactly sure how far they had come. If Randolph was right, and this road was shorter, they must be about halfway between Meriweather Hall and the church. None of them were in any condition to walk the distance.

"I saw something!" Miss Meriweather pulled back the loose curtain on the door.

"What?" Jonathan sat straighter.

"Look! A light!" She jabbed a finger toward a faint glow coming along the road from the direction of the village. "We have been found."

Jonathan smiled and quickly untied the curtain. He rolled it up so they could watch the lights come closer. "We still may get there in time for the wedding."

"By the motion of the lights, I would say they are walking." Miss Meriweather squinted through the snow. "They won't have any way to help us reach the church."

"If they are out in this storm," Cat said, "they must live close by. Maybe they will have a wagon or horses to hook to the carriage."

Miss Meriweather's smile returned. "I hope you are right."

"We should gather what we don't want to leave behind." Cat bent toward the floor, groping around the metal box that gave off less heat with every passing second.

Tearing his gaze from the lights, Jonathan asked, "Did you lose something important? Leave it for now. We can come back once the storm blows itself out."

"My book! It must have fallen out of my pocket when the carriage rocked."

He bent to join the search, and she had to draw back so their heads did not bump. He stretched out his arm to sweep the floor with one smooth motion. Was that her book back in the far corner?

"Cat, don't move!" Miss Meriweather screamed in terror.

He dropped what he had found. Straightening, he asked, "What...?"

He stared in disbelief at a pistol stuck through the window. It was aimed directly at Cat's heart.

Chapter Fifteen

Jonathan heard Cat's quick intake of breath. He kept his eyes focused on the men standing beside the carriage. Even if it had not been snowing so hard, he doubted he would be able to describe any of them other than greatcoats with raised collars and felt hats with brims that sagged over their faces almost to the kerchiefs covering their mouths and noses. Beneath the clinging snow on the wool coats were more white lines that could have been salt stains, but he did not need that clue to warn him that these men were some of the faceless Sanctuary Bay smugglers.

When the man motioned with the pistol for them to get out, Jonathan considered for a brief second begging the men to have compassion for the women. He said nothing. If the men cared about the Meriweather sisters, the pistol would have been pointed at him instead of Cat.

He stepped out of the tilting carriage, then helped both women. He kept his hands on their backs as they walked around the carriage and to the middle of the narrow road. A quick shove might be the only way he could save their lives if one of the smugglers decided to use a gun. When they stopped, facing the mob, he stepped in front of the women. He was one man against twenty or more, but he would fight to protect Cat and Miss Meriweather.

Be by my side, Lord. Turn the tide in our favor, and watch over us. Be our shepherd and hold off these sea wolves.

"What are you doing here?" demanded a muffled voice.

Jonathan wondered if it was only his imagination, but the voice sounded almost familiar. And why not? He probably had greeted each of these men at some point on the beach below the village. Then they had been pleasant, giving no sign of the treachery hiding deep in their souls.

"We slid into a snowbank on our way to Miss Meriweather's wedding." He saw no reason not to be honest. Maybe if they thought he was going to be straight with them, they would not suspect if he had to resort to lies to protect Cat and her sister.

The men conferred among themselves, surprising him. He clenched his hands by his sides. That not all the men knew about the wedding at the village church suggested that not every smuggler was from the Sanctuary Bay village. The network must be far larger and better organized than anyone at Meriweather Hall had guessed.

That was a disturbing discovery, not just for him, but for Cat who had clearly come to the same conclusion. Her face was so colorless that he could see a large bruise on her chin. He had not noticed it before, and she had not complained. Not that he would have expected her to.

For one minute, then two, the smugglers whispered so Jonathan could not hear. Were they arguing about what to do? Or were they debating how to do it?

He looked past them but could not see far into the snowstorm. Had they been missed at the church yet? Lady Meriweather had seen her daughters get into the carriage, so she knew they should have arrived right after her. How he wished he had Meriweather and Northbridge at his back now!

A man who had not spoken before stepped forward and said, "We will tek t' bride wi' wee."

"Pardon?" He could not understand the man's thick Yorkshire accent.

The man pushed his face closer to Jonathan's and snarled, "Ah sez we will tek t' bride wi' wee."

"Shout all you want, but I can't understand you. Speak the King's English, man."

The man pulled his hand back as his fellows egged him on, and Jonathan prepared himself to block the blow. It did not come because Cat stepped in front of him.

She turned to face him, then flung her arms around him. Snide remarks filled the air, but she whispered, "He said they want to take the bride with them. Don't let them take her, Jonathan."

"C'mun," growled the man. "We dooant 'av orl day. Wea'ar takin' t' bride. Naw!"

He did not need anyone to translate that for him. He understood enough to know the smugglers were getting impatient.

"Why do you want the bride?" he asked.

"So you and the other one will be mute as a fish until we are done with our business." That was the first man who had spoken; the man did not use the hard-to-understand Yorkshire pronunciations. "We will bring her back unhurt by morning's first light, if you do not try to follow us. Come after us, and she dies."

"Do you think I will agree to such an absurd offer?" He clenched his fists, ready to defend them.

The smugglers swarmed forward. He pushed Cat behind him but heard her scream. He whirled to see her in the clutches of a stocky man. He leaped forward to drive his fist into the man's face.

He stopped when he saw something flash behind Cat. A knife! A deadly knife aimed at someone he would give his life for.

Instantly the cold vanished, and sun blinded him. Shouts battered his skull. He could not grasp the words but recognized the sounds of panic and fury. Guns firing. Men screaming. Men dying. The odors of blood and death sickened him. He coughed, but the reek tainted every breath he drew. The roar of cannon fire escalated until he thought his ears would burst.

But he focused on the blade. He raised his gun to knock it away. Where was his gun? He did not have a gun! With a roar, he launched himself at the man holding it. This time, he would not trip over his own feet. This time, he would keep the blade away. This time, he would be a true hero.

Something struck him from behind. He heard Cat's scream. What was she doing on the battlefield? *Cat! Cat, run away!* Her horrified expression went with him into a black nothingness lit with bright flashes of pain.

* * *

Pain.

Flashes of red-hot pain.

Even thinking hurt.

He had to get out of there. Before the French over-ran their position and killed them all. He could not be dead. Not yet. He hurt too much.

"Slowly," a soft voice crooned. "Don't make any sudden moves until you are wide awake."

Sudden moves were the last things Jonathan would consider doing when his head was wrapped with fiery iron and someone was striking it with a hammer.

He faded in and out of consciousness, but the pain never diminished. Each time he was slightly awake, the soft voice offered comfort and never prodded him to do more than listen.

A soft voice that spoke in English.

A soft voice that belonged to a woman.

Then he opened his eyes.

He blinked, trying to make sense of what he saw. A low dark roof that seemed to be at an angle. He shifted his eyes and stared at a snowy branch sticking through a window. He raised his gaze to see Cat's pretty face above his, barely lit by the faint glow from the flickering lamps near the roof. He was lying with his head on her lap.

He pushed himself up to sit as memories burst into his head. Memories of the smugglers. Memories of the French. Memories that seemed to be a mixture of both. What had happened? Was any of it real? Pain rippled in the wake of the memories, and he had to support his head on his hands. Icy hands. The cold as much as anything else stripped away the last of the cobwebs in his mind.

The battles against the French were in the past. Not today. Yet he would have taken an oath that a knife had been aimed at Cat by a Frenchman. He remembered how Northbridge suffered from horrible nightmares. Had Jonathan had a waking one? Was that even possible?

He had no answers for that, and Cat would not, either. But there was one question he had to ask her.

"How long?"

Cat said, "At least a couple of hours. I have lost track of time, but the sun went down some time ago." Her words were bitten off by her chattering teeth. "I don't know how much longer the lamps will last."

As if on cue, the lamp closer to the hedgerow sputtered and died.

He looked outside the carriage. It was snowing so hard that he could not see the hedgerow on the other side of the narrow road. "Are you hurt?"

"No."

He glanced around the carriage, then wished he had made the motion more slowly. "Where is your sister?"

"They took her. Just as they said they would."

He moaned. Less from the pain than from his failure to protect those who depended him.

Again.

"They shoved you back in here," she went on, "and left after reminding me that Sophia's life depended on us complying with their orders."

Jonathan rubbed his cold hands together near the heat box which gave only a faint ghost of warmth. "Will you be all right here?"

"What do you mean?"

"I am going after them."

"Don't be absurd." She seized his coat sleeve so hard that he heard threads snap. "You can't go after them."

"Cat, I know how to take care of myself. I survived the war, after all."

"But I want *everyone* to survive this. Don't go after them. If you do, they will not hesitate to kill both Sophia and you."

He stared out the door. It would be simple to track the smugglers. Even though the snow had filled in their footprints, there were other ways to track them. He had refined his skills by creeping up on French camps to reconnoiter before a battle. So many men could not travel without leaving some signs of their passage. All he had to do was follow them to find the smugglers… and Sophia. He could rescue her, making sure she was uninjured, and he could unmask the smugglers.

At last, he would be the hero everyone already believed him to be.

He heard a sob and swiveled with care on the seat to look at Cat. She had her hands over her face, and her shoulders quaked with fear.

Putting a hand on her arm, he brushed her loosened hair back beneath the crushed brim of her bonnet. When had she put her bonnet back on? How had her bonnet been damaged? "Cat, I will be careful. I promise you. I will—"

"Didn't you hear them? If we give chase, they will kill her." With a sob, her voice broke. "On her wedding day, they will kill her. Please, Jonathan, I know you are a brave man and a great hero, but you are only one against all those smugglers. They mean what they say, just as they did when they hung that effigy of Jobby in the wood."

He almost told her that he must go after the smugglers, so he could prove he truly was a hero.

Then his shoulders sagged, and he sighed. No argument he could give Cat—or himself—would lessen the risk to both women if he chased after the smugglers. He had no doubts that, if he were caught, the criminals would come back and kill Cat.

He could not risk Cat.

He could not risk Sophia.

He could not be a hero.

The price of making the lie into the truth was too high.

Cat must have seen his decision on his face. "Thank you, Jonathan."

He ached to kiss her, but the thought of moving brought a fresh rush of pain. He had only enough strength to lean his head back against the tilted seat.

Lord, I hope I made the right decision. Watch over Cat and Sophia and keep them safe. What happens to the lie doesn't matter any longer.

Cat said nothing as Jonathan closed his eyes. She gauged the slow rise and fall of his chest. When that beast had struck him with a pistol, she had feared that Jonathan was dead. Her ears still rang with their malicious laughter, as they had tossed him into the carriage as if he were a net of fish. She had resisted when they had ordered her into the carriage, too, and she had paid with more bruises. Her left eye was sure to be black by the morning. She had gotten in a few blows of her own, but no satisfaction, because, while she was forced into the carriage by some of the smugglers, others took Sophia away.

How long would it take those curs to finish whatever business they had? And would they bring Sophia back when they were done? She had no reason to believe their promises.

But she had to believe them. Otherwise, she would have to accept that her sister might already be dead.

Staring at the storm, she leaned her head back against the seat. The wind did not blow so hard when she huddled into a corner of the carriage. It was a bit warmer. Not enough to be comfortable, but enough so that every breath she took was not an icy knife in her lungs. The box on the floor gave off so little heat she could no longer feel it through her pelisse.

She drew up her feet beside her and leaned into the carriage's wall. How much longer before Cousin Edmund and Charles found them? She closed her eyes. It would be for the best if they did not come until Sophia was delivered back to them. Otherwise, the smugglers might believe that the men from Meriweather Hall were hunting them.

How dismayed her family and friends must have been when their carriage never arrived at the church! Mr. Fenwick would have done his best to keep everyone calm, so the children were not frightened. Dear Vera would have sat with Mother, keeping her company while the men debated what to do.

Come now, Cat wanted to shout, but the words never reached her lips. Not that it mattered because her friends and her family were too far away as the storm roared around them. She wished she could see their faces outside the carriage, and they all could return to Meriweather Hall and get warm. Warm beneath a stack of blankets with a cup of hot chocolate.

She imagined holding the steaming cup in her hands. The rich aroma of chocolate made her mouth water. As she raised the cup, she heard, "Cat…"

She waited for the speaker to continue. When he did not, she started to take a sip again.

"Cat…"

Why wouldn't he just let her have a sip of the hot chocolate? Just breathing it in made her feel nice and warm.

"Cat…" Jonathan! Why was Jonathan keeping her from having her hot chocolate?

"Cat…"

"Cat…"

"Cat…"

At the repetition of her name, she tensed. Why didn't someone say something other than her name?

"Cat…"

Vexed, she whirled to face the man. Her cup flew from her hand and shattered. She jerked out of her reverie.

No, not reverie.

Dream.

She had fallen asleep. Sleeping in this cold would lead to freezing to death.

Every muscle protested as she tried to sit straighter and found herself held by strong arms. The frigid wind scoured her face, and she groaned.

Her ice-caked lashes fought her as she struggled to open her eyes. She reached up and rubbed her eyes, then wished she had not. Not only was her bruised eye tender, but she could barely open her eyes because the light was too bright. What light was that? The carriage lamps should have sputtered and gone out by now. When she opened her eyes again, tears trickled down her cheeks. She hastily wiped them away before they could freeze on her face.

Or she tried to. Her cold hands refused to move as she intended.

"Cat, stay awake." A deep voice rumbled beneath her ear along with an uneven heartbeat. Gentle fingers brushed the tears off her face.

She moaned.

"I am sorry. I didn't mean to hurt you more."

That was Jonathan's voice!

She was sitting with her head against Jonathan's chest!

That thought pushed aside the tempting tendrils that teased her to fade into the false warmth that she knew led to freezing to death. She started to sit up.

"Don't move," Jonathan whispered against her torn bonnet. His breath ruffled her hair. "I have blankets wrapped around us, and I don't want to chance any cold air seeping in."

"Blankets?" She sounded witless, but she was confused and so sleepy. She fought to stay awake and not succumb to the cold again.

"I found two in the boot, and I wrapped both around us." His voice caught. "So you would not freeze to death."

"But you were out in the cold longer than I was. Are you all right?"

"I am now that we have the blankets around us. Also I have a heavy greatcoat and boots. They have helped protect me from the cold."

"The lights?"

He smiled grimly. "I found two lanterns by the back of the carriage. I don't know if some of the smugglers had a morsel of compassion and left them for us, or if the lanterns were forgotten. Either way, I lit one and set it on the other seat to give us some light, and we will have the other when this one goes out. Too bad they don't give off more heat."

"Maybe if we talk, we'll be able to stay awake until morning." Her teeth began to chatter again. She was so cold. When his arms tightened around her, holding her closer to his chest, she knew he had felt her shiver.

"What should we talk about?"

She shrugged, then wished she had not when her stiff bones protested with aches. "Whatever you want to talk about." She peered past the blanket and out the window at the wind-swept snow. More snow had drifted into the carriage, blown onto the branches and then falling on the floor. "Anything except the weather."

"We could start with why you looked at me as if I were no better than a cur after I kissed you."

"I don't want to talk about that, either." Cat stiffened and pushed her hands against his chest.

"But I do." He held her tight to him. "Why did you ruin our kiss by running away?"

"I didn't ruin it. You did."

"Me? I ruined it. How?"

"By acting as if it were nothing special. You kissed me and then told me, that as tradition requires, you should wish me a happy Christmas. Just as anyone does who shares a holiday kiss under the kissing bough."

He put his gloved hand on her unbruised cheek. As

he gazed down into her eyes, she wondered what he hoped to see. "My sweet Cat, I kissed you because I could not bear *not* kissing you any longer."

"But you said—"

"I know how important traditions are to you and your family. I thought saying something about a tradition would make you laugh." He sighed. "My joke was only on me."

His voice was so sad that her heart threatened to break in midbeat. "I'm sorry, Jonathan. I thought—"

He put his fingers to her lips. "You have no reason to apologize. The truth is that I am envious of how many traditions your family has and how much you enjoy them."

His honesty gave her the courage to ask, "Doesn't your family have traditions?"

He leaned her head against his shoulder and made sure the thick wool blanket covered both of them. He stared into the snow that was falling even more heavily.

"We have traditions, but not ones I want to be part of." His voice hardened. "Our traditions have more to do with obtaining a better place among the *ton* than spending time together."

"Oh, Jonathan, that is sad. But surely there must be something that you shared that brought you joy."

"I thought so, too, then I got a hard lesson from Augusta."

A pinch of jealousy seared her, but she ignored it. "Who is Augusta?"

"She was my younger sister's best friend. We were always together as children. Even when I didn't want them along, Gwendolyn and Augusta found a way to tag along after me."

"As I did with Sophia."

"We remained friends as we grew. Even when I went away to university and began to read the law, Augusta sent me letters and was delighted to see me when I visited my mother's house." He paused. Each word sounded more difficult to speak than the one before it as he added, "Then one year, after her coming-out in London, I saw her at an assembly during the Season."

Cat bit her lower lip, remembering how he had disparaged the Season. She remained silent. Was *this* the secret that made his eyes fill with sadness?

Find a way to open your heart to God, Cat, and maybe you can find a way to help Mr. Bradby open his.

Vera may have had it backward. If Jonathan opened his heart, could he help Cat find a way to open hers? She had to take the chance that it would.

"What happened?" she whispered, her lip cracking from the cold. She put her glove to it to keep it from bleeding.

"She cut me directly."

Shocked, she blurted, "Why?"

"I asked myself that, and it puzzled me. Then I heard that she was going to marry a baron. I wanted to do whatever I could to halt the wedding. When I went to Gwendolyn to ask her advice, she laughed in my face. I can still hear her asking me why Augusta would want to marry a mere solicitor when she could marry a peer. *That* is what the Season did to my gentle sister and her kind friend. It altered them into fortune hunters." He put a crooked finger under her chin and tilted her head back. His intense gaze matched his words. "Cat, I don't want to see that happen to you."

"It won't."

"You can't be certain of that."

She smiled, as she stroked his cheek that was roughened by the cold and his whiskers. "I can. I saw what the Season did to Sophia, and I—" Her breath caught, and sobs overtook her.

Turning her face against Jonathan's coat, she wept. Would she ever see Sophia again? He let her cry, until she had no more tears to fall. She clung to his lapel as if it were her only lifeline out of the insanity surrounding them. Instead of sitting in the frigid carriage and struggling not to freeze to death while they waited to see if Sophia was brought back to them, they should have been raising toasts to the happiness of the newlyweds.

When her sobs had faded to hiccups, Jonathan whispered, "Have faith, Cat. God is watching over your sister just as He is watching over us. We must keep praying for her safety and ours. God will hear our prayers and protect her."

Her fear and frustration metamorphosed into rage as she snapped, "That is easy to say."

"It is just as easy to believe." His voice remained calm. "All during the war, God never abandoned me. He has a plan for me, and I only have to trust that He knows the road that lies before me."

"I used to believe that, too." She looked away from him, embarrassed by her outburst. She was not angry with Jonathan. She was angry with...with whom? God? Herself?

"But your belief in God has been shaken," he said in a tender tone.

"No. I believe in God. That belief has never faltered."

"But?"

Tucking the blanket more closely around herself again so she could avoid his steady gaze that seemed to see too much, she said, "I used to pray. I prayed for help through bad times and prayed with gratitude for good and happy events. When Papa sickened, I prayed harder than I ever had that he would not die." She shuddered as she recalled those difficult days. "I prayed and I prayed, but he died. I don't believe God hears my prayers."

"He hears everyone's prayers, but we must remember that His plans for us and those we love are something we can't always understand. His time is not our time. He sees beyond what we can."

"I understand that, Jonathan, but my heart doesn't."

"What is in your heart now?"

She almost said, "You," but she halted herself. "Fear. Loneliness because God is no longer with me."

"And anger."

"Yes. How did you know?"

"Because I have been angry at God, too. When I saw good men die in battle and from sickness, I was angry. Then I see my former commander laid low with terrors that stalk him during his sleep. I watch my good friend Edmund Herriott suffer from an invisible wound, and I'm angry. I want to shake my fist at the sky and demand that God explain how he could allow such things." His voice deepened with emotion. "Then I remind myself that faith is accepting that God's plan is a loving one, even if I cannot see it at the time."

"I want God back in my life, but He has moved away from me."

"Has He, or have you let your pain move you away from Him?"

Cat started to give him an answer and then realized she did not have one. Was it possible that *she* had pushed God away and stopped listening for His voice? She had been so filled with grief after her father had died that she had shut herself off from everyone, even Sophia and their mother for a short while. It had taken her weeks before she could bear talking to her very best bosom-bow, Vera. Slowly she had opened her heart to each of them again.

Except God. She had made some halfhearted attempts, but God wanted her to come to Him wholeheartedly.

Jonathan clasped her gloved hands between his and bowed his head. "Why don't we pray together?"

"I'm not sure—"

"*I* am. Let me start, and you join in as you wish."

She closed her eyes and laced her fingers through his. Then she opened herself to the words Jonathan whispered, words of hope and supplication for her sister, and guidance to help Cat feel God within her.

Keep Sophia safe. Keep us safe, she prayed silently. *Let me know Your love within my heart again. I miss You, heavenly Father. I need You now and always.*

Warmth flowed out of her heart. Not a great rush, but a trickle, so slight that she might have overlooked it. The bands of pain loosened, as she opened herself to welcome God back into her life. More tears sprang into her eyes, but these were tears of joy.

Jonathan embraced her. "I see the light inside you burning brighter."

She curved her hand around his nape and guided his mouth down to hers. As their lips melded, she softened against him. His fingers tangled in her hair as he kissed her again and again and again until she no longer felt the cold. He brushed her brow, her eyelids, her nose and her cheek with a flurry of light kisses, taking care not to touch any of her bruises. When he found her lips again, she knew her heart was lost.

She loved him.

The carriage shifted beneath them as it sank more deeply into the hedgerow. His arm over her head pressed her toward the seat as he threw himself over her. She grabbed the lantern before it could topple over and set the carriage on fire. More branches stabbed into the carriage, whipping once they were free and spraying them with snow. Wood cracked, and wind gusted through a hole that had not been there a moment before.

"If it keeps settling," Cat said as she steadied the lantern and then raised her head, "the carriage is going to fall apart like a ship on a shoal."

"It is our only shelter."

"And the smugglers will bring Sophia back here."

He nodded and flicked the blanket around her shoulders. "Let's hope they get here before the carriage is kindling." He looked down. "Say, what is that?"

Cat bent and picked up the leather book. "It's my sketchbook."

"I wondered if you had one."

She stared at him, astonished. "Why would you think that?"

"Because you are an artist."

"How did you know?"

Jonathan rested his cheek against her battered bonnet, and his words seeped through it to brush her face. "I am a solicitor, Cat. I look at the facts and see how they fit together. My first suspicion was when you chose to decorate the wedding breakfast tables with mermaid tears. Only someone with an artist's eye could look at bits of glass and see their potential beauty."

"I never thought of that."

"And I watched you with Mme. Dupont's sketches. You drew quick lines on them, and even those simple lines were elegant." He held out his hand. "May I see your sketchbook?"

Cat wanted to shove it back under her pelisse, but halted herself. She needed to know if she could trust him with her art. If she was willing to give him her heart, how could she deny him such a vital part of her soul?

Without speaking, she placed the sketchbook on his hand. She drew back her fingers and clasped them under the blanket. The light from the lantern flickered wildly. For a moment, she feared it was going out.

Jonathan moved the lantern so it was not tilting, and the light grew even again. He did not open her sketchbook. Her fingers quivered with more than the cold.

"Have you showed this to others?"

"Yes, my parents and Sophia have seen some of the pages."

"No one else?"

"Vera, of course."

"Of course."

She lowered her eyes, not wanting him to see the humiliation that still stung. "I showed it to a few callers, but they were not interested in my art. Roland was the only one who didn't think a woman should concern herself with keeping her house instead of drawing."

"Roland? Roland Utting?" Pain flashed in his eyes. "How do you know about Roland?"

"Your cousin told me that you were involved with him before the war." He glanced out at the snow. "And I heard people talking about him in the village. How heroic he was."

"He was a hero, and he was the only man, other than my father, who shared my love of art." She put her hand against Jonathan's cheek and turned his face toward her. "I loved him, and he loved me, but he felt a village boy must prove himself capable of extraordinary feats, if he were to ask the baron for his younger daughter's hand. He went to war, and he did not come back as he had promised."

"He could not have known what would happen."

"No?" Pain bubbled out of her heart as she spoke the words she had kept encased behind an icy wall, since she had heard that Roland was dead. "It was war, Jonathan. You cannot tell me that you did not know the risks."

"I knew them, but any soldier will tell you that death is something he believes will come for others on the battlefield, not for him."

"I know he wanted to keep his promise, which is why I am determined to keep the promise I made to him. We planned to see the Elgin Marbles in London together, once he was home from the war. Going to the British Museum is the only reason I am willing to travel to London. Please don't tell Cousin Edmund. He has been generous arranging for me to have a Season, but once I have seen the Greek sculptures, I plan to return to Meriweather Hall." A smile tugged at her lips. "So you don't need to worry about me being changed by the *ton*." She laughed. "Or the *ton* being changed by me."

"I am glad to hear that."

"What part?"

"All of it, and I won't divulge your secret to Meriweather." He looked down at her sketchbook but did not open the cover. He raised his eyes to meet hers. "Are you sure?" he asked quietly. "If you would rather I didn't—"

She slid his hand to the edge of the cover. "I'm sure."

Shivering as she wrapped her arms around herself, Cat watched as Jonathan opened the sketchbook, her most precious and personal possession. He turned the pages, pausing to look at each one. Some he went past quickly. Others held his attention much longer.

She yearned to ask why those drawings appealed to him but said nothing. Roland had chastised her more than once that she needed to let him look at her work without subjecting him to an interrogation of what he liked and what he did not and why.

"These are lovely," Jonathan said as he turned the last page of her work. "I see so much of you in them, Cat. Unlike Sir Nigel, who never reveals anything about himself in his art, you are there on the page. Knowing you, I would never doubt that this is your work. It is very good, Cat."

"You sound surprised."

He looked up at her. Was her nose as red with the cold as his? "Why wouldn't I be? You've kept this so well hidden that I never guessed you could do such amazing sketches." He went back several pages and tipped the book so, in the thin light, he could see the drawing of a grouping of sea glass in front of waves. "You have captured the power of the sea with a few lines. There's simplicity but so much depth. It is as well done as works I have seen at the Royal Academy of Arts."

"Really?"

He grinned. "Really."

"Thank you. I never expected such praise."

"I do have a question."

"What?"

He became serious. "Why are you showing them to me now?"

She opened her mouth to reply, but his hand covered it before she could make a sound. He held a finger to his lips. She nodded as she strained her ears to hear what he had.

Beneath the rumble of the wind, she heard voices. Male voices. Many of them.

Then a woman's voice called her name.

She tore Jonathan's hand away from her mouth and shouted, "Sophia!"

Chapter Sixteen

Jumping out of the carriage, Cat waded through the snow that rose above her knees. She ignored the men as she threw her arms around her sister. As the wind whirled their skirts through the snow, she repeated her sister's name over and over. She stepped back and touched Sophia's arm, her cheek, her other arm, her nose. She needed to make sure her sister was truly there, truly unharmed. That this was not another dream.

"Cat!" Sophia cried at the same time Jonathan shouted her name from behind her. "What happened to you?"

In amazement, Cat realized her sister was in better condition than she was. Sophia's dress was not torn, and the single bruise on her cheek was hardly noticeable in the light from the smugglers' lanterns. Her hair was still pinned in place, and her eyes were not puffy from crying.

"Praise God that you are here and safe," Cat said instead of answering her sister's question. She did not want to explain while they were surrounded by criminals.

Sophia looked past her, and Cat turned. Jonathan approached the smugglers with an easy confidence that spoke of his courage. He had no idea what the smugglers planned for them.

Quietly Jonathan said, "It would be for the best if the ladies returned to the carriage." His eyes were like twin pistols aimed at the smugglers. He was not asking their permission.

The man who had given orders before grumbled something, but nobody halted them as Cat took her sister by the hand and hurried her to the carriage. She looked back as she helped Sophia into the carriage which was in even worse condition than she had guessed.

Jonathan stood in the middle of the road. Arcing around him, the criminals carried weapons of all sorts. He crossed his arms over his chest, his gaze on the smuggler who had struck him over the head with a pistol. In astonishment, she realized Jonathan would not know that.

"Get in," Sophia urged. "Quickly. Before they change their minds."

"But if he hits Jonathan again…"

Sophia tugged her into the carriage. "He's a soldier. He knows how to deal with an enemy better than we do."

"He isn't armed, and this isn't a battlefield on the Continent." She peeked out the door and gasped.

With the smugglers behind him in a bizarre parade, Jonathan walked toward the carriage. Cat held her breath as she listened to the snarled orders from the lead smuggler. He wanted Jonathan to get into the carriage and to stay there with Cat and Sophia until sunrise. A guard would be left to watch the carriage. If any of them tried to leave before dawn, the guard's orders were to kill all of them.

Jonathan said nothing until he reached the carriage door. Looking in, he asked, "Miss Meriweather, were you injured in any way by these men?"

"No, Mr. Bradby," Sophia answered, her voice as emotionless as his.

"Very well." Jonathan faced the smugglers. His attitude suggested that he was in charge. "You have honored your side of the agreement," he said to them. "As Miss Catherine and I have honored our side. Therefore, let us part now. We will take our lamp and walk away from here. You do the same."

His words were met with jeers, but his expression did not change.

The man who gave orders repeated his command that they remain in the carriage until the sun rose over Sanctuary Bay. Jonathan did not relent, either. "The ladies must be allowed to find better shelter for the night."

"Cat," Sophia whispered. "Listen."

"I am."

Her sister tugged on her arm. "Not to Mr. Bradby." She gestured carefully toward the front of the carriage. "You understand the local cant better than I do."

Switching to the backward facing seat beside her sister, Cat leaned her head against the carriage wall. Through the broken wood, she heard a smuggler say, "Gerr ta 'is qualityship. Tell 'im everythin' is set, 'n t' bride saw nowt."

She bit her lower lip to keep from gasping. She pressed her head against her sister's shoulder, so if one of the men glanced in, he would not guess she was listening to the hushed conversation.

Go to his qualityship. Tell him everything is set, and the bride saw nothing.

That was what the man had said. The men must believe that, by using the thickest possible Yorkshire brogue, they could speak without an outsider realizing what they were saying. But she was no outsider, and, even though the villagers spoke to her without the accent, she had been around it enough years to be able to puzzle out the words. That could be why they whispered, not paying attention to the fact that she sat close enough to hear their conversation.

"Theur norrz 'is qualityship doesn't li' ta be disturbed int' middle o' t' neet," replied another man.

You know his qualityship doesn't like to be disturbed in the middle of the night, she translated automatically.

His qualityship. Both men had used that term. *Quality* could mean many things, but the tone they had used—both deferential and vexed—suggested they spoke of a landed gentleman. Was their leader a member of the peerage? That would explain why they had evaded capture and were bold enough to abduct a baron's daughter.

"Get in or die!"

At the smuggler's order, the carriage creaked as Jonathan climbed in and slammed the door closed. The frame had sprung so far out of shape that it would not stay shut. The men laughed as if they had never seen anything so funny.

Jonathan sat beside her. She put her hand on his arm to keep him from reacting to the insulting words fired in their direction. He patted her hand and gave her a taut smile. He would not risk them by responding to petty comments.

The laughter muted as the smugglers left them to the storm. She had no doubts that at least one guard was posted nearby.

"Jonathan," she whispered. "I heard—"

"Say nothing," he returned as quietly. "Not here. Not until we get behind the walls of Meriweather Hall."

She nodded. His advice was excellent. As always.

He handed one blanket to Sophia and draped the other over his and Cat's shoulders. At a normal volume, he said, "I know you must be exhausted, Miss Meriweather—"

"I think in light of all that has happened," Sophia said with a tired smile, "you should call me Sophia."

"I would be honored if you called me Jonathan. You are well?"

"Yes. They took me a short distance, shut me in a barn with a pair of guards, and then came back for me and brought me here. They never even tied me up."

"I am glad to hear that." His face grew grim. "Of other things that happened tonight, I believe the retelling of everything else that has happened to us should wait until after sunrise."

"I agree," Cat said at the same time as her sister. "But we need to talk about something so we don't fall asleep."

"I have just the dandy." He slipped his arm around Cat's waist and drew her sketchbook out from beneath his coat. "Before you arrived, Sophia, we were discussing Cat's excellent work. Would you like to join us in that discussion?"

"You were?" Sophia's eyes got big, then she smiled

at Cat who felt a blush climbing her face. "I think all of us have a lot to share about our adventures once we are home."

The sunshine was painfully bright on the fresh snow the next morning, so Jonathan kept his head down as he trudged along the road. The storm had ended just before dawn. He looked at Cat and Miss Meriweather who walked beside him. He had taken the blankets that had kept them from freezing to death and torn them into strips to wrap around the women's feet. The wool offered more protection from the cold than their silk slippers.

While they tied the strips in place, he jumped into the drift that had blown up against the carriage almost up to the base of the door. He was so fadded out that he could barely move. In addition, his head throbbed from where he had been struck, first when the carriage had tipped and then by the smugglers. He had made every effort to keep his pain hidden from the ladies, but he had seen how Cat glanced time and again at the dried blood in his hair.

He looked in both directions and discovered the carriage had overturned closer to the village than to Meriweather Hall. Even so, when he had helped the Meriweather sisters from the ruined carriage, he turned his back on the village. Neither Cat nor Miss Meriweather had protested his decision. He guessed, like him, they wanted to avoid villagers who had been among the men who had treated them so heartlessly during the night.

Nobody spoke as he broke a path through the snow to allow the ladies an easier walk. When Cat offered to trade places with him, he pretended not to hear. His eyes had a tendency not to focus at times, but with the hedgerows on either side of the road, he could not wander too far off the straightest path to Meriweather Hall.

Then the hedgerows ended, and he had no idea where the road was. He could see the cliffs dropping to the sea on his left and a wood on the right higher along the ridge. The road was somewhere between them, but he had no idea where.

He stopped, breathing hard. He could not chance leading Cat and her sister into a low wall or onto a pond hidden by the snow.

The quiet morning erupted with loud barking. Shading his eyes with his hands as well as the brim of his hat, he peered across the snow. Something large and dark was coming toward them. Two large and dark things. Were those men following?

He needed to hide the women, in case the smugglers had changed their minds. As he turned to motion them into the shadows of the hedgerows, Cat shouted.

"'Tis Jobby!" She ran as best as she could to the large dog. A sledge bounced in the dog's wake.

Jonathan was too tired to move. He watched as a half-dozen men appeared out of the glare. Sophia threw herself in Northbridge's arms. They clung to each other as if they never intended to let go again.

Words swarmed around him but made little sense. The pain along his skull seemed to drill into his brain. He forced himself to heed what they were saying.

"None of the wagons or carriages could move in the snow." Meriweather motioned for the other men to keep Jobby from jumping on them in his excitement.

"So you thought of putting a sledge behind the dog," Sophia said. "Brilliant!"

Meriweather and Northbridge cut their eyes toward each other and burst into laughter.

"Michael came up with the idea. Something he had seen in a storybook that their nurse read to them." Northbridge drew Sophia back into the arc of his arm. "Once he mentioned it, I had everyone in the stables looking for a sledge that might work."

"And it did work." She leaned her head against her fiancé's shoulder. "Thank the good Lord."

"What happened?"

"We should wait until we get back to Meriweather Hall to say much," Cat answered, glancing over her shoulder toward the hedgerows where one or more men could easily hide. "Suffice it to say, we encountered smugglers."

"Smugglers?" demanded Northbridge and Meriweather at the same time.

"Charles," Sophia said, "Cat is right. We should talk about this once we are inside and warm. As you can see, we survived the experience. Cat and Jonathan heeded the smugglers' request, and I was returned to them unscathed."

Northbridge's face reddened, and his eyes narrowed. "You let them take Sophia? I would have thought a hero like you, Bradby—"

This was his chance to be honest. His friends were already angry. The truth could not make them more furious.

Before he could speak, Cat said quietly, "You should not judge before you hear the whole story. Jonathan saved all our lives with his choices."

Meriweather winced at Cat's unfortunate choice of words. Jonathan knew she had not intended to remind her cousin of his inability to make the simplest decision as a way to deflect his anger.

"If he had gone after them," she continued in the same low, taut voice, "Sophia would be dead. Can't you see that it took more courage to wait for them to return her than to risk her life?"

Jonathan swallowed the bile rising in his throat as he realized he had a greater problem than telling his friends the truth. He had to tell Cat. Once his greatest worry had been losing Northbridge and Meriweather as his friends. Now, if he spoke the truth, he risked losing Cat.

Chapter Seventeen

Cat had never been happier to see the front door of Meriweather Hall. The men had insisted that she and Sophia ride on the dog sledge. By the time she had sat on it, she could barely feel her toes. Her fingertips burned. Her hands and feet ached when Charles set a box with heated stones between her and her sister. All the way back home, she had wished she could offer Jonathan her spot for a few minutes. He must be as cold as she was, and he was injured, but he would not admit that he needed help.

The sledge stopped, and footmen hurried out to assist them into the house. Cat paused long enough to pat Jobby on the head. The dog's tail wagged as his tongue lolled.

"Have Jobby taken to the kitchen," she said to Ogden as soon as she walked into the entrance hall. "Make sure he gets a bone with lots of meat still on it."

The butler nodded with an aplomb that suggested she gave such an order every day.

Charles assisted Sophia up the stairs. Cousin Edmund called for some of the footmen to help Jonathan while her cousin led Cat slowly toward the risers. At the top, the footmen led Jonathan toward his rooms as Cat and Sophia were guided to theirs.

Cat faltered, wanting to go with Jonathan to make sure someone tended to his head wounds. But she could not go with him to his rooms, and she knew the Meriweather Hall staff would take good care of him.

He glanced at her and then at the clock. He held up three fingers. She should meet him in three hours. That would give them a chance to get clean and warm, and take a nap.

Hot water was already being poured into a bath when Cat limped into her room. She dropped to her chaise longue, and was grateful when two maids knelt at her feet and began to loosen the snow-crusted blanket strips. Once they had removed the cloth and her ruined slippers, she let them undress her.

She sank into the hot water, and winced when pins and needles jabbed her fingertips and toes. It was a good sign but a painful one.

As the maids bustled around the room, taking away her ruined clothes and bringing clean items, Cat thanked God for bringing them through the trials of the previous night. The same sense of comfort that had filled her when she had prayed with Jonathan surged through her now. God had always been standing beside her, waiting like a patient parent, knowing she would return when her heart was ready.

Thank You, Lord. I won't forget that again. A smile spread across her face. *And thank You for opening Jonathan's heart so he understood why I was being so silly about both You and my artwork. Please heal his pain as You are healing mine.*

Telling the maids to make sure someone woke her up before the time she was supposed to meet Jonathan, she snuggled into her pillow, stretched her toes toward the warming pan beneath the covers and fell asleep.

Jonathan was waiting by her desk, exactly as Cat had expected. A white bandage circled his head, bright against his ruddy hair. She smiled when she saw he was wearing his usual garish clothes.

He did not return her smile as he crossed the room. "That eye is going to get very black."

"It won't be my first black eye." She tried to keep her tone light. "I ended up with one when Sophia dared me to ride a sheep. I tumbled off and landed on my face."

"But this is my fault."

She grasped his forearms. "Stop it, Jonathan! Sophia and I are alive because of your skill in the box, and your good sense in dealing with the smugglers."

"And by God's grace."

"Yes, because He gave you the skills you needed last night." She stared at the bandage. "How are you doing?"

"My head is hard." A smile raced across his lips. "Something I learned as a child when my sister dared me to ride a cow."

Cat laughed as she had thought she never would again. "And thank God for your sense of humor, Jonathan. It will help heal us."

He remained somber. "How are you faring, Cat?"

"I didn't think I would ever be warm again, but I am beginning to thaw. I hope I will be back to normal temperature by the time we need to leave to go to the wedding."

"When will it be?"

"Tomorrow afternoon. Christmas Eve. The wedding in the afternoon with the masquerade to follow tomorrow evening. The wedding breakfast will now be combined with Christmas. Sophia sent that message to me asking if I would be well enough to go. I suspect you will find a similar note in your room."

He took her hand and led her to a chair by the hearth. He turned the screen so the full heat from the fire washed over them. Pulling up a footstool, he sat on it. Again she had the unusual experience of looking *down* into his eyes.

He started to speak, but she halted him by saying, "I must tell you what I heard in the carriage."

"You heard the smugglers say something that will betray their identities?" His predatory grin startled her, and then she wondered if he had worn the same expression each time he went into battle.

"Not them but possibly their true leader." She told him how she had heard the smugglers discussing *his qualityship*.

Jonathan slammed his fist into his other palm and jumped to his feet. "Brilliant! They did just as I had hoped they would." He squatted down in front of her. "Cat, I got the one spouting orders to argue with me in hopes that his fellows would get bored and start talking among themselves. This is amazing information." He sprung back to his feet. "We must let Meriweather know."

She grasped his hand. "Don't say anything to cousin Edmund until after the wedding and Christmas."

"But—"

"Jonathan, the smugglers have been in Sanctuary

Bay since before my father was born. They will be here after the New Year begins." She smiled sadly. "Sophia and Charles and the children are eager for the wedding. They have waited long enough."

"And you have done so much work for it. Now everything must be changed."

"I can do it. With your help."

"Ask of me whatever you wish, Cat."

Tell me that you love me. She bit back the words that battered against her lips.

Instead, she forced a smile. "Let's start in the kitchen. I want to make sure Jobby got his reward."

"I pronounce you man and wife." Mr. Fenwick closed *The Book of Common Prayer* that he had cradled in his hands during the ceremony. "You may kiss your bride, my lord, if that is your wish."

"It is my wish."

Cat laughed along with the other guests as Charles swept her sister into his arms and kissed her. Beside them, Charles's children squealed with excitement as they waited their turn to kiss their new mother.

"At last," Cat whispered.

Not quietly enough because Jonathan leaned toward her and asked, "Did you think either your sister or Northbridge would let a small thing like an abduction or a blizzard halt their wedding?"

"Absolutely not." She smiled as Charles, now her brother-in-law, thanked Mr. Fenwick for holding the wedding on Christmas Eve.

Cat thought it was the perfect time for a wedding. With the church bedecked with greens interspersed with white and red candles, it was the most beautiful setting she could imagine for a wedding. Her sister wore the dress made for her by Mme. Dupont, but Cat's gown had been torn beyond repair. She had selected a light blue gown that she wore often to church. Only when she came down the stairs to see Jonathan waiting with the other men did she realize the silk was the exact color of his eyes.

No one among the guests, who included many from the village, mentioned Cat's black eye. Her sole attempt to try to lighten the bruise with powder had been futile, so she had not bothered for the wedding. She had seen many shocked looks exchanged, and she wondered how many were real and how many were feigned because some of the smugglers were among the guests in the pews.

"What a beautiful bride Sophia is!" Vera said. "The next Meriweather wedding will be yours, Cat."

"Or maybe Cousin Edmund's."

Vera's brows lowered. "Is he courting someone?"

"No, but Sir Nigel mentioned his great-niece will be attending church here. That makes it clear to me that he hopes Cousin Edmund will offer for Lillian."

"Time will tell." Vera smiled. "Anyone with two eyes can see that Lord Meriweather will not allow Sir Nigel to tell him what to do."

Cat laughed along with her friend.

When it came time to leave the church, Cat followed behind the newlyweds. She stepped outside, and the wind pummeled her. She grabbed the children's hands and hurried them to a waiting carriage. As she waited for them to climb in, she looked out over Sanctuary Bay.

Small boats were heading out to sea. Legitimate

fishing trips or were they smugglers bound to pick up more untaxed cargo?

She turned her back on the sea and stepped up into the carriage with the help of a footman. There was nothing she could do to stop the smugglers, and it was her sister's wedding day. She was going to forget about smuggling and concentrate on joy.

"Mrs. Porter, you have worked wonders," Cat said as the cook placed the multitier wedding cake in the middle of a preparation table in the kitchen. "It looks as fresh as if you made it this afternoon."

"The cold weather is a blessing in a few ways." The cook motioned for the waiting footmen to carry the cake upstairs and have it ready to be brought into the great hall.

Mrs. Porter shooed Cat out, telling her that, after all her hard work, Cat should enjoy the masquerade.

Cat hurried up the stairs, the flounces on her shepherdess costume fluttering around her ankles. She grabbed her crook that was decorated with a white ribbon to match the ones in her gown and in her hair.

The great room was filled with guests in a variety of costumes. She saw several other shepherdesses, but none of them had a black eye, so she knew she stood out among them. Ogden was conversing in a corner with Cousin Edmund, so she went toward them. If the butler needed a decision made, she could offer her cousin help. The orchestra was playing, and the music provided a soft background to conversations.

She veered away when she saw Sir Nigel and Lillian walking straight toward her cousin. It was not very neighborly of her, but she did not want to have to listen to more of Sir Nigel's veiled suggestions that her cousin marry his great-niece.

Where was Jonathan? She should be able to see him towering over most of the guests. The newlyweds and their children would not arrive for a half hour. At that time, the dancing would begin.

Over and over, she greeted guests and then asked, "Have you seen Jonathan Bradby?"

She got the same answer from each one. Nobody had seen him.

He had been quiet at the wedding, and she wondered if his head ached too much for him to join in the party. She looked around for a footman to send to his room to check on him. All of them were busy with other tasks.

She went to the entrance hall. She might find a footman there who could set aside his other duties long enough to check on Jonathan.

Then, as she stepped into the entrance hall, Cat saw Jonathan bending over to pat Jobby. He stood and faced her, and she saw his packed bags beside the dog. She stopped, unable to take another step.

"I was just going to come and look for you, Cat," Jonathan said. When the dog leaned heavily against his leg, pain rushed through him, reminding him of every bruise from head to toe. But it was nothing compared to the anguish in his heart as he gazed at Cat.

She said nothing.

He looked down at the dog. "I was saying goodbye to Jobby. He will be better off here than in Norwich. One wag of his tail in my sitting room and everything would be on the floor." He forced a smile.

She continued to stare at him without saying a word.

"I assume Jobby can stay here."

She remained silent.

"My work for Meriweather is done. I figured I should start back for Norwich before another storm comes. I haven't had much luck in dealing with North Yorkshire blizzards. I know I should have mentioned this to you this afternoon, but I really didn't plan to leave tonight until after I heard some of the guests talking about another storm brewing." He could not seem to halt the words that usually were so indispensable to him as a solicitor. "By leaving now, I may be able to get to East Anglia without getting stuck in another storm."

"So that is that?" Her voice was as icy as last night's wind.

"Cat, you must understand. I planned to stay for the masquerade. My wolf costume is upstairs, but I could not put it on. I am no wolf."

Her eyes slitted. "Is this about last night? I—"

"Cat, I told you that the weather is why I am leaving now."

She walked closer to him, and her tone became even colder, if possible. "Stop interrupting me! And you may believe that out-and-outer, but I do not!"

"It is not a lie."

"But it's not the whole truth, is it? Isn't that what a solicitor is required to deal with? All the truth, not some portion of it?" She drew in a ragged breath, then said in a gentler voice, "I understand what last night cost you."

"I don't know what you mean." *That,* at least, was completely the truth.

"You don't? By not giving chase after the smugglers, you went against your own best instincts. You put my sister's safety before your wish to unmask the smugglers. You set aside the acclaim that could have been yours so you could protect us. All of us." She leaned her crook against the newel post. "I have seen how important it is to you to continue being a hero."

"By trying to rescue a child who didn't need rescuing on the pond?" He hated the self-contempt in his question, but he clung to the emotion. If he pushed it aside, his pain at leaving Cat would increase a hundredfold.

"But, Jonathan, don't you understand? It took a lot of courage to make that choice when you did not chase after the smugglers. You dared to believe that God would see all of us through the night."

"Heroes don't sit back and do nothing. They make a difference."

She took another step closer to him, standing so near that Jobby could not squeeze between them. Raising her head, she gazed at him. She was so beautiful, so loving, so forgiving that his heart broke.

"But, Jonathan, by staying with me in the carriage, you became *my* hero when you urged me to pray again and believe that God hears all our prayers, even when He doesn't give us the answer we hoped for. You made a difference for me."

"You would have discovered that on your own."

"I hadn't. You helped me realize that it isn't God I need to forgive. I need to forgive myself. Not just for doubting Him, but for being ashamed of the gift He gave me."

"The gift of your art?"

Her eyes sparkled with unshed tears as she nodded. "I let the judgment of others carry more weight in my heart than God's blessing. I saw myself only as others saw me instead of listening to the truth in my heart." She wove her fingers through his. "Just as you do. Jonathan, you are a great man. You don't have to prove that to us. We all know that."

He whipped his hand away from hers. "You don't know anything about me."

"I know—"

"Nothing!" he spat before he turned away from her. He could not face her when he revealed the truth, and he could not hide the truth any longer. She deserved to know why he was leaving. Maybe then her heart would know he was not as honorable as he had pretended to be.

He stared at the door while he said, "I am no hero, Cat. I saw the Frenchman raise his knife toward Northbridge. That much is true. What nobody knows is that when I went to halt him, I stumbled over someone else. My shot went wide, and I bumped into the French soldier, knocking him away from Northbridge so the knife only cut Northbridge's cheek, not his throat.

"After the battle, I was proclaimed a hero. By Northbridge and Meriweather. They spread the word before I had a chance to speak the truth. I should have been honest right then and there, but, for the first time in my life, I was appreciated for something I had done. I wasn't the useless son who read the law against my mother's wishes. My father helped me achieve that dream but only to spite my mother. Both of them live a life of illusion, pretending to be a happily married couple when they cannot tolerate being in the same room with each other or with us. My siblings have re-made themselves to obtain a title or wealth or both, believing that was the route to the happiness we never knew as children."

"Which is why you did not want me to go to London," she said to his back.

He whirled to face her. "But don't you see, Cat? I have hated them for living an illusion, and then I became just like them. Living a lie."

She closed the distance between them. "You silly, silly man!"

His eyes widened in shock. He had imagined her saying many different things when he told her the truth. Telling him that he was a worthless liar. Telling him to get out of her life. Telling him that he should leave Meriweather Hall and never return. He had never guessed she could call him silly.

"Do you think," she asked quietly, "that it makes any difference to my sister or Gemma and Michael *how* you saved Charles? Do you think he and Cousin Edmund will be any less fond of you?"

"I lied to them. If they hated me for that, I would understand." He picked up his bags. "I would understand, because I hate myself for allowing them to believe this lie for months and months, even though I have had plenty of chances to be honest with them."

"How odd."

He looked over his shoulder at her. "I don't know what you mean."

She crossed the entrance hall to stand in front of him again. "Surely you have heard that opposites attract."

"Yes. What is your point?"

"My point is that I am most definitely attracted to you, and you are attracted to me." A blush climbed her face. "Or I assume you are attracted to me."

He bent to place his bags to the floor once more. "More than words could express, Cat." His fingers rose to brush her hair back from her cheek, but he quickly pulled his hand away. "More than a man like me should."

"There." A hint of triumph rang through her voice.

"There what? What are you talking about, Cat?"

"What you just said. 'More than a man like me should.'" She put her hand on the center of his chest, and his heart thudded to a faster pace at her touch. "Do you know how many times since I have met you that I told myself I should not allow myself to have feelings for you, because they were not appropriate for a woman like me who had lost my connection to God?"

"But you have not been false."

She smiled sadly. "Of course I have. I have blamed God for what was my own fault. I have denied His gift to me, and I let the opinions of others sway me from the truth."

"But I am no hero. Not like your Roland."

A shadow of grief dimmed her eyes. "Yes, Roland was a hero. Both you and he displayed great courage by defending England. The difference is that he didn't survive, and you did. Not only that, but you saved the life of your commanding officer who is also your good friend. Roland may have saved lives, too. I don't know. What I do know is that both of you, along with Cousin Edmund and Charles and all the other men who served, have no further need to prove your bravery."

The pain around his heart faded. "Thank you, Cat. I never thought of it that way."

She leaned her head on his chest and splayed her fingers across the front of his waistcoat. He held her close, savoring the quiet moment when both their hearts beat in unison.

"Stay," she whispered.

"I will." He pressed his face to her dark curls and drew in a deep breath of her light fragrance. "But only if you promise me one thing."

"What is that?" she asked, looking up at him.

He dropped to one knee and clasped her hands. As her eyes and her mouth grew round, he said, "Promise me that you will be my wife, Cat. I love you with all my heart."

Tears flowed down her face. "Yes. Yes. Yes! I promise that I will be your wife. I love you, Jonathan. I have since you were so patient about teaching me to handle the accounts for the wedding and ball. I knew you would never expect me to be the perfect wife."

"How could I expect you to be a perfect wife when I am far from perfect myself?"

She tugged on his hands to bring him to his feet. "But you are perfect for me."

Just as their kiss was, he thought, as he held her in his arms. Soon he would be able to kiss her whenever he wanted and welcome her kisses whenever she offered them.

"Well, I think our wedding is about to be overshadowed by another," Sophia said as she came down the stairs on Northbridge's arm. She walked around Jobby and kissed Jonathan on the cheek before giving Cat a hug. "I'm glad you two have finally come to see what the rest of us already knew."

Northbridge offered his hand and shook Jonathan's firmly. "Welcome to the family, Bradby. Who would have guessed when we wallowed in the mud that one day we would marry sisters?"

"Tonight is your night," Cat said, smiling. "We can make an announcement tomorrow on Christmas Day."

It was agreed, and the four of them walked to the great hall. The Yule log burned brightly on the largest hearth, and candles brightened every corner of the huge room. Cheers went up as Northbridge and his bride entered. Jonathan and Cat hung back to let the newlyweds bask in the excitement and happiness of friends and family.

"Don't forget you promised me something else," Cat said with a smile for Jonathan. *Her* Jonathan.

"What is that?"

"The first dance tonight."

"I have not forgotten." He drew her with him out to the area set aside for dancing.

As others lined up for the first set, the men facing the women for the country reel, he smiled and gestured to the orchestra. Bewildered gasps sounded as the orchestra began to play in three-quarters time. He held out his hands to Cat.

"What sort of music is that?" she asked as she looked from the orchestra to his hands.

"A waltz."

"I don't know how to waltz." She had read of it in magazines from London, but she had never seen anyone dance it.

"Then let me show you." He put one hand on her waist and drew her hand to his shoulder. Taking her other hand, he spun her into the pattern of the dance.

People stared at them as they whirled around the

great hall. When Charles swung Sophia into the dance, all eyes turned to the bride and groom. A few other brave couples joined in.

"You need to be careful," Cat said as she smiled with her delight as she danced with her future husband.

"Did I step on your toes?"

"No, but you told me you are not a great dancer. If you keep telling such tales, I will never know what to believe."

"I am a poor dancer in reels and other country dances." He laughed. "I always forget which way to go and who is my partner for each step. The waltz is simpler. The way is clear, and I only have a single partner. The only one I'll ever want."

When Jonathan drew her even closer, Cat leaned into him. It might be scandalous, but she did not care. She wanted to be in his arms. Closing her eyes, she lost herself in the music and the joy of having the man she loved love her.

Then they stopped, though the music had not.

"Look up," he said.

She did and saw the kissing bough over their heads. Laughing, she said, "It's a tradition, you know."

"A wondrous tradition. One I think we need to keep all year round."

She agreed by giving him a quick kiss. With a laugh, he pulled her to him, and that kiss was not quick.

* * * * *

Dear Reader,

Thanks for returning to Sanctuary Bay to share Catherine and Jonathan's story. I hoped you enjoyed a chance to celebrate Advent at Meriweather Hall. So many of the holiday traditions we enjoy now were begun in the Victorian age, which makes it fun to explore how Christmas was celebrated during the Regency. Medieval traditions, like the Yule log, were commonplace, and the carols might have the same melodies as the ones we know and love, but the words were different. Yet some traditions remain the same: wanting to be with loved ones, and enjoying our special traditions that come from our hearts and our families.

The next visit to Sanctuary Bay focuses on Edmund Herriott, the indecisive Lord Meriweather. Look for Edward's story in March 2014. As always, you can contact me by stopping in at www.joannbrownbooks.com.

Wishing you many blessings,
Jo Ann Brown

Questions for Discussion

1. Jonathan Bradby has let his friends believe what he knows is a lie. How would you feel if you discovered a friend had lied to you about something important?

2. Catherine Meriweather has lost her connection with God. What would you do if you or someone you cared about felt the same?

3. When a dog crawls into Jonathan's carriage, he makes an effort to find the dog a home. That doesn't work out, so he brings the dog along to Meriweather Hall. If an animal or a person looking for a family came into your life, what would you do to help?

4. Edmund Herriott struggles to make decisions. Which decisions are the hardest for you to make, and how do you make them anyhow? Or do you avoid making those decisions?

5. Meriweather Hall has a lot of traditions for Advent and Christmas. Which traditions are important to you throughout the year? Why?

6. Catherine is determined to make her sister's wedding perfect, but she fails over and over. What do you do when you are faced with failure?

7. Jonathan and Roland, Catherine's late fiancé, both feel that they have to prove something to

the people they love. Do you think that's necessary or important?

8. Catherine hides an important part of herself—her love of art—because she thinks other people will consider it worthless. Is there something important to you that you find difficult to share with others?

9. Jonathan and Catherine have to make some tough decisions to protect the ones they love. Have you ever had to make decisions like that? Did you find it hard or simple?

10. Catherine learns she must forgive herself as well as others. Do you find it easier to forgive yourself or the other people in your life?

REQUEST YOUR FREE BOOKS!

2 FREE INSPIRATIONAL NOVELS
PLUS 2
FREE
MYSTERY GIFTS

Love Inspired.

HISTORICAL
INSPIRATIONAL HISTORICAL ROMANCE

YES! Please send me 2 FREE Love Inspired® Historical novels and my 2 FREE mystery gifts (gifts are worth about $10). After receiving them, if I don't wish to receive any more books, I can return the shipping statement marked "cancel." If I don't cancel, I will receive 4 brand-new novels every month and be billed just $4.74 per book in the U.S. or $5.24 per book in Canada. That's a saving of at least 21% off the cover price. It's quite a bargain! Shipping and handling is just 50¢ per book in the U.S. and 75¢ per book in Canada.* I understand that accepting the 2 free books and gifts places me under no obligation to buy anything. I can always return a shipment and cancel at any time. Even if I never buy another book, the two free books and gifts are mine to keep forever.

102/302 IDN F5CN

Name	(PLEASE PRINT)
Address	Apt. #
City	State/Prov.	Zip/Postal Code

Signature (if under 18, a parent or guardian must sign)

Mail to the **Harlequin® Reader Service:**
IN U.S.A.: P.O. Box 1867, Buffalo, NY 14240-1867
IN CANADA: P.O. Box 609, Fort Erie, Ontario L2A 5X3

Want to try two free books from another series?
Call 1-800-873-8635 or visit www.ReaderService.com.

* Terms and prices subject to change without notice. Prices do not include applicable taxes. Sales tax applicable in N.Y. Canadian residents will be charged applicable taxes. Offer not valid in Quebec. This offer is limited to one order per household. Not valid for current subscribers to Love Inspired Historical books. All orders subject to credit approval. Credit or debit balances in a customer's account(s) may be offset by any other outstanding balance owed by or to the customer. Please allow 4 to 6 weeks for delivery. Offer available while quantities last.

Your Privacy—The Harlequin® Reader Service is committed to protecting your privacy. Our Privacy Policy is available online at www.ReaderService.com or upon request from the Harlequin Reader Service.

We make a portion of our mailing list available to reputable third parties that offer products we believe may interest you. If you prefer that we not exchange your name with third parties, or if you wish to clarify or modify your communication preferences, please visit us at www.ReaderService.com/consumerchoice or write to us at Harlequin Reader Service Preference Service, P.O. Box 9062, Buffalo, NY 14269. Include your complete name and address.

LIH13R

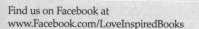
Jayne Gardiner is determined never to be a damsel in distress again. But when her shooting lesson goes awry, she must nurse an injured cowboy back on his feet. Will he walk away with her heart?

COWBOYS OF Eden Valley

Claiming the Cowboys Heart

by

LINDA FORD

is available January 2014 wherever Love Inspired Historical books are sold.

Bygones's intrepid reporter is on the trail of the town's mysterious benefactor. Will she succeed in her mission? Read on for a preview of COZY CHRISTMAS by Valerie Hansen, the conclusion to

THE HEART OF MAIN STREET *series.*

Whitney Leigh rolled her eyes. "Romance! It's getting to be an epidemic."

Because she was alone in the car she didn't try to temper her frustration. Fortunately, this time, the editor of the *Bygones Gazette* had assigned her to write a new series about the Save Our Streets project's six-month anniversary. If he had asked her for one more fluff piece on recent engagements, she would have screamed.

Parking in front of the Cozy Cup Café, she shivered and slid out.

As a lifelong citizen of Bygones she was supposed to have been perfect for the job of ferreting out the hidden facts concerning the town's windfall. Too bad she had failed. Instead of an exposé, she'd ended up filling her column with news of people's love lives. But she was not going to quit investigating. No, sir. Not until she'd uncovered the real facts. Especially the name of their secret benefactor.

She stepped inside the Cozy Cup.

"What can I do for you?" Josh Smith asked.

Whitney was tempted to launch right into her real reason for being there. Instead, she merely said, "Fix me something warm?"

"Like what?"

"Surprise me."

LIEXP1213

She settled herself at one of the tables. There was something unique about this place. And, truth to tell, the same went for the other new businesses on Main. Each one had filled a need and become an integral part of Bygones in a mere five or six months.

Josh Smith was a prime example. He was what she considered young, yet he had quickly won over the older generations as well as the younger ones.

He stepped out from behind the counter with a steaming cup in one hand and a taller, whipped-cream-topped tumbler in the other.

"Your choice," he said pleasantly, placing both drinks on the table and joining her as if he already knew this was not a social call.

"I see you're not too busy this afternoon. Do you have time to talk?"

"I always have time for my favorite reporter," he said.

"How many reporters do you know?"

"Hmm, let's see." A widening grin made his eyes sparkle. "One."

Will Whitney get her story and find love in the process?
Pick up COZY CHRISTMAS to find out.

Available December 2013 wherever
Love Inspired® Books are sold.

Love the Love Inspired book you just read?

Your opinion matters.

Review this book on your favorite book site, review site, blog or your own social media properties and share your opinion with other readers!